CONTENTS

To Cynthia and Donald Firth

CHAPTER 1 - THE WASTELANDER

◆◆◆

Across the wheat field, down the hill, through the yard of rusting cars. West moved slowly, kept low. Using the tightly-packed wrecks, he was able to get within twenty feet of the house – a crumbling cube of bleached timber and corrugated iron. One section of the roof had come loose and hung from a corner, squeaking in the quiet wind.

Hunched behind the hood of a long, low vehicle, West surveyed the place where his prey dwelt. The window left of the door was closed, beyond it only gloom. The door had once been red but had now faded to a thin pink. That was shut too. The window frame to the right had been lifted two or three inches. Eyes narrow beneath his hat, West peered into the darkness. Was something moving there?

Yes. It had to be Tom Jericho.

As far as West knew, Jericho lived here alone. If he could get to that window and take a shot, this might be his easiest job so far. According to the townsfolk who were paying West to kill him, Jericho had been an upstanding citizen once upon a time. But his wife had died a while back and the previous year his daughter had succumbed to a snake bite. Jericho was angry at the world and he was taking it out on the people of Hexton. Two men and one woman had been beaten and another man shot; he was lucky to survive. The townsfolk were offering a healthy horse and six weeks of provisions to rid themselves of the man. Quite a reward.

West had gathered what information he could. Jericho owned a shotgun but wasn't particularly handy with it. Crucially, he didn't own
a dog, which explained how West had been able to get so close. Jericho lived four miles out of town and the townsfolk had only decided on the bounty this week. They thought it unlikely that he knew what was coming.

West watched the window. It had to be Jericho in there but the house was not easy to get to without breaking cover. There were several outbuildings but none were close. The best route he could see was from the nearest of the cars, under the timber fence of the yard and to the left side of the house. Given his location, it was unlikely Jericho would see his approach. West could then slide along the front to the right window and take his shot.

Almost doubled over, he made his way past two wrecks to the front of the yard. Here he paused, eyes once again boring into the gloom. Someone was definitely moving around in there. West reached down and pulled his heavy sixer out of the holster. When he cocked the hammer, he felt a chill run down his back.

Gun in hand, eyes on the house, he crawled under the lowest beam of the fence, then got to his feet. One wary step at a time, he tiptoed across the dusty ground to the left corner of the house, breathing a sigh of relief when he made it. Sixer out in front of him, he moved past the left window, then the door, grimacing as his right boot scuffed the ground. West halted beside the window, checking over his shoulder just in case. Then he peered inside, looking along the barrel of the sixer.

It took a moment for his eyes to adjust. He saw a section of wall and a strip of curling wall paper. He saw floorboards covered in dust, marked by footprints. He saw a lone chair facing the window. And then he saw the grey cat sitting upon it.

So, Jericho didn't have a dog but he had a cat. And when its yellow eyes saw the face staring in from outside, the feline unleashed a piercing howl. Jericho might as well have had a dog.

Footsteps: quick and heavy.

West considered diving in through the window – taking the initiative – but that seemed like a gamble too far. Judging by the footsteps, Jericho was coming from the back of the house; which meant West still had a little time.

He bolted for the yard, fingers tight on the sixer. Jericho was spitting curses which became shouts as he wrenched the front door open. By then, West was into the yard and veering right towards the closest vehicle.

'Son of a bitch!'

The last word of the sentence coincided with the first blast of the shotgun. As West struck the ground behind the car– almost losing his grip on the sixer – he knew he'd been hit by something. But the pain wasn't bad so he told himself to ignore it.

Once up on his knees, he peered over the trunk of the car. There was Tom Jericho: barefoot and heavily-bearded, wearing only grimy pants and a leather waistcoat. His eyes were manic, mouth full of broken teeth. The shotgun was an automatic: most likely six or eight shells. Jericho saw West, adjusted his aim, fired again.

The impact did no more than blast flakes of rust into the air. West had already ducked down. He drew in three deep, long breaths, settling himself. He wanted to end this quickly; before Jericho realized he was facing an armed man and needed to take cover himself.

He could have fired over the trunk or the hood but there was a better choice. The middle section of the car between the windows offered the best protection – however much rust there was – and only the top of his body would be exposed. He crawled over to it and stood up. His right arm came down on the car's roof.

Eyes wide, Jericho was already adjusting.

West didn't rush: he aimed, squeezed the trigger. The men fired at the same time.

The shotgun blast hit only the car, peppering the decayed metal.

The sixer bullet hit Tom Jericho in the neck, toppling him backwards and sending the door slamming into the wall.

West waited to be sure he was down, then walked around the car and up to the door. The shotgun slid down onto the doorstep, Jericho's fingers already lifeless. From his bloodied, torn-up throat came a quiet gurgle.

West lowered the sixer and let out a long breath.

He was surprised to see the cat reappear. It walked up to its owner, licked blood from his throat, then disappeared into the house.

It wasn't until he looked down that West remembered he'd been hit. He sat on the lower rung of the fence and examined his right leg. Fragments of glass from the car's tail light had struck his boot and a few had gone through his sock and into his leg. Seeing instantly that none had caused major wounds, West elected to get on with his work.

The first task was to turn over Jericho's body and drain out as much blood as possible; he needed proof of his kill and he wanted to be back in Hexton to claim his reward before sundown. Any place in the Wasteland could be – or *become* – a dangerous place and he was new to the area. The second job was to check the outhouses, where he found the mule the townsfolk had mentioned. He put a bridle on the animal and led it around to the front of the house.

Having scoured numerous *empty* houses and properties, West felt a touch ashamed about searching Jericho's home but, in the Wasteland, such opportunities could not be passed up. He had to be quick but was quite happy with his haul of a small cooking pan, a dozen candles, a hand saw and a few bits of cutlery. West never took much – he only possessed one large backpack after all – but he claimed anything he could use or trade, which in this case included the shotgun. His pack was currently under lock and key back at the inn where he was staying in

Hexton.

Jericho was not a small man. Having bandaged the neck with a table cloth, West lifted the body onto the mule. The animal didn't seem too keen on its load and West had to make several adjustments. But with a final glance at the house, he led the mule away and along the trail back to Hexton.

Sunset was perhaps two hours away but the Eastern Glow had already tinged the distant sky with purple. The Glow was visible on any clear night and sometimes there were also strange flashes that resembled lightning. West didn't know what it was or what caused it. As far as he could ascertain, neither did anyone else.

Hexton wasn't much of a town. Only main street and a few others were occupied and West doubted there was more than two hundred residents. The sun was close to the horizon as he led the mule along a deserted backstreet, past crumbling houses where he saw not a single light. There was seldom much point investigating such places; most had been picked clean long ago.

The Rider's Retreat inn was situated on main street and West approached from the rear. Tying the mule to a wreck inside a shadowy carport, he walked to the inn, entering through the back door. He moved carefully, not wanting to show himself to those at the bar, who usually numbered at least a dozen. He stuck his head into the kitchen, where a large lantern was alight. Mrs. O'Reilly, the innkeeper's wife, was chopping something on the counter.

'God, you scared me!'

West said nothing.

'Well, I guess I'll go get him.' Keeping her chopping knife in her hand, Mrs. O'Reilly moved warily past him and into the bar area. The smells of the kitchen were enough to elicit rumbles from West's stomach, despite the evening's grisly work.

O'Reilly was a short, stocky man with a stubbly beard. He ushered West to the back door.

'You did it?' he whispered.

'I did it. Brought him on the back of his mule.'

'Show me.'

'Not yet. Get Fowler – meet me at the house three doors down on the right. Bring the reward. And a light.'

Fowler seemed to be some kind of leader. West gathered that he ran the store opposite the inn and also traded in livestock, which made him far wealthier than most. Apparently, the man Jericho had shot was his brother.

After he and O'Reilly arrived carrying two weighty sacks, Fowler produced a flashlight and knelt beside Jericho's body. West had pulled him down off the mule and laid him out. The yellow light illuminated the bearded face that now looked oddly peaceful.

'Well, that's him all right,' said Fowler, who looked and sounded like someone who preferred a quiet life.

'Good,' said West. 'Wouldn't want to shoot the wrong man.'

'Give you much trouble?' asked O'Reilly.

'No more than expected.' West moved over to the two large sacks the men had brought with them.

'The light.'

Fowler obligingly turned it so that West could open the sacks and look inside. 'Dried meat, dried peas and dried fruit. You've also got a leg of pork in there.'

West surveyed the food and swiftly concluded that it would indeed last him six weeks, maybe even more.

'Appreciated. How much would you take back in return for that flashlight?'

'Not for sale. Almost as hard to find as batteries.'

West wasn't surprised by his answer. He'd been looking for both for months.

'And the horse?'

'I'll take you to it in the morning,' said Fowler. 'A kind donation from one of our concerned-'

'-I'll take it *now*.'

O'Reilly didn't seem all that happy about leaving his wife in charge at the inn but he agreed. West grabbed his pack from his room and pulled it onto his back. He waited for the innkeeper outside with the mule, glad that no one else had noticed him leave. Over at the house, he could still see Fowler's flashlight as he showed other interested townsfolk the body. Apparently, Jericho would be buried in the morning.

When O'Reilly arrived, they loaded the two sacks onto the mule. The innkeeper then led the way along the near-silent main street before turning onto some open land. The pair passed a six-legged water tower that was leaking noisily.

'I'll admit I'm a little jealous of you travelling types,' said O'Reilly as they walked on. 'Hexton ain't a bad place but it does get boring.'

West wasn't much for conversation but O'Reilly continued talking: 'You ever seen a crater? There used to be cities there, you know. Huge places. With millions of people.'

'So they say.'

'What's your thinking on it?'

'No idea.'

'Must have been some kind of war, right? We have a few travellers come through the Retreat. Not one of them ever seen a big settlement that wasn't more than a ruin.'

'What about Woodhaven?'

'Bigger than Hexton, no doubt about it. But most of that's been built in the last few years. Wasn't much more than a village when I was a kid. I don't go that way no more. Nobody from Hexton does. You headed there?'

'No.'

'Biggest slave market in these parts. You could buy yourself a girl with all you got here. Think about that – your own personal slave girl.'

It seemed to West from the way O'Reilly said it that maybe *he* liked to think about it. He decided to change the subject.

'Ever get any raiders in Hexton?'

'Not for a while, which suits us fine. Were you a raider? You sort of seem the type. No offense.'

'I'm no raider. Never was. Never will be.'

The horse belonged to an old couple who lived on the edge of town. While waiting outside the barn where they kept it, O'Reilly explained their involvement to West:

'Their daughter is married to Sonny Lopez. He's still laid up with a broken arm thanks to old Jericho.'

With the wife holding a lantern, the husband led a tall grey horse out of the barn.

'We saddled him for you too,' said the man.

'We're grateful for what you did,' added his wife. 'That bastard Jericho didn't deserve to live no more.'

'Let's tie your mule on too.' Grabbing a length of rope out of the barn, the old man did just that. West was glad to see that neither animal seemed to mind the arrangement.

'Here,' he said, handing over the shotgun. 'There are four shells left in there. Couldn't find any more but I hate those things anyway. Too heavy.'

'Much obliged.'

The woman patted the horse affectionately. 'Why don't you get that feed, Donald? We've no use for it now.'

'I will.'

While he headed into the barn once more, the wife spoke to West.

'She's called May on account of that's the month we got her. I believe she was two then. She's six now. Stamina is nothing to write home about but over a mile or so, there are none faster. Wonderful temperament too – unless she sees a snake, that is. Where you headed, Mister ...'

'West,' interjected O'Reilly.

'Not sure yet.'

'You're welcome to stay here tonight,' she offered.

'Thank you but I'd like to get on the road.'

The old man had just finished roping a sack of feed onto the mule.

West tightened the straps of his pack and prepared to mount up.

'The southern road?' asked the husband.

West nodded.

'Watch out for those strangers.'

'Strangers?'

'You didn't tell him?' said the old man to O'Reilly.

'I didn't know. Been down cleaning out the cellar most of the day.'

'Young Fisher ran into them late afternoon a few miles out of town. Three of them. They were interested in the Jericho bounty. Fisher didn't like the look of them so pretended he didn't know nothing about it. I guess they might go into Hexton tomorrow. Well, they missed their chance.'

'Why didn't he like the look of them?' asked O'Reilly.

The old man spat on the ground. 'Reckoned they were raiders.'

CHAPTER 2 -THE AMBUSH

◆ ◆ ◆

The building looked like it had been used for storage. One end of the isolated concrete structure had collapsed but the other was intact, the crumpled door half open. A light rain fell as West tied up the horse and the mule. He fished the newly-acquired pan out of his pack and filled it with water, letting each animal take its turn. West knew he'd need to find a larger container. He'd had a horse the previous year and now understood how much food and water they got through in a day. He'd never given that horse a name and it was probably just as well. It had been shot out from under him by two raiders. At least the poor animal had cushioned his fall.

The horse and the mule pressed themselves close to the building, sheltering under the overhanging roof. West unleashed three firm kicks to knock the door all the way in, creating enough space for him, his pack and the three sacks. He was very glad to have the food but he wondered if he'd taken on too much. Had he made himself a target?

Though there was a three-quarter moon, it was obscured by the cloud and rain, so he had to feel his way as he settled in. The first sack he opened contained the dried fruit. He didn't have the energy to start a fire so washed down several handfuls with some water then laid out his bedroll and the folded-up towel he used as a pillow. Just as he was drifting off to sleep, the horse stuck its head in and nosed his bootless feet. West reckoned it was good to have some companions again. As the horse was named May, he decided to call the mule June.

With the dawn came a bright, warm sun. West reckoned the road wasn't far away but was glad not to be in sight of it. He poured some more water for May and June and put out some feed, soon realising he was in desperate need of a hot meal. He retrieved his fire-starting kit and found some dry wood inside the building, along with straw to use as kindling. Once the fire was going, he heated water for coffee then used the rest to heat through the dried beans. When these were cooked, he ate them with a bit of the dried meat, adding flavour from a jar of spices he'd bought in the town before Hexton.

With his stomach full, West packed up. In daylight he could give May and June a good look over and he was relieved to find that both seemed in good condition. Tying the mule to the rear of his saddle once more, he mounted up and headed off to the east, knowing he would eventually strike the southern road.

He found it in less than an hour, this particular stretch adorned by a burnt-out truck and several wrecks covered in bird shit. Bearing in mind what he'd heard about the raiders, West decided to stay off the road but use it to navigate his way. His aim was to return to the town of Bethesda, where he'd heard of a man who provided security for mines. These mines were some distance away but now West had the transport and the provisions for such a journey. Bethesda was close enough for him to make it by nightfall.

Staying off the road created a number of difficulties. The ground was waterlogged and he had to go around numerous obstacles, including a reservoir, power pylons and a chain of low hills. But from the top of one of the hills, he was able to spy Bethesda and continue on without needing the road.

After halting briefly at a stream to water the horses and eat some lunch, West pressed on, soon finding himself on a trail that ran through another area of rolling hills and patchy forest. Spring was well underway and the vivid leaves upon the trees held every imaginable shade of green. Such areas were rare in the Wasteland; the Cataclysm had turned most places into arid, lifeless plains where nothing would grow. West had sometimes spent an hour or two crossing such areas without seeing a single living thing except the odd insect or hardy weed. Towns like Hexton remained occupied because they still had enough viable land to make farming possible.

But here, today, the air was crisp and clean and there was not a cloud to be seen in the sky. With his new stash of provisions, West felt as good as he had in a while.

As he approached a pass between two hills, the space between the trees on either side of him narrowed. The thought was beginning to form in his mind that this was the perfect place for an ambush when May suddenly pulled up. West had sensed no tension in his mount but when he turned, he saw that something had disturbed June.

West gazed out from beneath his hat. The trees to his left were fractionally closer, perhaps no more than a hundred feet. The leaves were thick and low on the trunk; they could obscure riders and men on foot. But when it arrived, the danger came from his right.

Movement dragged his eyes there and he saw four riders burst out of the trees. Once on open ground, the men whipped at their mounts, driving them into a gallop. Two were already ahead of the others. West had only encountered one type of group in the Wasteland who attacked on sight: raiders.

He pulled his hat down tight, wheeled May around and gave her a kick to set her away. He hadn't yet tested her speed but she accelerated with impressive ease. The decision to untie June was an easy one: the mule would never keep up and the temptation of the visible supplies might distract the raiders. It would be a damn shame to lose the provisions but they could be replaced. West kept one hand on the reins and turned, using the other hand to untie the rope on his saddle. As he threw it back, May veered away and slowed to a trot.

The raiders didn't follow her, which surprised West. Then again, they could kill him and still return to catch the mule if they wished. He decided the time had come to really try May's speed. Hunching low and gripping the saddle with his thighs, he urged the tall grey into a full gallop and soon she was sprinting across the grass, her stride and breathing remarkably even.

Gambling that at least some of the pursuing mounts wouldn't possess the young horse's speed and agility, he led it into an area of fallen trees. May slowed; weaving and jumping through the greying timbers. West looked back and saw one of the horses baulk at a jump. The hapless rider cried out as he was thrown forward, barely staying in the saddle.

Once out of the fallen trees, West guided May onto a section of flat, open ground. Now the first shots rang out, one coming close enough for him to duck. Looking back, West saw that the unfortunate rider had turned and was heading back towards June. Though he'd abandoned his newly-acquired supplies, the prospect of losing them suddenly enraged him. He hated the thought of just riding away; losing what he'd earned to these greedy bastards. He also doubted they would expect what he was about to do.

West eased May left into an increasingly tight turn. By the time it was complete, the speedy horse was making straight for his three pursuers. They were already slowing.

Two hundred feet.

By the time West had drawn the sixer and cocked it, the distance was down to one-fifty.

The first man pulled up. West didn't want his foe to fire from a stationary horse – that would give him too much of an advantage. As he would be firing while moving, West decided to aim for the larger target – the raider's mount.

A hundred feet.

His first shot was wide. His second hit the animal. The raider had been about to fire and the resultant jolt – as the horse stumbled – knocked the pistol from his hand. As West bore down upon him, his horse staggered, spittle foaming at its mouth.

Fifty feet. Forty.

The raider was reaching for a second weapon when West's third shot hit him in the chest. With a silent cry he fell backwards out of the saddle, coming down hard on his neck.

The next rider had a rifle and was skilful enough to keep his horse moving and fire with both hands. West was lucky. His enemy's first shot thudded into the thick leather of the saddle, an inch from his thigh. As the riders closed on each other, West returned fire, his fourth shot catching the second raider on his knee. The man cried out and let go of the reins as he came past. As his horse decelerated, West turned May towards him. At a range of no more than thirty feet, he shot the man between the shoulder blades. The raider slumped forward, pawed once at his back, then fell limply to the ground.

West had lost track of the third man entirely.

When May shrieked, he knew she'd been hit. Her jerking head almost pulled West out of the saddle. The poor animal leaped away from the danger but then planted a hoof on a branch. She somehow kept her balance for another couple of steps, giving West a chance to jump clear. He came down on his side in the grass and heard the horse land with another shriek and the splintering crack of bone.

Staying low, West spun around and saw the third rider charging towards him. A bullet nicked his hat. Up on one knee, he fired back. His sixth shot tore into the rider's arm and the raider pulled up, clearly in considerable pain. With his hands off the reins, his horse ambled along, then slowed to a halt.

'Want another one?' said West, reaching into his coat pocket for more of the sixer's heavy rounds. 'Or you gonna be smart?'

Evidently too preoccupied by his bleeding arm to have counted West's shots, the third man threw his gun away. He then brought his leg over and dropped to the ground, his face already pale.

West slotted three bullets in then flicked the cylinder back into place. 'Turn around. On your knees.'

West advanced to within ten feet of the man, then looked around. In the distance, the two riderless horses sped away in different directions. Back towards the trees, the last raider was on the ground holding his horse and June, watching.

The injured man somehow pulled his arm out of his coat. When he saw the ragged mess near to his shoulder, he fainted, falling on to his side.

Had the circumstances been different, West might have laughed. As it was, he hurried back to May. He saw the bleeding bullet hole on the horse's rump. She might easily have survived that. But the front right leg was broken above the ankle, the bone visible. May lay there, breathing hard, eyes rolling. West knew enough about horses to know she was done.

He walked up to her, bent over and aimed the sixer at a point two inches above her eye.

'Can't believe I only had you a day. Sorry, girl.'

With two of his enemies still alive, West didn't bother to check on the others; he could see no way they would have survived. The third man regained consciousness swiftly and West ordered him to his feet. Now up close, he had no doubt this was a raider. Upon his neck, were swirling black tattoos, upon his fingers many rings, doubtless claimed from numerous victims. The man had a wolfish look about him and a thin, well-kept moustache that suggested vanity. He seemed more interested in his wounded arm than West. Blood was seeping from the bullet hole.

'You'll live.'

The raider now looked past him. The fleeing horses were out of sight.

'What about the others?'

'What about them?'

'They may still be alive.'

'If they are, they ain't getting up. Start walking.' West jutted his jaw towards the remaining man who – oddly – was still watching.

Once the raider had set off, West grabbed his horse's reins and walked behind him. When he thought about May, he was tempted to shoot this one in the back of the head.

As they approached the last man, West made sure he was directly behind the injured raider, his sixer at the ready. The last raider had June's reins in one hand, those of his mount in the other. Unlike the other three, his was a pony. He was a short, slender man with fine blonde hair and a patchy beard that was in places red. He wore military-style boots, dark pants and a baggy camouflaged jacket with a large hood. There was also a black tattoo on his neck, though it was quite small.

He was frowning and anxiously chewing the inside of his mouth.

'Fetch,' said the wounded raider, 'you are one useless piece of shit.'

The man called Fetch shrugged. 'I ain't got no gun, Silvera.'

He did, however, have a large knife in a scabbard strapped to his thigh.

'Want me to bandage that?' added Fetch.

Silvera turned to West.

'Once you've taken out that knife of yours and thrown it to me.'

'Yes, sir,' said the raider, obediently complying.

This prompted Silvera to shake his head in disbelief.

Fetch tethered June to his pony; neither seemed to mind.

Silvera sat down on the grass, whimpering with pain.

West moved around in front of him, watching as Fetch came over with a small bag retrieved from his saddle. As the skinny raider knelt down in front of Silvera and examined the wound, West reached into his own pack and took out a water bottle. If she was affected by the passing of May, June didn't show it.

West could feel his breath slowing, his body gradually relaxing after the fear and exertion of the chase and the gun battle. He wasn't entirely sure why he generally came out of such encounters well, though he'd noticed that he was able to keep calm and make better decisions than most men.

'Which raider gang you with?'

'Reapers,' said Silvera in between pained gasps. 'So, you'd be well advised to let us go.'

'Never heard of them,' replied West.

'*Him*. Reaper is a man.'

'Are all his employees as clueless as you two?'

'You got lucky,' countered the raider. 'Who are you anyway?'

'Name's West. Were you the ones heading for Hexton, looking for that bounty?'

Silvera nodded towards the sacks still on June's back.

'That bounty was *ours*. Three days ago, we heard about it. When we got to Hexton, everyone denied all knowledge, apart from them old folk that gave you the horse. The old hag spilled everything when I stuck a gun in her husband's face.'

West didn't much like what he heard. Especially as these bastards had caused May's death. He walked up to Silvera and pushed Fetch aside. He aimed the sixer between the raider's eyes.

'Lucky for you I have something in mind or I'd shoot you right now.'

The two raiders looked at him as he explained.

'Thanks to you, my horse is dead. I need something in return and as luck would have it, Woodhaven's not far. Reckon it's time I got into the slave trade.'

West knew Woodhaven was at least ten miles away, which meant he'd have to watch the two men all night and some of the following day: not a pleasant prospect but worth the effort if he could turn a profit. He first allowed Fetch to treat Silvera's wound; a long process during which the tough-talking raider fought back tears. The bullet had passed through his arm but had taken some of his shirt material in with it. They all knew that this could lead to infection and it took Fetch some time to pluck it out. He cleaned the wound with pure alcohol then bandaged it as best he could, reassuring Silvera that there would be a surgeon in Woodhaven who could take on the complicated task of stitching him up. Despite Fetch's efforts, the raider was not appreciative.

'You couldn't even do *that* properly, you idiot,' he snarled as he pulled his bloodied shirt back on. 'Hurts like hell. In fact, give me the rest of that alcohol.'

'Don't,' ordered West.

'You bastard,' hissed Silvera.

'Careful now,' said West. 'If you keep going like this, you'll need that alcohol for the hole in your *other* arm.'

Silvera now pulled on his coat, which was also a struggle. Fetch silently helped him, again without a word of thanks. West had kept his gun in his hand throughout, and he'd decided on how they would travel.

He first aimed the barrel at Fetch. 'You're going to lead the pony and the mule.'

The quiet raider nodded.

West turned the sixer on Silvera. 'Go behind him. You so much as turn your head without asking, I'll put a bullet in it. Know the way to Woodhaven, Fetch?'

'I do.'

'Good. No tricks.'

Silvera snorted. 'You think he's got the wit to come up with a trick?'

Ensuring that he kept his eyes on the raiders and his hand on the holstered sixer, West set off with his captives. Fetch led the way through the pass and – as the afternoon wore on – they crossed a grassy plain now coloured by pretty yellow flowers. At one point, Fetch stopped to look at a vast patch of the blooms, which were a rare sight in the blighted landscape of the Wasteland.

Silvera complained of exhaustion several times and West eventually allowed him to rest. He also gave the pair some water and took the opportunity to check Fetch and his gear for any hidden weapons. He had already commandeered the raider's knife and found only equipment and provisions. While Silvera and the other two had carried light packs, Fetch's smaller pony was laden with supplies. It seemed he had fulfilled a very different role to the other three.

West also patted Silvera down for a second time and found nothing. The raider snarled more threats, suggesting to West that he had made a major mistake by taking on Reaper's Boys. Somehow, West resisted the temptation to crack the man on the head with his sixer.

As evening approached, the trio approached a lone crag, which looked to be at least a thousand feet high. West recalled it from his trip north, though he had only seen it at distance. According to Fetch, the crag was known as Edgar's Rock and Woodhaven was located on the other side.

Sunset was close when West called a halt. He had spotted a dense stand of trees in the shadow of the crag which seemed like a safe place to spend the night. Once there, he swiftly located a small clearing with space enough for three men, a pony and a mule. Silvera slumped down against a tree, refusing Fetch's offer to check his wound. His thin face still pale, he watched West for a while then gazed morosely at the ground.

'Can't believe all those flowers,' said Fetch to no one in particular while tethering June and the pony. 'So beautiful.'

West was beginning to wonder if he was a bit simple.

'Any plans for dinner, Mr. West?'

'I have some, yes. Am I going to offer food to two men who tried to kill me earlier in the day? No. You see to it that the animals get some water and feed. Feel free to have some water yourself and give some to Silvera. That's all you'll be getting tonight.'

'Fair enough, sir. But I must say that I didn't actually try to kill you. That was the others.'

West took off his hat and ran his fingers through his hair. 'What are you telling me? You're a peace-loving raider?'

'I'm proud to say I've never killed anything bigger than a deer. I've seen enough killing to know I don't want to do it.'

'Why'd you think we call him Fetch,' added Silvera with a sour look. 'That boy's only good for fetching and carrying.'

When he heard this, Fetch started chewing the inside of

his mouth again.

Once he had dealt with the mounts and the two raiders had drunk some water, West took out some rope and told Fetch to sit against a tree close to Silvera.

'Cruel son of a bitch,' wailed the wounded man when he saw what was happening. 'I'm in pain – how the hell I'm I going to spend the night like this?'

West said nothing; he had no choice if he wanted to get any sleep himself. Once he'd roped Fetch, he pulled Silvera's arms back behind the tree and tied his wrists together. He imagined it hurt greatly but by that point he was past caring.

With his captives secure, he delved into his pack to find some dinner. He cut several slices off the pork leg and savoured every mouthful. Little moonlight penetrated the trees and the two men on the other side of the clearing were no more than dim shapes.

'Feeling faint,' said Silvera after a time. 'Don't reckon I'll make it until morning. Maybe if you give some of that meat.'

West ignored him; instead finishing his meal and laying out his bedroll. Without shelter, the spring nights were cold, so he also retrieved his blanket. He lay out on his back, facing the raiders, sixer at the ready.

Before long he could hear snoring, though he wasn't sure which of the raiders it was coming from. Then the pony came close, chewing grass. Shortly after he waved a hand to move it away, West fell asleep.

When the face emerged out of the darkness, he at first thought he was dreaming – but the sight was accompanied by someone shouting his name. West lifted his arms and blocked an attack he didn't even see coming. Something hard and heavy slammed into his left arm, knocking him onto his side.

Despite the darkness, he knew it had to be Silvera. He'd lost track of his sixer but kicked out with his left foot, connecting with what felt like a knee. Silvera cried out and fell back, landing heavily.

Though the pain in his arm still burned, West scrambled around with both hands. With his right he located his sixer, with the left he found the rough surface of a branch, presumably the same one Silvera had struck him with.

Once up on his feet, he could see a little better, specifically the face and eyes of the sly raider, who was lying on the ground, whimpering.

'What a shame – you fell on your wounded arm.' West threw the branch at him for good measure.

To his surprise, the raider's first words were not aimed in his direction.

'Fetch, I swear I'm going to cut your balls off!'

West bent over Silvera. He grabbed his hair with his left hand and pushed the barrel of the sixer into his neck.

'I have had just about enough of you. My trigger finger's getting itchy. Any more bullshit and I'll scratch it. Do we understand each other?'

'All right,' uttered Silvera between gritted teeth.

West dragged him back to the tree by his collar, gun still at the ready.

'How'd you get loose anyway?'

Silvera didn't answer so West gave him a little knock on his head with the sixer barrel.

'Ring. Got a blade on it.'

'Nice move.' West kept the gun against the raider's neck as he carefully removed the ring along with three others. He felt the triangular blade on the inside.

'You don't cut yourself?'

'There's a cover. Dropped it.'

'Very neat. I'm definitely having that.' Once he'd used the remaining rope to bind Silvera to the tree again, West fetched some more and also tied his neck. As he finished up, he realised how much his arm still hurt. It wasn't broken but he expected to find a nasty bruise by morning. The thought of it caused him to lash out a couple of kicks into Silvera. The raider grunted with the pain but said nothing more.

On his way back to his bedroll, West almost thanked Fetch for the warning. He decided against it; surely the raider had only done so to save himself.

CHAPTER 3 -THE MARKET

◆ ◆ ◆

While only a quarter of Hexton had been occupied, Woodhaven looked to be a hive of activity. The first sign of it was the unpleasant smell, which West had detected once they were beyond Edgar's Rock. Then they came upon the muddy road that led into Woodhaven, and it was busy, with numerous people entering and leaving the town, many upon horse-drawn carts. From the outside, it was hard to see exactly what the settlement looked like because it was surrounded by an uneven wall of timber, brick and metal. Several thin columns of smoke drifted up into the sky.

Standing guard at the entrance were four men, each armed with a wooden stave and wearing a sleeveless armoured jacket painted red. Though he didn't know much about the place, West was reluctant to ask his captives.

'Never been here before, have you?' said Silvera, as if sensing his unease.

West grabbed the raider by his injured arm and checked the rope binding his hands in front of him.

Silvera's grimace turned into a smile. 'You're out of your depth, West. This is a dangerous place. Easy to make a wrong move.'

'So maybe I'll just shoot you instead.'

That shut him up so West then checked Fetch's ropes too, not that he thought he'd cause him a problem. After tying the raiders together, he attached the rope to his belt.

'Let's go,' he said, urging the pair towards the gate while

leading the pony and mule. He felt sure there would be a decent stable in Woodhaven, and he planned on leaving the animals there while he arranged the sale – once he'd found out how to do such a thing.

The gate was a high metal arch with two hefty open doors. Once there, West found himself behind a trader with a handcart who was arguing with the guards. Accompanying the four enforcers was a smaller official who wore a cloth cap with a red hexagon on the front. It seemed the trader hadn't paid a levy on a previous transaction conducted in the town and couldn't enter until he had. When he responded angrily, the smaller man withdrew and one of the guards ordered the trader to leave. Once he'd manoeuvred his vehicle out of the way, West moved up.

'What's your business?' asked the official, who wore a jacket with numerous pockets.

'Selling these two as slaves.'

The man perused Fetch and Silvera briefly then took out his notebook and pencil. 'Do you have guild sterling?'

West knew that Woodhaven used its own currency and he'd taken some of the coins as payment for a previous job. He reached into his pocket and retrieved a handful. All were thin, roughly-made and hexagonal in shape. They were different sizes but all displayed a 'W' on one side and an elaborate imprint on the other.

'How much?'

'A crown buys you trading rights for a week – meaning you can buy and sell here until sundown.'

West looked down at the coins. 'A crown ...er...'

Silvera loosed another disdainful snort.

'The biggest coin,' said the man.

As West handed it over, the tallest of the guards pointed at his sixer. 'No weapons can be openly carried. Any use of a weapon within the city will land you in the church.'

'Church? That doesn't sound so bad.'

The locals chuckled, as did Silvera.

'You won't think that if you end up there,' replied the

guard.

'Where can I sell these two?' asked West.

'Straight ahead then left for the slave market,' said the official. 'What's your name?'

'West.'

The man made a note of it. 'A word of advice, Mr. West. Judging by his tattoos, this fellow is a raider.'

'They both are.'

'You may have difficulty finding a buyer. Even slave traders aren't all that keen on antagonising raider gangs.'

Though he didn't look at Silvera, West could feel him smirking.

'As long as I get them off my hands.'

The official shrugged and stepped aside, turning his attention to those next in line. West pointed Silvera and Fetch forward. The pony resisted for a moment but a sharp pull on its reins changed its mind. On his way past the guards, West asked about a stable and one man told him to take the first left. Directing his two captives that way, West followed them, now finding himself walking through more thick, clinging mud. It was hard to know where to look first and he swiftly reminded himself to keep his attention on Silvera, who would surely be prepared to take a risk if it meant escaping slavery.

Despite the mud and the stink and the noise, Woodhaven was organised around straight, wide paths which divided stalls and small buildings offering numerous services. Within the first minute, West spotted advertisements for medicine, beer, saddle and tack repair, blades, guns, clothes, leather, timber and precious metals. Though such stores were often seen in settlements, he'd never seen such a variety in one place. He was looking forward to spending his earnings.

There were hundreds of people too, the visitors all striding around in a purposeful manner. As usual, West felt uneasy about the sheer number of them; he spent most of his time out in the countryside, alone. Pairs of guards were patrolling, all armed and armoured.

One building had a row of chairs outside, where three people were sitting. As they passed, a woman standing with them pointed to Silvera.

'Hey there, you sick? Your colour's no good at all.' She gestured at the door. 'My husband will see you right in no time!'

West pushed his captives on, glad that Silvera was wearing his coat. He guessed his wound would reduce his value.

'Pies! Fresh pies!'

A rotund man came around a corner, holding a tray with a strap around his neck. West reckoned he needed it: there were at least a dozen large pies on the tray. Fetch stopped and stared at them but the vendor sidestepped him and winked at West.

'Feeling hungry, sir? I've got beef and onion or turkey and vegetable.'

'Maybe later.' They had passed three junctions by now and West still hadn't seen any sign of a stable. He nodded back at June and the pony. 'Do you know a place where I can leave these safely?'

'Sure thing. Old Mackey's place. Second right, then left and walk all the way to the wall.'

'Thanks.'

It turned out that 'Old Mackey' was long dead but his daughter – Michelle – ran one of the cleaner-looking stables in a row of six. She charged West four 'scraps' to look after the pony and June for the day, explaining that these were the smallest coins of the guild currency, ten of which made up a bit. Ten bits was equal to one crown.

Michelle had given him a suspicious look when he arrived with his captives but her attitude changed when she learned they were raiders. In fact, she even recommended a trader named Echeverria: according to her, he was 'the best of a bad lot'. Before leaving the stable, West grabbed his pack and asked Michelle to think about a price for the pony. He would only need June to carry his gear.

Once past the stables, they came to another large structure. It looked quite new and – like all new buildings in the Wasteland – barely half as good as the best preserved of the old buildings. Even so, it had three storeys, glass windows and a red flag hanging from a pole over the door. Due to the lack of wind, the writing upon the flag was illegible. But across the top of the front door was a sign made of what looked like silver: *MERCHANT'S GUILD*. Two guards were posted outside and a group of six men and women nearby were examining some papers. Like the man at the gate, they wore the red hexagons, though theirs were on their jackets.

'Who are they?' West asked Silvera.

'Why should I tell you anything?' countered the raider.

'Guild inspectors,' said Fetch.

'You've been here before?'

'Once.'

'What's the Guild?'

'Don't know exactly but they run this place.'

'Just Woodhaven?'

'Think so.'

Continuing along the street, they passed more stalls and a long, low building guarded by the only men West had seen in Woodhaven carrying guns.

'The church,' said Silvera, apparently now eager to share information.

'I still don't get it,' replied West.

'That's where the Guild puts anyone who causes trouble. And they ain't that keen on letting you out once you're in. They call it the church because all you can do is pray for salvation.'

West looked up at the roof, and the two sentries. As well as the rifles, they were equipped with metal helmets and armour.

'Listen, West,' said Silvera. 'My arm feels like it's about to drop off. No one buys injured slaves. Get it seen to and I'll tell you everything I know about this place. Knowledge is power.'

'Is that right? Well, if you're so smart, I guess slavers will be falling over themselves to buy you. I'm looking forward to getting a good price.'

West had only seen slaves and slave-traders once before; a column of chained men being marched along a road. When they entered the area where slaves were kept, bought and sold, he began to realise the realities of what he was getting into. He couldn't think of a dirtier, nastier, crueller business.

After receiving directions to Echeverria's, the trio walked past roughly-made buildings where slaves – male and female – were kept in cells of various sizes. Most looked filthy and many had iron collars around their necks. But what struck West the most was their forlorn, hopeless expressions. They reminded him of a dog he had once found chained to a fence post with not a human for miles around. Some of the traders called out to West, offering him prices for his captives. Silvera informed them that he was one of Reaper's Boys, which did seem to put some of them off.

When they reached Echeverria's place, the man himself came out to greet them. He was about fifty, his angular face pockmarked and dominated by a thick black moustache that reached down to his jawline. His establishment was basically a shack and a collection of stalls that might easily have housed animals. He spotted Silvera's tattoo instantly, then listened to West's explanation before replying.

'Well, Reaper ain't really known around these parts but a raider is a raider. I got enough troubles – don't want to invite any more. And you said he's injured?'

West pulled Silvera's coat off. The wound had earlier soaked through the bandages but had now stopped bleeding.

Echeverria leaned forward and sniffed it. 'Least it ain't gone bad. We can get that stitched up easily enough. Does he have any skills?'

'Definitely *not* ambushes,' said West.

The slave-trader raised an eyebrow and turned to the raider. 'Can you fight?'

Silvera ignored him and stared at West. 'You're a dead

man.'

Echeverria bobbed his head from side to side. 'A raider should be half-decent in a fight. If I sell him for the pits, most likely he'll never be seen of again – not much chance of any comeback from his gang.'

'The pits?'

'Fighting pits. There's one over by the quarry, a few elsewhere. Usually slaves or desperate men. Sometimes just fist fights, sometimes weapons. People bet on it. I know one man who buys just for the pits and I believe he'll be passing through soon.'

While Echeverria had been talking, Silvera's pallor – along with demeanour – had changed significantly. 'Hold on now. That's a death sentence.'

'Not if you win,' replied the trader. 'The best fighters sometimes even go free.'

Silvera gulped. 'West, come on now, I know we've had our differences but-'

'Yeah, couple of differences,' agreed West, 'like that time you tried to kill me in my sleep.'

'What about this one?' asked Echeverria, turning his attention to Fetch. 'He a raider too? Ah yeah, there's the tattoo. That's a small one.'

'He has skills, though,' said West. 'Knows a bit about medicine. Good with animals. And he was no trouble. He'd be useful to someone.'

'That's as maybe,' replied Echeverria, 'but he's a raider. And I ain't going to keep him around to tell his mates what happened to this one. Better I sell them both for the pits. Don't look like much of a fighter but you'd be surprised – most men can do pretty good when their life is on the line.'

Fetch was hanging on the slave trader's every word. West was not surprised to see him chewing the inside of his mouth again.

'If I can offload them quick, I can make some money on them,' continued Echeverria. 'Best I can offer you is ten crowns for the pair.'

West had little idea if that was a good price but the man seemed to have been open with him and he wanted this over with. He thought the fighting pits would be a perfect place for Silvera to end up. The look on Fetch's face, however, was hard to ignore.

'Can you do twelve?'

'Ten's my best.' Echeverria nodded at Silvera. 'I've got to pay to have this one stitched up.'

The trader offered his hand. West shook it.

'Candy! Bring me ten.'

After a moment, the shack door opened and out came a woman who was taller than West, which meant over six feet. She also possessed a set of unusually broad shoulders and was armed with a studded cudgel hanging from her belt. She handed her boss the coins.

'Put these two in cell four then go find Doc – I got a job for him. Here you go, Mr. West. Nice doing business with you.'

It was only when West looked down at the collection of big hexagonal coins that he realised he'd changed his mind.

'Just five.' West pointed at Fetch. 'Not him.'

Echeverria shrugged and handed back half the coins. 'No problem.'

The trader then pulled a flick-knife out of a pocket and used the blade to cut the rope connecting Silvera to West. Candy already had a hand around his neck and now guided him towards a cell.

'You're going see me again, West,' said the raider. 'I guarantee it.'

'Enjoy the pits.'

West beckoned Fetch over and borrowed Echeverria's knife to cut the man free. Fetch rubbed the back of his head and just gazed at West.

'See you around,' said Echeverria before returning to the shack.

'Why?' asked Fetch eventually.

West didn't say anything. But as he walked away – Fetch right behind him – he reckoned he knew why. The man hadn't pleaded with him, hadn't mentioned the fact that he'd saved his life. For all his limitations, he seemed to have a quiet dignity about him. Raider or not, he didn't deserve to die.

West had his mind set on one of the vendor's pies but he never got that far. Passing another shack with LUCY'S painted on the timbers in white, he caught a whiff of fresh bread. Going up to the door he was greeted by Lucy herself, who told him that the day's special was beef stew. That was enough for West, who took a seat at a table in the corner. Fetch sat opposite him, wringing his hands anxiously.

There were only five other tables in the place but all were occupied, which West took as a promising sign.

Lucy called over from the counter. 'Stew for both of you? For two scraps, you also get bread and a mug of beer.'

Fetch kept his eyes on the floor as West raised a thumb.

'Thanks, Mr. West.'

'Just West is fine. Happy to buy you lunch but after this we go our separate ways.'

Though sure he'd made the right decision, West had never travelled in the Wasteland with anyone else and he wasn't about to start now. He'd done pretty well on his own and he couldn't see any reason to change.

'Okay,' said Fetch.

West rubbed his arm, which was still sore from the previous night. He then let out a long sigh and reminded himself of the few things he wanted to get done in Woodhaven before he left. He intended on keeping a few coins but the rest he would spend.

'Guess I'll keep moving,' said Fetch, now scratching at his patchy beard.

'Where to?'

'North maybe – less chance of running into Reaper's Boys.'

'How long were you with them?'

'Seven or eight years, I think. There weren't all that many of us in the beginning. Couple of dozen, maybe.'

'And now?'

'Couple of hundred.'

West didn't much like the sound of that.

As they sat there, others eating and talking around them, he found he wanted to ask Fetch more questions. But what was the point? Soon they'd go their separate ways and he'd likely never see the man again. And yet he was curious.

'What about Reaper himself?'

'I made him angry once,' said Fetch. 'Never made that mistake again. He's mean – real mean – but clever with it. He's not like most leaders – he doesn't just kill for the sake of it. If he takes prisoners, he'd rather use them than kill them. That's how he's added so many boys over the years, that's how he built up Spring Bay.'

'That's his base?'

Fetch nodded. 'On a lake. I think it was a hotel or something before the ... well ...before. Reaper's got it just how he wants it now. Got himself a harem – you know what that is?'

'Can't say I do.'

'That's a group of women – just for him, if you know what I mean. I felt sorry for them though. They were slaves, I guess. And he's got plenty of male slaves too. They do the work around Spring Bay – fix the machines, farm the land. That way the Boys have time for raiding.'

'What about Silvera? Was he close to Reaper?'

'They go back aways but Silvera made a few mistakes. Guess he's not one of Reaper's favourites any more. They are related though – cousins.'

'What about before? Where did you live?'

Fetch looked away for a moment before replying. 'A place called Archer's Ford. When I was growing up there were four families but later on there was only us.'

'Us?'

'Me, my dad, my mom and my sister, Gabrielle.'

West could tell from the way Fetch spoke that something had happened to them.

'Are they-'

'Dead. All dead. Wasn't a lot of food around. Dad killed one of them strange elk – the blind ones with no fur. I guess it poisoned them.'

'Not you?'

'I wasn't there – I'd taken some hides over to Spring Bay to sell. When I got back, they were all in bed. All dead. Took me 'til sundown to bury them. Couldn't think of anywhere else to go but the Bay.'

Fetch reached under his camouflage jacket and took out a package wrapped in plastic. He removed the plastic and showed West a surprisingly good picture in coloured pencil: him and the rest of his family.

'Gabrielle drew that. Mom always said she was real talented.'

'Looks that way.'

Fetch carefully replaced the picture in the packaging and put it back under his jacket. 'Sure am glad I ain't no slave. I heard they take all your belongings from you. I don't have anything else I care about but I couldn't bear to part with that picture.'

Lucy then arrived with a tray; smiling as she handed the pair their bread, stew and ale. West smiled back: with her red hair and freckles, he thought she was very pretty.

'What about you?' said Fetch after she'd left. 'I guess you've got a tale too.'

West grabbed his spoon. 'Let's eat.'

CHAPTER 4 - THE JOB

◆ ◆ ◆

The stew, the bread and the ale were as good as West had tasted. He told Lucy so when she came to collect their plates and the pair exchanged a few words. West didn't get many chances to talk to pretty girls so he found himself in a fine mood as he left, pledging to himself that he would come back and see her again. Being in such good spirits, he couldn't see any immediate need to cast Fetch adrift.

'You know this place better than me. Want to help me out with a couple of things before you go?'

'Sure,' said Fetch, wiping crumbs off his collar.

'First thing I need is a gunsmith.'

Fetch shrugged. 'There are a few. Can't say I know which is best.'

In fact, they found one just around the corner. West didn't want to stay in Woodhaven any longer than necessary and he figured the man would know his trade. One customer was already present so he and Fetch waited while the smith replaced a rifle butt. His place was as much workshop as store, with the left side containing shelves, cabinets and boxes, the right side occupied by a hefty table and racks of spare parts and tools. Within the cabinets were various types of ammunition and a small selection of guns. West had already taken out the sixer but held it by the holster in case any of the Guild enforcers appeared.

'How come you use a spinner?' asked Fetch. 'Less bullets, right?'

'Right. But most guns are as old as the Cataclysm or rough versions based on those designs. Unreliable. Sixers misfire less often than quicks,' West used the name most commonly used for semi-automatic pistols. 'This takes a heavier round too. Not often I need a second bullet.'

Fetch nodded. 'I know a man who was shot seven times and survived.'

'Seven? Shit.'

'Then again, he's very big. Name's Rock – he's Reaper's bodyguard. I guess he's another reason why people generally do what Reaper tells them.'

The gunsmith had at last finished the repair. He took payment from the other customer, who pronounced himself happy with the work before departing. The smith wore a greasy apron and a pair of circular spectacles perched on his nose.

'What can I do for you?'

West took his sixer from the holster and handed it over, having already unloaded it. 'Trigger's felt a little loose for the last few weeks.'

'That shouldn't be too much trouble.' The gunsmith took the weapon over to his work table.

'I need some ammunition too.'

The artisan nodded as he began taking the sixer apart. 'Two scraps a bullet for this.'

Fetch pulled a face that suggested this was expensive. West didn't much care; the sixer had served him well and he couldn't think of anything more important to spend his money on. He only had about twenty bullets left and began calculating what to buy.

When Fetch drifted off to look at the cabinets, West joined him. His aim was to eventually buy a rifle but he couldn't afford one yet. He always carried a knife in his boot but he also wanted a decent second gun in case he lost the sixer.

He recognised some familiar models within the cabinets.

'After a quick?' asked the gunsmith.

'If the price is right.'

'How much you looking to spend?'

West had already decided that. 'No more than a crown.'

'In that case, I'd suggest the Browning. Nine bits. It's from a batch that was kept in storage – all wrapped in plastic and perfectly preserved.'

The gun did look in good condition but West had heard such claims from sellers before. Because newly-made guns were notoriously unreliable, everyone was after well-preserved originals.

'If it breaks on me, I'll be coming back for a refund,' said West.

'Naturally,' said the gunsmith. 'But if you look after it, it won't.'

'I'll do nine bits for the Browning if you throw the repair in free.'

'Fine by me.'

A quarter of an hour later, West left with two guns and plenty of ammunition. The bullets for the Browning were comparatively cheap and he'd also bought twenty for the sixer.

'That quick looks brand new,' said Fetch once they were outside. 'Hard to believe it's eighty years old.'

'Eighty-one now.'

'Is it? I'm not very good at keeping track of time.'

Just about everyone West had discussed the matter with knew the year of the Cataclysm. And though most were clearly not sure of the cause, many proclaimed theories, few of which made much sense to West.

They continued along the street towards the stable, though there was another stop he wanted to make first. A mule up ahead had stopped to relieve itself. As he took evasive action, he was struck by another thought:

'If anyone ever finds a way to recreate a factory that can make guns, they're going to be very rich.'

'Maybe someone will rebuild Factory Row.'

'I heard of it. You've been there?'

Fetch nodded vigorously. 'While back, with the Boys. Never seen anywhere like it. Massive buildings – all off this one road. Some of them have collapsed but we pulled some useful stuff out of there. I think there was even a couple of lights – the bright ones with the big bulbs.'

Other than medicine and weapons, lights – any kind that functioned – were of immense value in the Wasteland. As with Fowler back in Hexton, anyone who got hold of one tended to hang onto it. Some enterprising people made their own lanterns (and West owned one) but powerful flashlights and batteries were very rare.

'I guess you cleaned the place out?' he added, imagining that this would have been one of Reaper's more profitable raids.

'No,' replied Fetch, 'We weren't there very long. We had to clear out on account of the rats.'

West frowned. 'I've seen some big rats, but none that were nasty enough to send me running.'

'Oh, they're big,' said Fetch. 'But that's not the real problem. They're *blinds*.'

'Ah.'

West had heard of these creatures but was yet to encounter one in the flesh. The condition seemed to affect certain animal populations and it was generally agreed that it had been caused by the Cataclysm.

'And you know how blinds can be.'

'Actually, I've never seen one.'

'Count yourself lucky, said Fetch, suddenly animated. 'I told you about the elk my dad killed. I've also seen blind wolves, even a blind bear once. They might not be able to see but they can sniff you out well enough and they're more dangerous than any normal animal. Real aggressive, much quicker and stronger too. And they look damn strange. Not a piece of regular fur or hair on them – their skin is all red and pink, kind of scarred.' Fetch actually shuddered. 'And those eyes. White. Dead.'

West couldn't help dwelling on the thought of these creatures but his attention moved on swiftly when he spied a jewellery trader. Here he was able to sell most of Silvera's rings, making himself another crown. While there, he enquired about purchasing a flashlight and the trader directed him to a store run by a husband and wife named Novak.

When West and Fetch approached the place, a trio of guards were inside so West decided they would wait for the Guild enforcers to leave. The Novaks also employed their own bodyguard, a tall, heavy-browed fellow with muscles bulging through his shirt. He was currently munching his way through an apple and, by the looks of him, he didn't need a weapon to do his job.

Once inside, West could see easily why the Novaks required security. Their store contained not only a large number of lanterns but at least a dozen well-maintained flashlights and several varieties of battery. All had clearly been polished and presented to impress.

'What are you after, mister?' asked the wife while her husband fiddled with some device on the counter.

West pointed at a cabinet behind her. 'How much are the flashlights?'

'That depends.' Like her husband, she was at least seventy. Unlike him, she had dyed her hair an unlikely shade of red.

'What's your cheapest?' asked West, taking his hat off.

'That little black one is two crowns. Battery for that is eight bits.'

Fetch let out a long breath and West admitted to himself that it was an eye-watering price. One thing about Woodhaven: when you dealt in money, at least you got a clear idea of value. No wonder Fowler and the others hadn't wanted to give up their lights. A lantern did a fair job but a flashlight created a beam you could control and enabled you to see a long distance. West had been caught in a few nasty situations at night when such a piece would have been invaluable.

'And how long would that last me?'

'Er...' The wife didn't seem sure.

'About six hours solid use,' answered Mr. Novak without

looking up.

West wasn't sure. It would mean spending just about all he had.

Mr. Novak came over to join his wife. 'It's a lot, I know. But working flashlights ain't easy to find – batteries neither.' He paused for a moment, as if appraising West. 'Say, you look like a man who don't mind a bit of danger.'

'This again?' snapped the wife, throwing up her hands in disbelief. Do you believe this man, Leon?' She retreated into the rear of the store.

Leon – the enforcer – just grunted. He seemed more interested in finishing his apple.

'What sort of danger?' asked West.

Novak placed both hands on the counter. He was a broad, bald-headed man with a white beard. 'The sort that keeps most men away. I'm looking for someone prepared to take a risk – for one hell of a reward.'

'Go on.'

'What if I told you I know a place where there is a big stash of lights *and* batteries?'

'I'd ask you where it is.'

'I can't tell you *exactly* where – not yet anyway. Usually when I tell people the area, they don't want to hear any more.'

'Let me guess – Factory Row.'

Novak seemed genuinely shocked. 'How did you know?'

'I know it's close, dangerous and the most likely location for lights and batteries. Didn't take much working out. So, what do I have to do to get the *exact* location from you?'

Novak grinned.

Five minutes later, West and Fetch were on their way to the stable. Having become quite talkative since lunch, the former raider was now strangely quiet. Despite his mention of heading north, West guessed Fetch would have preferred to stay with him. West still didn't much like the idea of travelling with someone else but Fetch had been where he was going; he might be useful.

'Lucky for you that you're heading north,' he said. 'I guess you wouldn't much fancy another trip to Factory Row.'

'Mr. West, I don't suppose you'll listen to me but I really don't think you should go there. I bet Novak has asked dozens of people and nobody's said yes to him.'

'No doubt it's a risk.' West tapped his shirt pocket. Inside was the map Novak had drawn for him. 'But if this is accurate and I can get the stuff out, even half the profits is going to be a serious number of crowns.'

'What would you do with it?'

'I have some ideas.'

'What if you never come out of Factory Row?'

'You got out of there. Listen, Fetch, what if I offer you a third of my take? That would be enough to get you as far north as you want to go.'

West was glad to see that Fetch wasn't chewing the inside of his mouth again. He was however wringing his hands, and staring down at the muddy puddle between his feet.

'Tell you what, you help me and you can have that pony back – whether we get the stuff or not.'

West offered his hand. Fetch was smiling when he shook it.

*

Fetch also smiled when Michelle brought his pony out along with June. He'd told West that the animal had been rounded up by Reaper's Boys but the raiders all wanted horses so the pony became his. Fetch called him Sandy due to his colouring and reckoned he was about seven or eight. West had decided not to buy a horse. If he needed a mount in an emergency, he could use June. But after what had happened to May, he just didn't want another one right now. After all, he'd always spent most of his time on foot.

If Michelle was surprised by the fact that West had freed one of his slaves, she didn't mention it. But, as they were leaving, she did ask where they were headed. Fetch sensibly stayed quiet and West was purposefully vague.

From the stable, they led June and Sandy towards the main gate. Judging by Novak's map and what he'd told them, Factory Row was about twenty miles away. West wanted to cover a few of those before sundown and arrive there the following day with plenty of time to search. Considering what he'd heard about the blind rats, it didn't seem like a place to spend the night.

Close to the gate, they passed some kind of religious group. A dozen or so followers were gathered around an elderly man. He was standing on a box, ignoring the protests of a Guild official.

'Listen all, to the keepers of the Secret. We are the Servants of Messenger, Slaves to the Divine, Believers in the Revelation ...'

West had occasionally seen such groups before; and preachers who tried to recruit anyone they encountered to their cause. From what he'd gathered, many of these religious groups believed the Cataclysm was a punishment from God; and that only obedience to his will could restore the Earth to its previous state.

He and Fetch picked their way through the followers and onlookers, many of whom seemed more amused than intrigued by the preacher. With his unblinking eyes and wild gesticulations, he seemed rather unhinged. By now, the guards were also getting involved and the departing pair passed under the arch without attracting any attention.

West had memorised the first part of the route. They would follow the road to the east then head north across country before eventually picking up the old road that ran straight to Factory Row. As they turned left, rain began to fall. Fetch lifted his hood, West pulled his hat down lower, and they trudged through the mud.

Though he cursed the rain as it worsened, West soon had cause to be thankful for it.

They were no more than a mile from Woodhaven when they heard a shout away to their right. A line of six riders emerged from another forest of dead trees, galloping despite the rain. The first man pointed at the road and for a moment West thought he was coming straight at him. But in fact, the riders veered away, aiming for the road, which they reached about a hundred yards behind West and Fetch's position. From there, they rode hard towards Woodhaven without a second glance at the two men on foot.

When he turned to West, Fetch's eyes shone with fear.

'Reaper's Boys?'

Fetch gulped. 'The man out front is called Kinney. Reaper sent four groups to scout new territory, looking for fresh sites to raid. Silvera's was one of them. Kinney's was another.'

'You think he's up here looking for Silvera?'

'Probably.'

'Lucky we're leaving then.'

But West knew this was bad news. Most likely the raiders would track down Silvera and free him. Far from being consigned to the fighting pits, the sly bastard would now be seeking revenge.

'What if they find out where we're going?' added Fetch.

'Only Novak knows – and there's no way he's going to tell them. Relax.'

But West didn't get close to feeling relaxed until they were off the road. By then, the rain had intensified and the two men and two animals ploughed on with heads bowed, the ground increasingly sodden and unstable beneath their feet. They were heading for a landmark – an old church on top of a hill – but navigation was difficult in the rain and West was wary of damaging the map. So, with only an hour or two of light left, he began looking for shelter. They were now on a track edged by brambles that wound its way through low hills. There were isolated patches of trees but nothing that would offer decent protection for the night.

Eventually, however, Fetch spotted a shack surrounded by old fencing, much of which had collapsed. By this point, West was grateful to find anywhere at all. Tying the mounts up outside the shack, the men removed their gear and hurried in under the roof. They had to throw out some junk but soon cleared enough space to sit down and eat. June and Sandy would have to endure the rain but they got some food and water too.

By then, the sun had long set. West lit a candle and soon the pair were laid out on their bedrolls, snugly fitted into the little shack.

'I think that rain's settling in,' said Fetch as he stretched his soaked jacket over his saddle to dry.

'Fine by me,' answered West, who was squeezing water out of his hat. 'Gives your friends no chance of following our trail.'

In fact, the rain eased off after a couple of hours. The hammering on the roof of the shack had been loud and West slept soundly – until the sound of a scream woke them both.

'What the hell?' breathed Fetch.

'That was a woman,' added West. Looking outside, he could see that both the pony and mule were unsettled.

When it came, the second scream enabled him to identify the direction – at a slight angle from the front of the shack. The noise was followed by a bark of laughter; not as loud as the scream but clearly made by a man.

'Not good,' said Fetch.

West would usually have minded his own business; but if there was someone so close, he wanted to know who they were, particularly given their pursuers and onward destination.

'Bring your knife,' he told Fetch, having returned it to him that evening. He supposed it was a risk but he didn't believe the man would betray him. His instincts on such matters generally served him well.

West pulled on his belt, along with holster and gun. He didn't bother with his lantern, reckoning that the three-quarter moon would be sufficient.

'Stay close,' he told Fetch as he set off, carefully taking a path that would avoid the worst of the fencing. Even so, they both stumbled a few times before reaching open ground. Once clear, West followed a shallow ditch that led to a hill dotted with trees. Few had any leaves on them and he detected the familiar smell of rot as he ascended a slope. Reaching the top of a ridge that ran up the flank of the hill, he spied the orange bloom of a fire ahead and to his left. It was about half a mile away and even at that distance he could see several moving figures close to the flames.

He turned to Fetch. 'Quiet and slow.'

West now took one step at a time, using the cover of the old trees when he could. Gradually, the scene emerged.

The fire was a large one and around it was at least a dozen men. One was now playing an accordion and some were dancing along in time. At least half were holding bottles and all seemed to be enjoying themselves. The one person clearly not enjoying herself was a young woman. She was wearing only underwear and trying her best to cover herself. Suddenly, one of the men darted forward and pulled at her bra. She screamed again, prompting the man to whoop triumphantly and his compatriots to cheer.

Squatting beside a tree stump about twenty yards away, West ran his eyes over the rest of the camp. He reckoned there must be a road close by because the group had at least three carts and a horse per man. Despite the moonlight, his vision had been affected by the fire and he was wary of advancing any closer.

'Slavers,' said Fetch, coming up beside him.

'How can you tell?'

'See there – between the trees.' Fetch pointed to the left and after a while West realized he was looking at a large cart with an angular structure in the back. Shapes moved within.

'A cage.'

'Yes,' replied Fetch. 'Maybe two or three people in there.'

'I guess they're aiming to sell them at Woodhaven tomorrow.'

West watched the slavers again. Another man approached the woman, grabbed her around the neck and kissed her. She simply covered her face and stood there, sobbing. West didn't want to watch any more.

'Let's go back.'

He half-expected Fetch to protest but guessed the man had seen much worse while riding with Silvera and the others. If there'd been one or two slavers, it might have been possible to intervene. But West had counted at least fourteen: taking them on would have been nothing more than a quick way to commit suicide. He finally had some money together and every prospect of making more; he wasn't about to throw it away for a stranger. People suffered every day in the Wasteland.

And so, the two of them turned and walked away in silence as rain began to fall again. As they neared the ridge, West stopped, sighed and took off his hat. Despite the circumstances, he enjoyed the cool water on his face.

'Ah, what the hell. Won't be able to sleep with that going on anyway.'

'What are you going to do?' asked Fetch.

'Don't know yet. Something.'

"Something" involved creeping around the outskirts of the camp, checking there were no sentries. When they reached the cage, West sent Fetch forward a few yards to keep lookout then approached the prisoners. There was no danger of being heard by the slavers: the accordion was once again playing, the men singing along cheerily.

'Who are you?' asked a woman, sitting up in the back of the cage.

'Don't worry about who I am. Do you want to get out of here?'

West couldn't figure a way to help the woman beside the fire but at least he could do this.

'Of course.'

'There's no point,' came a weak male voice from the cage. 'They'll just capture us again.' West could make out another man lying beside him but this one said nothing at all.

'I'll take my chances,' said the woman, who sounded young.

'Listen, you don't even need to pick the lock, just undo the bolt at the bottom there. We can't reach it from inside.'

West ran his hand down the rear of the cart, fingers moving from a metal bar onto the wooden surround, then to the bolt. Looking up, he checked that none of the slavers were close, then pulled the bolt. Once he'd opened the door, the woman hurried to the edge and dropped onto the ground.

'Thank you,' she whispered, grasping his arm with one hand. 'We're close to Woodhaven, aren't we? How do I get out of here?'

'That's up to you,' said West. 'Wait a moment.'

He hurried along the side of the cart and grabbed Fetch, glad to see the slavers were still preoccupied. The pair of them were almost back to the woman when Fetch spoke: 'Down.'

As the three of them ducked into the shadows behind the cart, West looked for what had caused such alarm. Then he saw – and heard – the slaver. Weaving a drunken path and whistling tunelessly, this man had evidently wandered off and was now heading back to the camp. He seemed to be heading straight for the fire but suddenly lurched towards them.

The young woman cursed under her breath. West reached for his sixer, though he knew that firing it would likely be a death sentence. Still whistling, the slaver ambled towards the cart. West wondered if he was coming to take out the woman. He was close enough to Fetch to feel his companion trembling. He kept his eyes on the slaver who now arrived at another cart only a few yards away. The man reached into the back and, after some rummaging, pulled out a bottle. With a belch, he continued away, still whistling.

The woman let out a long sigh of relief.

'Let's go,' said West.

The three of them walked then jogged away until they were over the ridge.

'Do you have shoes?' asked West.

'Yes,' she replied. 'But where do I go?'

'Not with us, I'm afraid. We've already got one set of bastards on our tail. But the rain will cover your tracks. You've got at least three hours of darkness left. Just get as far away from here as you can.'

Though they hadn't travelled far, she was breathing hard. In the moonlight, West could see only her eyes.

'All right then,' she said, sounding determined.

To West's amazement, the young woman grabbed Fetch and planted a kiss on his cheek. She then did the same to West.

'What's your name?'

Though there was absolutely no reason to tell her, he did so without a second thought. 'West. You?'

'Isobel. I remember reading about the good Samaritan but I've never seen one in the Wasteland. So, thanks, West. I'll see you around.'

CHAPTER 5 - ISOBEL

◆◆◆

By the time they reached the shack, West had already made the decision to move on. When the slavers discovered they had lost one of their prisoners, they were sure to search the area. Worse still, the captive who'd refused to leave had witnessed the whole thing.

Fetch clearly agreed and they were soon plodding north through the darkness. The rain relented again after an hour or so and when dawn broke, West was relieved to see that they weren't far from the hill-top church on the map.

He was determined to get within sight of Factory Row before stopping and so they rounded the hill and kept walking. By now, there wasn't a cloud left in the sky and West took off his hat to enjoy the sunshine. They then came to a difficult section where a forest of downed trees presented quite an obstacle. West had seen such areas before. The trees were old and grey, rotten and hollow, and appeared to have been knocked down by some great hand.

Not long after escaping the maze of wood, they spied the road. And there, in the distance, were the high towers and blocks of Factory Row, standing stark against a vivid blue sky. West called a halt and – as he delved into his supplies for food – Fetch stood there, gazing at their destination. Having cut some more off the pork leg, West invited his companion to eat then gazed back across the ruined forest, eyes narrow as he scanned for pursuers. As far as he could tell, there were none.

'That's *good,*' said Fetch when he tasted the meat. 'Damn good.'

'Sure is.'

Fetch also surveyed the forest. 'Wonder where Isobel is now.'

'As long as she's not back in that cage.'

'I think she was pretty.'

West chuckled. 'It was dark, Fetch.'

'I didn't say she *was*, Mr. West. I said I *think* she was. She just ... sort of ... seemed pretty.'

'Maybe. She definitely seemed sure of herself.'

'We did a good thing.'

'Yeah, well, doing good things can easily get you killed.'

Chewing on his second piece of meat, Fetch turned back towards Factory Row. 'Lots of things can get you killed. Is it just the lights and the batteries you're after, Mr. West?'

'I'm curious too. I want to see the place. I want to know more about how the world was before.'

'Have you read any books?' asked Fetch. 'I don't know how to read. But I know you can find out a lot about the old world in books.'

'I've read a few,' replied West. 'But I haven't met a single person who can explain the Cataclysm to me. Not in a way that makes sense.'

'My father said it was best not to think about it. A person could send themselves mad thinking about how the world changed. But everyone has ideas, I guess. Reaper says it was a war – he reckons the enemy got their attack in first and we didn't get a chance to fight back.'

'There were aircraft in the old world,' replied West. 'If other places were doing better, they'd fly over and help, right?'

'I guess that makes sense. Did you ever see an airplane?'

West shook his head.

'I don't mean in the sky,' added Fetch. 'I don't think anyone's seen that. I mean on the ground. I saw this place way down south where they left all the planes to die. They were so big, Mr.

West. Huge. And so much metal in them. I couldn't understand how something so big could get into the sky.'

West hadn't had very long to explore the Wasteland. Just over two years. Perhaps that was why he was desperate to see more and know more.

'I told you. Don't call me mister. Just West. And what's your real name? Just because the raiders called you Fetch, you don't have to keep using it.'

Fetch scratched at his beard. 'Family name was Gibson. I'm Jake Gibson.'

'So, should I call you Jake?'

'Fetch is fine.' He shrugged. 'I guess I'm just used to it now.'

*

There weren't only factories. As they approached along the road – one of the widest West had seen – they passed gas stations and old tankers and yards full of wooden pallets and plastic barrels and mouldy tyres. And before the first of the factories, they came to a railroad station with an ancient train still on the tracks. Much of the paint upon the locomotive and six cars had faded but one section of lettering was still visible: *ALMONT CHEMICAL AND FUEL*. Most of the track itself had been obscured by earth, dust and trash.

West had seen most of these sights before in the Wasteland but never in one place. The old maps he'd studied showed that there had been a few big cities in this part of the country. Now there were only the craters – evidence of their destruction. West had seen some of those craters and he guessed that most of the built-up areas like Factory Row had gone the same way. But somehow this one had escaped that fate.

Towing June and Sandy along the middle of the road, West and Fetch gazed warily around them. Passing the railroad station, they soon found themselves hemmed in by large structures on both sides. To the left were three immense globes connected by a pipe that must have been as tall as a man. West imagined they must have stored some kind of liquid or gas. Towards the top, the original white paint was visible; close to the ground, the tanks were coated with dust. To the right were four huge identical buildings, each at least a hundred feet high and with a chimney at one end. Two of the chimneys had partially collapsed, as had some sections of the buildings. All the various parts were connected by chutes, pipes and cables.

West consulted Novak's map. 'Second building along. Towards the back.' On the other side of the paper was a more detailed map of the building's interior and the basement where the stash could apparently be found. When they reached the entrance, Fetch began chewing the inside of his mouth.

'Did you go in here?'

'I believe we did,' replied Fetch. 'And some place further down.' He pointed past the three tanks, towards the next complex, which was a blocky building with hundreds of small windows.

'Where'd you see the rats?'

'I don't remember exactly. It was only a few to begin with but once they started going for us, more of them turned up. One horse got bitten up so bad we had to shoot it.'

'We'll leave them here,' said West, leading June over to an old sign and tying her to the post. They hadn't seen anyone all day, which was not an unusual occurrence in the Wasteland.

As Fetch tethered Sandy and prepared some water for the pony and mule, West grabbed his pack. He didn't plan on carrying all that heavy weight into the factory so picked out a few items he might need: a coil of rope, a sack and a lantern. The lantern ran on oil and – though not one tenth as powerful as a flashlight – it gave out a decent glow. West didn't use it often because oil was pricey and hard to come by. He also took his coins and the second gun in case anyone robbed their gear.

'Some food might come in handy,' said Fetch, 'Distract the rats.'

'Won't they smell it?'

'Not if we wrap it right.'

'Go ahead.' While Fetch grabbed some of the meat, West ambled out onto the road. Taking his hat off to cool his head a little, he used it as a shade while checking they were still alone. Other than some squawking vultures on top of one of the white tanks, there was nothing moving.

'Ready,' said Fetch. He had taken off his camouflage jacket and now placed it in one of his saddlebags. Underneath he wore a grimy grey t-shirt and only now did West realise how slim and wiry his companion was. He guessed Fetch was about thirty, a little younger than him. The former raider patted down his fine, fair hair and adjusted the scabbard which held his hunting knife.

As he was also feeling hot, West left his black coat behind. Underneath he was wearing one of his two pairs of black jeans and a long-sleeved blue shirt he'd picked up in Hexton. He threw his spare gun, the lantern and the rope into the sack and offered it to Fetch. 'Carry that for me?'

'Sure thing, Mr... sure thing, West.' Fetch took the sack and chucked in the packet of meat along with a flask of water.

'Now,' said West, drawing the sixer, 'as I'll be trying to find this stash, you can keep an eye out for our four-legged friends. Let's go.'

*

The closest way into the building was through a set of swinging double doors. Once inside, West was pleased to find that sufficient light came in from the high windows, though he knew that wouldn't be the case in the basement. Entering a massive space packed with walkways, gantries, tubes, tanks and valves, he and Fetch halted near some kind of control room with windows darkened by dust. Only a few feet away was an old wasp's nest hanging from a yellow pipe.

West consulted the map and led the way past the control room, listening as keenly as he was looking. 'Memorise the route,' he told Fetch quietly, 'in case we have to leave in a hurry.'

West was relieved to find a stairwell exactly where it was

indicated on the map. The clank of their boots on the metal stairs was all that could be heard as they descended to the first basement level. The ceiling was surprisingly high – at least twenty feet – and here were yet more pipes and tanks. Little light reached this area from the windows but West could still see his way and make out the map. Following Novak's lines and arrows, he soon reached another stairwell which led to a sub-basement. According to Novak, this is where the stash could be found.

On several of the steps were piles of droppings that gave off a pungent odour.

'Those are pretty big,' said Fetch.

'Can't say I'm an expert,' replied West. 'You recognise this area?'

'No. I think we went in one of the other buildings.'

As West glanced around at the endless nooks and voids where rats – blind or otherwise – might be hiding, he felt his initial courage fade. He looked down at the sub-basement below, which was cloaked in gloom. As if reading his mind, Fetch retrieved the lantern. Taped to the side was a pack of matches that West had obtained a while back. Apparently, some enterprising individual manufactured them in a town far to the south (it was rumoured that a greedy raider had recently taken over the concern). Fetch struck a match and lit the lantern's wick, then half-closed the shutter and handed the lantern over.

West already had his sixer in his other hand. 'Feel free to take the quick.'

When Fetch retrieved the gun, West was surprised to see him give a lop-sided smile.

'What?'

'You trust me.'

'I guess I do. Don't make me regret it. Know how to use that?'

Fetch nodded. He' switched the sack to his right hand and held the gun in his left.

With the lantern out in front of him, West slowly descended the steps until he reached the floor. The ceiling here was low – just above his head – which did little to ease his nerves. Apart from the rats, there was something about the sheer size of this place that put him on edge.

'Hold on.' He consulted the map a final time, memorizing the final few directions, then replaced it in his pocket. He wanted to be able to keep his full attention on whatever lay ahead.

From the bottom of the stairwell, West turned to the right, the glow of the lantern casting a pool of thin, yellow light upon the floor. He could see very little beyond it and took each step slowly, relieved when he came to a door wedged open by a bucket full of green water. Keeping his gun at the ready, West advanced through the doorway and turned left. Ahead was a narrow corridor with a series of metal doors on the right side. Water had leaked in somehow, leaving shallow puddles across the floor. Stepping over one, West skidded and almost fell. He aimed the lantern at the floor and spied another stinking pile of rat shit.

According to the map, the stash was located behind the fifth door along and West was determined to get there quickly. He could hear Fetch's breathing accelerating behind him and feel his heartbeat getting faster. He passed the fourth door. So far, they had all been left shut.

Novak hadn't actually been here himself. He'd been given the map as a form of payment but seemed convinced that the information was correct. West was beginning to wonder if this job was worth the reward; after all, Novak wasn't the one down here risking his neck.

He reached the fifth door, which was also shut.

'Here.' He handed Fetch the lantern then gripped the metal handle. Easing it open, he watched the lantern-light spread into the room. It was a small, confined space, with shelves on either side. West could already see that there was a considerable number of boxes upon those shelves. With a grin forming on his face, he took the lantern from Fetch and stepped into the room. The light lurched forward and what West saw directly in his path froze him.

Lying there was a man; or what had once been a man. He

was on his back, still wearing a cap, under which was the toothy grin of a skeleton. Eyeless hollows gazed up at West. Finger bones poked out of his sleeves. Beneath him, the floor had been stained brown. There was no trace of flesh left. Even the clothes were beginning to rot.

'God,' whispered Fetch, as he came forward to see it.

'He's been here a while,' said West.

He moved past the skeleton, eager to see the boxes. There wasn't so much dust inside the room and he could read the handwritten labels on the plastic boxes: *FUSES, BULBS, TOOLS (SMALL), ASSORTED, BULBS, TOOLS, BATTERIES.*

'Ha!'

West put the gun and the lantern on a shelf, grabbed the box and lowered it to the floor. He tore off the top and saw dozens of little cardboard boxes containing batteries of various sizes, some of the same brands he'd seen proudly displayed in Novak's shop.

'Er ...,'

West looked up to see Fetch point at the body then at the door. He wasn't sure what was up with the man but he had other priorities.

'Look at this. I can't believe it! Now let's find those lights.'

This turned out to be easy. Two boxes labelled *FLASH-LIGHTS* had been stacked at the far end of the room. West ripped the lid off the top one and saw at least ten yellow flashlights in their original boxes. Even if some of the parts had decayed, he knew they would be hugely valuable.

'We did it, Fetch. Look at all this!'

West heaved the second box off the first but underestimated the weight. It fell to the floor a couple of feet from the skeleton.

'Er...' Fetch was looking back at the door.

'What's wrong with you, man?'

'I think those holes in his clothes are *bites*.'

'Nah, it's just...' But now he looked closer, West saw that Fetch was right.

'And aren't those droppings?' Fetch pointed to another pile below one of the shelves.

'Looks like it.' West was going to ask what Fetch was getting at when the answer finally came to him: 'The door was shut. So, if the rats killed him, how did they get in-'

Open-mouthed, Fetch pointed past him, at the wall behind where the second box had been. There was a waste chute. It was open and clearly visible upon the metal were scratch marks. And now West could hear them: the frantic scraping and squeaking told him that at least one was coming up the chute. He reached over the top of the lower box but wasn't quite close enough to get a grip on the chute door. And it was then that he realised he'd made a terrible mistake. He'd put down his gun.

The rat came flying up the chute and leapt at him. West saw only the beady white eyes and the outstretched claws before he turned away. The thing landed on his side, claws piercing his shirt. Flailing at it with a fist, he somehow knocked it off. From there, he went straight for his sixer, plucking it from the shelf as Fetch backed towards the door, the rat nipping at his ankles. Only when it gripped his pant leg was it still enough for West to risk a shot.

The bullet tore into its fat, pale body, propelling it off Fetch and into a wall. West was astonished to see it was still moving but after a couple of spasms it stopped. The thing was at least a foot long, the tail adding another six inches. The white, hairless skin was marked by pink scars and patches of yellow pustules.

Just as West turned back to close the chute, he heard the scraping and squeaking once more. Now he had time to aim and as this blind leaped out of the chute, its trajectory was halted immediately by the sixer shell. The head was blown clean off and the body thumped heavily onto the floor. West stepped past it, around the box and rammed the chute door shut.

'Told you they were nasty,' stammered Fetch.

'Next time one's trying to bite your leg off, you might want to shoot it.'

West was all set to start hauling the boxes out into the corridor when he heard the tapping of claws on metal once more. The noise wasn't just coming from the chute. It seemed that the rats were somehow both below the room *and* above it. He glanced at the corridor and was relieved to see that none of the afflicted rodents had appeared there. Yet.

'Open that sack. We'll just take what we can carry.'

Fetch shoved his gun into his belt and grabbed the sack. West retrieved the first pair of flashlights and threw them in. With the sound of the rats growing louder with every passing moment, he claimed ten lights in all then moved onto the batteries. Hauling the box up, he emptied half of it into the sack.

West grabbed the lantern. 'Time to leave. You first. I'll watch our backs.'

Fetch didn't need to be asked twice. Holding the sack with two hands, he threw it over his shoulder and hurried out into the corridor. West followed him out and aimed the lantern to the right. He immediately wished he hadn't.

Bounding through the puddles, tails flying high, were dozens of blind rats, apparently racing to reach their prey first. The squeaking had combined into one piercing screech that reverberated along the corridor.

West sprinted after Fetch, soon reaching the door held open by the bucket of water. Fetch was doing well, already at the top of the stairwell. Taking the stairs two at a time, West glanced back to see that this presented no obstacle to the rats. The first of them was soon leaping up after him. Their speed was incredible.

'Go! Go!' he yelled, catching up with Fetch and grateful that he could now see without the lantern-light. Running side by side, they ducked under a low pipe, bolting for the stairwell that would take them out of the basement. About halfway up the second set of steps, Fetch stumbled. West had the lantern in one hand and the sixer in the other, so couldn't help him. By the time Fetch was moving again, West felt the closest of the scampering rats touch his legs and suddenly his feet went from under him. He came down on his left side, the lantern glass shattering.

Abandoning the light, he tried to get to his feet but his

left boot was trapped awkwardly between two steps. He fired a random shot downward but knew that, even if he hit one, there were plenty of others. His scrabbling left hand caught the brittle whiskers of one rat as more surrounded him. He felt claws on his legs and on his back, surprised by their power and weight. Then one of them scampered along his right arm. He threw it off but another landed on his neck, scraping his skin.

West heard himself shout, a mixture of fear and revulsion running through him. Then he felt a hand on his collar and the rats abruptly leapt off him. He turned his foot and was able to pull it clear. Free of the blinds, he let Fetch help him up and soon they were running once more through the building.

Relieved that he'd kept hold of his sixer, West glanced back and saw that only a few of the rats were still coming. Fetch was running so quickly with the heavy sack that he almost overbalanced. West returned the earlier favour by steadying him with a hand under his arm. He then took the lead, shouldering through the double doors. Suddenly they were outside and safe, panting and half-blinded by the sun.

'Thank God,' said Fetch, lowering the sack to the ground.

'Owe you one,' said West. 'How'd you get them off me?'

'Remembered that pack of meat.'

'Good thinking.' West felt a little embarrassed that he hadn't thought of it himself. He'd fought plenty of men but when those awful things had almost overwhelmed him, he had frozen.

'You're cut up a bit,' said Fetch, pointing at his neck.

'I'll be okay.'

'I wouldn't be so sure about that.'

The man was one of seven standing with their horses not far from West's mule and Fetch's pony. They looked like they'd been there some time and now walked casually forward, guns at the ready.

Leading the way was Silvera, and that wolfish face of his was smiling.

CHAPTER 6 -BLINDS

◆ ◆ ◆

West soon forgot about the scratches inflicted by the rats. He and Fetch were told to drop their guns and Silvera wasted no time in getting to work on him. He ran up to West and tried to club him on the head with a newly-acquired pistol. West parried the blow and reckoned he'd get a bit of retaliation in early. But Silvera proved himself agile enough to duck under his punch. One of his compatriots joined in, kicking West on the knee and giving Silvera an opportunity. The raider's punch caught West on the ear and sent him reeling. West landed heavily on the ground and soon found himself assailed by kicks from his nemesis and several others. He covered up as best he could but took one very hard blow to his head and another to his groin. At this last strike, he rolled over and threw up. Thankfully, this had the effect of breaking Silvera's rage and the raider actually laughed.

'Not so tough after all, eh, West? Thought you could sell me as a slave? *Me*?' With one last kick, Silvera withdrew and turned his attention to Fetch.

West's relief at being left alone soon evaporated when he saw his companion knocked to the ground. The others helped Silvera out here too, only stopping when a short but bulky man ordered it. West assumed this was Kinney, leader of the other group. Silvera told him he had no intention of stopping but Kinney insisted that it was up to Reaper to decide the pair's fate. West was glad to hear it; and glad that they weren't subject solely to Silver's desire for revenge.

He got to his knees, still feeling sick but more concerned about his head: his vision was clouded and blurred. He could, however, see that Fetch was also trying to stand; and that motivated him to get up.

'You all right?'

'Will be,' murmured Fetch.

'Not if I have anything to do with it,' said Silvera.

Kinney, meanwhile, was more interested in the contents of the sack. 'Well, well. Looks like our time up here wasn't entirely wasted.' He showed it to Silvera. 'Might persuade Reaper to go easier on you.'

Still feeling shaky, West put out his hands to retain his balance. He sucked in some long, deep breaths and was relieved when his vision began to clear.

Silvera had just claimed his gun. 'I think I'll take this.'

'We'll take it *all*,' added Kinney.

'I'll tie these assholes to my horse,' said Silvera. 'Drag 'em back to the lake.'

'That'll slow us down,' countered Kinney sternly. Despite his lack of height, he was very muscular and possessed a presence that suggested he could best Silvera with ease. 'We'll bind their hands, stick 'em on the donkey and the mule.'

Silvera didn't seem too happy about this.

West caught his eye. 'How'd you know we were here?'

Silvera seemed to enjoy telling him: 'After these fellas came and got me, Kinney here ran into an old friend of his. Used to be a raider. Name's Leon. Works for a man named Nowak. In return for a couple of bits, he had a real interesting story to tell.'

West had rarely felt so hopeless; and the irony of his reversal of fortune was not lost on him. As the raider party set off south towards their base at Spring Bay, Silvera often looked back at his prisoner with a smug grin. As promised, West and Fetch had been bound at the wrist, then put on June and Sandy. The mule was tethered to Kinney's horse, while the pony was tied to another man's mount. Not only that, a rider had been stationed behind each prisoner. There was no possibility of escape.

Somehow West had lost his hat and the bright sun did little to ease a pounding headache. He was at least relieved that his head had stopped bleeding. Riding for hour after hour only exacerbated his aching groin, however, and as the afternoon wore on, he grew so weary that he almost fell out of the saddle. On more than one occasion, he glanced over at poor Fetch, who looked to be in no better condition. His right eye had swollen up badly and there was a livid red cut across his forehead. West couldn't avoid a feeling of guilt that he'd landed them both in such trouble. What hurt almost as much was the knowledge that all the effort they'd put into claiming the lights and batteries had benefited only his enemy.

West had once heard a woman use the expression "count your blessings". He reckoned there were only a couple to count but they did provide him with a little hope. The first was that Silvera hadn't killed him on sight. The second was that he and Fetch hadn't been hurt too badly. That meant that if there was a chance at escape, they'd be able to take it.

From listening in to the raiders, he knew they were aiming to reach this Spring Bay place by the next morning. That night, the raiders camped out close to the road they'd ridden along for much of the day. Unlike West and other lone travellers, the raiders clearly felt they had little to fear. Upon the road, they'd passed only a couple of small groups, who were clearly relieved when Reaper's Boys rode past and left them alone.

West was hugely relieved when he was allowed down off June and he guessed the poor mule was glad too. Kinney instructed that he and Fetch be given some water and taken to the hollow that the raiders had chosen for their latrine. The pair were then told to sit back to back and tied together. While Kinney and Silvera examined the lights and batteries, the remaining raiders gathered firewood and prepared food.

'Hanging in there, Mr. West?' asked Fetch.

'Yes. You?'

'I'm all right. What about that head of yours? Lot of blood.'

'Head wounds bleed a lot. I'm fine. And I told you – just West.'

'Right. I realised today that I don't know much about you. You don't say anything about yourself. You got a family?'

West didn't reply.

The truth – the crushing, unavoidable truth – was that he had woken up in a field two years ago and could remember nothing before that. He didn't know his true name, anything about his family, anything about the earlier years of his life. And he couldn't tell Fetch what he didn't know.

So he said nothing; and it was Fetch who eventually spoke again. 'My picture. I've got it here in my pocket.'

They had earlier both been searched thoroughly: West had lost the knife in his boot and Silvera's nifty blade-ring, which would have come in extremely handy at this particular moment.

Fetch continued: 'When they kill me, ask them to leave the picture where it is, would you? I want it close to me.'

'They're not going to kill you.'

'They will. I don't know about you but I went against the Boys and Reaper takes things like that to heart. Can't say I blame him. It's a shame. It was nice to be...'

His voice drifted off.

'Free?'

'Yes,' replied Fetch, his voice cracked by emotion. 'Free.'

West knew it was a strange word to reflect on, given their present situation.

His relief at the end of the journey didn't last long. Now he was still, all the various injuries he'd sustained that day seemed to hurt all the more. He had scratches on his hands and neck from the rats and who knew what diseases they might carry? The head wound still ached though that sick feeling caused by the blow to his groin had at least faded.

The trials of the day were not over. Some of the flashlights and batteries didn't work but most did and soon Silvera, Kinney and the others were shining them all over, whooping and cheering at the beams of yellow light that sliced through the darkness. West assumed raiders must have seen such devices before but their jubilant reaction confirmed to him just how valuable the find was. Silvera had some fun shining his flashlight in the captives' eyes but then moved on to swigging from a bottle. He invited his fellow raiders to join him in celebration but Kinney remarked that Silvera hadn't done much to earn it, having only been saved from slavery by he and his men.

As the evening wore on, the men cooked up some meat. West was so despondent that he didn't even feel hungry. Later, as most of the raiders settled down for sleep, Silvera kept drinking, his bottle fixed in his grasp. With the camp almost quiet, he walked off to relieve himself then came back and stood over West.

'It's good in a way,' he said, words slurring. 'A quick death would have been too easy. You'll suffer a good deal more before you die, West. And I'll enjoy every minute of it.'

Reaper had chosen an isolated location for his base. Led by Silvera and Kinney, the group negotiated the spur of a steep, grey mountain then followed a winding trail down to the shore. The lake was wide, a couple of miles at least by West's estimate. From a distance, the waters appeared blue but, when closer, he saw that the lake was as cloudy as most in the Wasteland. Like a healthy tree, clean water was the exception rather than the rule.

The riders rounded the lake, crossing beaches of pebbles and little streams running down from the slopes above. Blinking under the bright morning sun, West noted a fish jump high out of the still water before splashing back down. It seemed odd to him that on such a lovely day he might meet his death.

Having overheard the raiders talk, he knew that Reaper's base was called The Lodge and before long the building came into view. It had been constructed at the centre of what was presumably Spring Bay. As Fetch had suggested, it did look like a former hotel. It was a very large timber building with various sections all topped by sloped roofs. An area at the rear had been cleared to corral dozens of horses. Two slender piers ran out into the lake and a number of small boats were moored at each.

Around a quarter of a mile from the Lodge, they encountered the first guards. The path ran between two enormous boulders and standing atop each of them was a raider. The men glowered down, both armed with long barrelled rifles. One of the guards fixed his gaze on Silvera.

'You on your own? Oh no, there's Fetch. Looks like there's a story to be told.'

As they rode between the boulders, Silvera glanced back at the prisoners. 'There is at that.'

West hadn't expected there to be so many of them. By the time they reached The Lodge, he'd counted at least fifty of Reaper's Boys. Every last man bore the extravagant neck tattoos and many of the curling shapes extended onto their faces. Every one of them had a gun. While a few stood around in small groups, most were at work. On the beach side of the path, a couple of them were supervising a group of slaves bringing in nets. West was surprised to see how much fish came out of the lake. On the other side of the path, land had been cleared for several fields of crops where more slaves laboured. And closer to the hotel were half a dozen roofed workshops. Here slaves appeared to be repairing guns and pulling apart salvaged items. One sprawling workshop contained cars and motorbikes. Engines and other parts had been removed and were being worked on. Most of those they passed paid little attention to the new prisoners, though Silvera and Kinney exchanged a few remarks with their compatriots.

Eventually they reached the rear of The Lodge and West saw that the building was very clean and well maintained. Supervised slaves were making some kind of repair to a window and others were sweeping the ground. Reaper clearly liked to keep his headquarters orderly. Away to the left was the corral West had seen earlier and there a young stallion was being broken in. Once they'd all dismounted, Kinney's men led the horses in that direction.

Fetch stood with his head bowed, as if not wishing to make eye contact with anyone. After a minute or so, a short man with lank, greasy hair came out of the hotel's rear entrance, which was in the middle of a long porch. He hurried down the stairs and ran his eyes over the new arrivals. He wore a bulky leather jacket and a high, circular hat, as if trying to make himself appear taller.

'How we doing, boys?' He looked down at the saddlebags and the provisions removed from the horses. 'I ain't seeing a lot of treasure.' When he glanced at Fetch, the frown on his lined face deepened. West wondered if this was Reaper but he didn't seem like a leader.

'Not a lot,' said Kinney. 'But what we've got is quality.' He nudged a nearby sack with his boot. 'Lights. And batteries.'

'Is that right? And what about these two?'

Silvera spoke up: 'Antonio, it's probably best if I speak to the boss directly. It's a long story. Complicated.'

West noticed Kinney roll his eyes and the man called Antonio seemed equally unimpressed.

'Why is that you still think you're special, Silvera? Even if you ever were – and you weren't – you definitely ain't these days. So how about you tell me what happened and I'll talk to the boss. That's how he likes things done. If he had to listen to every tale of every raider that works for him, he wouldn't have time for more important things.'

From a higher floor of the hotel came a women's laugh.

Kinney grunted with amusement at the timing.

'Wait here,' said Antonio before returning back up the stairs.

Fetch was still gazing at the ground, his jaw trembling. West couldn't think of anything that would make the man feel better. He glanced at the sack and shook his head, reflecting that the risk had *definitely* not been worth the reward.

Silvera came up behind him and hissed over his shoulder: 'Whatever the boss says, I'll make sure you get what's coming, West. Count on it.'

'Still think you're something special?'

Silvera hammered his fist into West's back, sending him staggering forward. With his hands bound in front of him he almost lost his balance but just about stayed on his feet.

'Cool down,' advised Kinney. 'You don't want to make the boss any madder than he's going to be.'

A couple of minutes later, Antonio reappeared at the top of the stairs. 'Bring Fetch. The other one goes to the pool for now.'

Silvera grabbed West by the shoulder and turned him around, apparently now a lot less keen to see Reaper.

'No,' snapped Antonio. 'You bring Fetch, Silvera. Boss wants to talk to you right now.'

West took a little satisfaction from the fear that washed over his foe's face. Silvera untied both prisoners then guided Fetch up the stairs.

'Hang in there,' was all West could get out before Kinney took charge of him and walked him away.

They passed under a wooden arch covered with climbing plants then reached an open area behind the hotel. Several more vehicles had been stored here and a group of raiders were taking turns with what looked to West like a sniper rifle. The men were shooting at a brightly coloured railroad sign. West had never seen anyone with so much spare ammunition that they could afford to practice.

Kinney pushed him to the right and, once past the vehicles, they reached an empty swimming pool. The tiles were cracked and discoloured and weeds had taken root at the bottom. The shallow end had been bricked off and the deep end built up by at least five feet. One small hole in this surrounding wall was covered by a metal door which Kinney now unbolted and opened.

The raider drew his quick and aimed it at West. 'See the ladder over there. Put it in and climb down.'

West did just that and soon found himself standing at the base of the pool. The wall looked even higher from inside. He didn't have to be told to pass the ladder back up.

'Any chance I could have some water?'

Kinney grunted with amusement again as he recovered the ladder and shut the door. The metal was flush with the brick; there was no hand hold and therefore no chance of escape.

From the bottom of the pool, West could see little but the sky. He heard Kinney walk away and could also make out a distant metallic clanging. He was stiff from the ride and decided to walk around his prison, partly to take his mind of his raging thirst. Every so often, he would hear the low report of the sniper rifle and either a cheer or a groan from the raiders.

West's spirits rose considerably when he saw Fetch. He had been sitting against the edge of the pool but jumped to his feet when the door was unbolted and the ladder put down. Kinney and another man were with Fetch, who descended the ladder swiftly. West was very relieved to see that he looked unharmed. Once the ladder was back up and the door shut, Kinney threw down two plastic bottles full of water and a little metal box.

Before saying anything, West unscrewed the top of the bottle and glugged down a third of the contents. He was also ravenously hungry and tore open the box. Inside were some cuts of meat, slices of bread and some dried apple.

'Pretty good service at this hotel,' he said with a grin. He stuffed some of the meat into his mouth and then offered it to Fetch. Only then did he realise that the man hadn't even taken a sip of his water. There wasn't a mark on him and yet his face betrayed unalloyed fear.

'Kinney called it a last supper.'

West stopped chewing. 'What?'

'I don't know what Reaper will do to you but I'm to be executed tomorrow. As I was with him a long time, I thought he might go easy and hang me.'

'Go easy?'

'Traitors don't get an easy death. I'm getting the drag.'

West put a hand on Fetch's shoulder. 'What ...what's that?'

'Reaper will go first. They take it in turns, tie a man to their horse, drag him up and down the road until ...until it's over.'

West couldn't bring himself to eat the food, though he'd almost finished the water by the time Fetch spoke again.

'I didn't dare mention my picture. I thought he might burn it or something.'

Once again, West didn't know what to say.

Fetch continued: 'He was interested in Factory Row – that we got the stash out of there. And he's angry with Silvera. I think that might go in your favour.'

'You mean he'll just hang me?'

West hadn't expected a smile and he didn't get one. He lowered his voice, on the off-chance that any of the raiders above were still listening. 'We'll get out of here.'

Fetch looked around the pool. 'A couple of people escaped before. That's why they added the wall. There's no way out of here.'

'I'll think of something.'

Fetch gazed up at the cloudless sky and shook his head.

West grasped his arm. 'I promise you. I'll think of something.'

To his surprise, West actually dozed off. Fetch had kindly used a little water to clean his head wound and reported that it would be all right without stitches. Fetch's eye was still badly swollen but he said it wasn't overly painful. West reckoned he had plenty else to worry about.

It was late afternoon when Kinney returned and put down the ladder.

'Let me guess,' said West. 'Now I've sampled the pool, you want to show me the hotel's other facilities.'

'Just get up here, numb nuts.'

West winked at Fetch but the man simply watched him, once more chewing the inside of his mouth.

Once out of the pool-prison, West found that Kinney was accompanied by a woman. She had spiky blonde hair, narrow features, and a scar down one cheek. The pair of them took an arm each and escorted him towards the hotel. West shivered at the spring cold; the raiders had never returned his coat or hat.

'So, you killed Redwood, huh?' said the woman, exposing a mouth full of sharp, yellow teeth.

West shrugged as they took him up the steps.

'Redwood and Thomson,' replied Kinney. 'Then he sold Silvera to a slave trader.'

The woman found this hilarious and didn't recover herself until they were up another set of stairs.

'Weren't all that funny,' remarked Kinney. 'Especially as we had to go and rescue him.'

'Word has it you got some batts, though? Right?'

Kinney sighed as they led West along a wide corridor. There were framed pictures on the wall, several showing the hotel in the past, before the Cataclysm. West was always interested – and bemused – to see that everyone in the past always seemed happy. Hardly anyone in the Wasteland was happy.

'You know your trouble, Lindsey?' said Kinney.

'I'm too good-looking?'

West had seen enough of her to establish that this was not true.

'You talk too much.' Kinney stopped outside a set of broad wooden doors and knocked.

'Yep!' came the loud reply.

Lindsey seemed to know her duty was over and she walked back along the corridor.

Kinney shouldered the doors open and led West inside by the arm. West found himself in what had presumably once been a large bedroom. To his left, two pretty young women in long, flowing gowns were playing cards at a table. West had only ever seen a few women wearing makeup and, as ever, he was amazed by what a difference it made. They were sitting on delicate wooden chairs. The third card player was sitting on a sturdy bench that nonetheless groaned when he turned to glance at West.

The man was immensely broad and tall, with long, straight black hair. He wore a woven waistcoat decorated with images of animals. The pale green eyes within his weathered face observed West for only a moment before he turned back to his game.

'I'm guessing you've heard of Rock?'

West's attention was drawn to the right. Sitting there behind an immense desk was a man in his forties. He was wearing a black suit with thin white stripes. His hair was short and grey and narrowed to a V. He wore a pair of spectacles with one clear lens and one black.

On the desk was a huge map that had been taped together from smaller maps. Pins identified certain sites and from them lengths of twine led out to the edges of the desk and piles of paper, some several inches high.

'I have,' said West. 'And you must be Reaper.'

'Hope you're enjoying the pool.'

'Delightful.'

'Shame about Fetch.' Reaper pushed his chair away from the desk and casually plucked something from his sleeve. 'Dumb son of a bitch but I always liked him. Been in the Bay longer than most.'

'I don't see that he's done much wrong.'

Reaper fixed West with a cold, one-eyed glare. 'You'd be well advised to think about saving your own skin. I got two men dead. You owe me.'

'You've got the batteries and lights. Silvera and his pals ambushed me. What was I supposed to do? Hand everything over and wish them a good day.'

'Dolores.' Reaper tapped an empty glass sitting on the edge of his desk.

One of the young women stood and fetched a bottle from

a nearby cabinet. She poured her master a generous measure of what looked like whiskey. He winked at her and watched her walk away.

When he turned back to West, his expression had changed. 'Most people *would* have given up. But judging by what I've heard, you're not most people. Seems like you're good at getting in places and taking what you can. Seems like maybe you're a bit of a raider.'

West was genuinely offended by that. 'I don't take what's not mine. Only what I find.'

'How noble. I suppose I did get a bit back for my losses but you tried to sell one of my men into slavery. Now that's just rude – even if it was Silvera.'

West felt that one sharp eye still appraising him.

'Can you read?'

West nodded.

'I'm getting there but it's slow,' replied Reaper. 'They say it's easier to learn when you're young. I've got a couple of bright sparks – present company excepted – but only five readers.'

If Kinney was offended by the remark, he didn't show it.

'Trouble is,' continued Reaper, 'readers don't tend to be the bravest souls. I got some brains, and some brawn, but not too many that you'd called ...enterprising. Seems to me maybe you could be useful.'

West shrugged. 'Beats staying in the pool, I guess.'

Reaper stood up and sipped his drink. 'Come and have a look at this map.'

Rock cleared his throat and stood. Despite Reaper's instruction, West didn't move as the big bodyguard approached him. The floor actually shook with each footstep. Rock put one great paw on West's neck then began patting him down.

'So sweet,' remarked Reaper. 'Always looking after me. You know his people live not far from here. They've gone back to their old ways. Some of them even think the Cataclysm was a punishment for those who took their land all those years ago. I'm assuming you know a bit of history too?'

'I've heard about that bit.'

Rock had finished his check and now shoved West forward, hard enough that he almost fell over. Now close to Reaper, West could smell his aftershave.

'I guess he doesn't know his own strength. I've seen him kill a man with one punch. Don't know if he can't speak or just doesn't want to. Loves the cards though. And the girls.'

'You need me, boss?' asked Kinney

Reaper shook his head and spoke as his underling reached the door. 'Find out if the Cutters are back yet.'

West approached the map and looked down at it. He'd seen a few in his time and immediately gathered that this represented a large area. Reaper sipped more of his whiskey then put it down and leaned forward, both hands planted on the map.

'I've been doing this a while. Things come to me. People. Weapons. Information. Whatever it was that screwed up the world, it hit the surface. Wiped out all the cities and just about most else. But there's a world *under* the surface.'

West knew that.

Though he remembered little else, he could always recall the place under the ground. All he knew was that he'd spent time there – a lot of time.

'And I'm not talking about basements,' continued Reaper. 'They called them bunkers. Big places, built well, some of them deep, deep under. I met this old timer who was obsessed with finding them but he was on his way out and the best he could give me were these locations.'

Reaper gestured towards one of the pins. 'They're not precise. I've had my men check out the areas but we've not got inside one yet.' Reaper put his finger on a green-topped pin which was situated close to a river.

'This here is called Twickstan Bridge. Heard of it?'

West shook his head.

'About sixty miles from here. The old timer reckoned he'd got close in this area. He reckoned there was a stash of weapons in there. And he meant military grade stuff. Heavy shit.

Whenever I've had the time and the man-power I've had a good look for it but nothing yet. Maybe a fresh pair of eyes can find the place for me. You do that, West, you can consider our debt settled.'

West didn't mind the sound of that at all. He was as curious as Reaper about these underground bases, or 'bunkers' as he called them. And while he had no doubt that the raider would be providing him with an escort, getting away from Spring Bay greatly improved his chances of survival. But there was one problem.

'What about Fetch?'

Reaper shook his head. 'That's not up for discussion. Two separate matters.'

'Not for me.'

'Alternatively, I could just have you both killed.'

West chose his next words carefully: 'You're a good leader. Any fool can see that. So, I know you understand the idea of motivation.'

Reaper grimaced but let West continue.

'Right now, I'm motivated. I'll do my best to get you what you want. If I do, we both go free. Everybody wins. You kill Fetch – maybe I'll do what you ask because you'll make me. But you think I'm going to give it my best? Risk my life for the man who killed my friend?'

'Your friend. How adorable.'

West didn't care what Reaper thought about that. The truth was that Fetch had got him out of a mess in that factory.

He made sure he kept his tone calm, logical, reasonable: 'You think you need to kill him to make a point, follow your rules, make an example. I get that. But don't *you* make the rules?'

Reaper looked annoyed at that but still didn't interrupt.

'I have a deal,' added West. 'I'll find the bunker in ten days. I want Fetch to come with me. If I don't find it, you can kill us both. Put on a real big show if you like.'

Reaper sniffed noisily then straightened up and swigged more of his whiskey.

'Glad to see I was right about you, West. You are pretty smart. I'll take that deal. But I'm going to need insurance. You're going to have some company.'

CHAPTER 7 -SPRING BAY

◆◆◆

Once back in the pool-prison, the first thing West did was tell Fetch the good news. Fetch seemed greatly relieved but as the chilly hours of darkness wore on, they both became silent. West began to wonder if Reaper had changed his mind. They lay there in the cold, their breath visible, gazing up at the stars, waiting for the sun. It was one of the longest nights West had endured and he was thankful for the arrival of dawn. Some time later, the door clanged open and Kinney threw down two more bottles of water.

'You must be one persuasive son of a bitch, West,' said the muscular raider as he lowered the ladder. 'In fact, I'd be tempted to say you're both very lucky sons of bitches. But then I saw who you'll be travelling with.'

While Kinney chuckled to himself, West and Fetch downed half their water then climbed the ladder. Kinney was accompanied by Lindsey again, and this time she had a crossbow over her shoulder.

She smiled at West. 'You're handsome.'

Kinney shot her a glare. 'Keep your ugly mouth shut.'

Lindsey seemed to think about snapping back at him but held her tongue. The two raiders pushed their charges towards The Lodge. West felt a brief surge of happiness when he saw June and Sandy tied to a rail outside. He was surprised to see that most of their supplies had been returned, along with his black coat and hat. A young man arrived with a tall grey horse that had been saddled. As he tied it to the rail, Fetch hurried over to Sandy and rubbed her snout. West gave June a pat.

'Where's Silvera?' he asked.

'The boss sent him off on some errand,' replied Kinney.

'I guess he didn't want him around to see you go free,' added Lindsey.

'Free's not exactly how I would describe it,' said Kinney, a smug grin on his face.

Four horses trotted in from the track that led past the hotel to the corral. Reaper was on one of them, still wearing his distinctive glasses. Sitting in a neat holster on his saddle was a double-barrelled sawn-off shotgun. Beside him, riding one of the largest horses West had ever seen, was the bodyguard, Rock. His grizzled face remained as impassive as the day before.

Reaper reined in and looked down at West. 'All ready?'

'I don't suppose I could get my gun back too?'

Reaper grinned. 'You suppose correctly. Allow me to introduce the Cutters – Theodore and Thea.'

The pair trotted their horses forward and halted beside Reaper. Both wore sleeveless green vests stuffed with weapons including quicks, grenades, throwing knives and several other blades. They were without doubt brother and sister, both slightly built and wearing wide-brimmed hats similar to West's. They might even have been twins with their defined cheek bones and beady, deep-set eyes. Theodore was missing two fingers on one hand. Thea's neck was heavily scarred. West had no doubt that they would watch him like hawks and kill him without hesitation.

'They seem like a lovely family,' he said, hoping to appear fearless.

No one dared laugh at this but their leader leaned forward, that one eye sparkling. 'Cutter isn't their name, West. It's what they do.'

Before they left, Reaper handed over a smaller scale map, with crosses marking possible locations for the bunker. He also reminded West that he had precisely ten days to return to Spring Bay; and that he was expected not only to locate the bunker but get inside.

By then, West had realised that the Cutters communicated in a language he didn't know but soon learned was French. According to Kinney, the pair had grown up 'north of the border'. As if it wouldn't be bad enough having the brother and sister watch him, they could communicate without giving a single thing away.

The route to Twickstan Bridge was to the north. Passing the corral and the piers, the four riders followed the path around the lake's edge. Though glad to be away from Spring Bay, West had little doubt that he was now dealing with a different level of opponent. The Cutters communicated infrequently but there was something about those small, dark eyes that made West put all thoughts of escape to the back of his mind. If an opportunity arose, so be it, but for now he was satisfied to get a measure of the pair. He thought it naïve to assume that success would ensure his freedom from Reaper but he had found the man more reasonable than expected. There were other dangers at the Bay. Silvera aside, some of the raiders had cursed and spat at Fetch as they left. Even if they somehow got Reaper what he wanted, could either of them really expect to escape the place alive for a second time?

About a mile from The Lodge, they came to a wooden bridge built over a spur of rock that would have been impassable for the horses. The spare horse had been allocated to West. It didn't mind being roped to June and the mule trailed along as dutifully as ever.

Once over the bridge, the path met a fork and Theodore took the left. Before long, they were climbing up a steep, zigzagging trail that eventually took them through a pass. On either side were snow-topped mountains and twice West saw eagles soaring high above. The air was notably thinner and colder here but – unlike the previous night – he now had his coat to warm him.

He found himself third in line behind Theodore and Fetch. Bringing up the rear, Thea never got too close or too distant. For much of the path, there was thick forest on one or both sides. West reckoned he could dismount and make it to cover in about ten seconds. He also reckoned that if he did make it, he'd do so with a bullet or a blade in his back.

Around noon they stopped to rest the horses and eat. Ever-efficient, the Cutters took it in turns to watch their charges. West exchanged a couple of words with Fetch but neither could find much more to say while being monitored so closely.

They were about to set off once more when they heard a noise in the trees. Already some distance from the pass and now heading downward, they'd stopped in a small clearing close to the path. Charging towards them was a fully grown stag, covering the ground with remarkable speed.

The Cutters drew their guns. While Thea ordered West and Fetch to freeze, her brother advanced, ready with his quick. A shot rang out from the trees behind the stag. This didn't affect the creature but when it saw the humans, it skirted the clearing and bolted away across the path. A second shot came so close to Theodore that he took cover, spitting curses.

Seconds later, West spied a man coming through the trees, a rifle in both hands. By now the stag was long gone. Shaking his head as he reached the clearing, he lowered the gun when he saw the others.

'Sorry about that. Didn't see you there.'

Theodore stepped out from behind the tree, gun trained on the new arrival.

The man – who was not young – threw the rifle onto his shoulder and put up both his hands. He was out of breath.

'Son, I'm not looking for a fight.'

Theodore lowered his quick. 'You know where you are?'

The hunter looked at the other three. 'I'm not sure what you mean.'

'This is Reaper's land. You can't hunt here. You can't even come here.'

'I …er …I thought that was on the *other* side of the mountains. I …guess I made a mistake. I'll get going.'

The hunter forced a smile, turned and walked away.

The Cutters exchanged a couple of quiet comments in French. West half-expected Theodore to pull out a knife and throw it. He didn't move.

His sister did. The narrow throwing blade flew past West and stuck between the hunter's shoulders with a sickening thud.

'What are you doing?' thundered West.

The hunter staggered, his gun falling to the ground. Theodore's knife landed just below his sister's. Even through the horror, West acknowledged a remarkable display of skill.

The hunter took three more shaky steps then fell into a patch of fern. Theodore turned and gave his sister a satisfied smile. He then walked towards the hunter, presumably to recover their knives.

'Why?' whispered Fetch.

'Target practice,' said Thea in her heavily-accented English. 'You want to be next?'

*

West had seen his share of suffering and death in the Wasteland. He'd seen people fight over land and possessions, even over food. But at least those fights had been *about something*. The Cutters had killed the hunter on a whim. Because it amused them. Because they liked to throw their knives. Perhaps even because they wanted to show off; leave West and Fetch in no doubt about who they were dealing with.

As they rode on, leaving their victim lying there alone in the trees, the random nature of the encounter occupied West's mind. *Why hadn't the stag run in a different direction? Why hadn't the man hunted in some other area? Why there? Why today? And why hadn't he simply fled as soon as he saw them?* West reckoned he should have warned him; he could have done that at least. So much was unpredictable in the Wasteland and there was still so much he didn't know. That was what made it so dangerous.

The four riders reached level ground in late morning. It seemed that Reaper's enforcers had memorised the route because they didn't ask to see West's map. They picked up a well-used trail around midday and spent most of the ensuing hours on a broad road. One section contained more wrecks than West had ever seen: hundreds of them, a couple containing skeletons. There was a brief delay after Thea's mount stepped on some glass but the horse recovered itself and they continued on at a steady pace. West and Fetch barely exchanged a word, even when dusk came and the Cutters halted at a ruined gas station.

The siblings made West and Fetch prepare dinner, both smoking cigars while they rested. They seemed to enjoy doling out orders and – after their captives had tidied up – Theodore retrieved some chains and locks from a saddlebag. West and Fetch were allowed bedrolls and blankets but each was chained by an ankle manacle to a fuel pump. Having locked these, the Cutters retired to a warmer, more sheltered spot within the station itself.

West was glad that he and Fetch had the blankets for it was a cold, windy night. The two of them lay there only a couple of feet apart, the ageing panels of the station roof shaking and rattling above. A wolf howled in the distance. West had lost count of the times he'd heard wolves howling at night. Yet he had only seen one once.

'That man,' said Fetch after a time. 'Someone will be waiting for him. Wife maybe. Children.'

The same thought had struck West many times. Imagining the now cold body lying in the clearing, he shook his head, desperate to dispel the image.

'What else do you know about them?'

'Not a lot,' replied Fetch. 'They came to work for Reaper a couple of years back. One of his old chiefs, a guy called Dietrich, decided he'd disappear with some of Reaper's guns. Unfortunately for Dietrich, him and his friends ran into the Cutters. When they realized they had Reaper's stuff, they offered to sell it back to him. That's how they met.'

'What about Dietrich?'

'The Cutters killed his four men. Kept Dietrich prisoner. There are ...stories.'

'About what?'

'Dietrich was tough. Apparently, he put up quite a fight. He's the one that gave Thea those scars on her neck. So, they had their fun with him. By the time they gave him back to Reaper, he had no fingers and no toes.'

They reached Twickstan Bridge in late afternoon. The structure was made up of four great arches that crossed a dried-up river bed. Between those broad arches was a lattice of metal-work that gave the bridge a certain elegance. Despite the rust and wear, it looked very solid, as if defying the elements, the years and the Cataclysm.

They had approached along a road that passed one of the larger craters West had seen: a deep bowl of dark earth several miles across. Nothing grew within it and the countryside around it was just as lifeless and bleak. Passing the edge, West also spied the remains of several helicopters, another type of flying craft he had seen in pictures. In the closest of them, the glass had fallen out, revealing two skeletons clad in green uniforms and metal helmets.

'So now what?' said Theodore, easing down off his horse.

West dismounted with the others and took out the map. 'There are five potential sites already marked on here – three on the east side of the bridge, two on the west. All within a mile.'

Theodore's beady eyes turned to his sister and he spoke to her in French. After a short conversation, he approached West and examined the map. 'We're not following you around all day playing hunt the hole. We'll stay on the bridge with this idiot while you do the legwork. Just don't go out of our sight. If you find anything, shout.'

'Bring the horse and mule,' Thea told Fetch.

Fetch gave a nod to West and followed the raiders towards the bridge.

He had already examined the map and was confused by the fact that Reaper had identified five points but apparently made no progress. The reason for this became obvious fairly soon. After half an hour of searching through knee-high grass on the east side, West found a circular hole four feet wide. The hole was almost full of water, the interior made of some tough, plastic tubing. Unable to uncover anything else of use, West moved to the next location, which was about half a mile away. This took him further from the bridge but he made sure the Cutters could see him the whole time. They had stationed themselves in the middle of the structure and Theodore was standing at the rail, watching through binoculars.

The second hole was also almost full of water and it looked identical. Close by was a hatch that had evidently been forced off. After scrubbing some mud away, West spied writing printed on the metal: *SOUTHERN DISTRICT WATER AUTHORITY*. This meant nothing to him but the third hole gave him another clue. It had also been opened and was again flooded. However, just above the water was the top of a narrow slot. West stretched down and found that slot continued as far as he could reach.

Checking the surrounding area, he initially found nothing. But then he widened the search and it soon paid off. Half buried in mud was a long tube made of plastic and metal. West hauled it out and took it down to the river's edge. Here he cleaned it up, revealing numbers etched on the plastic part of the tube. It was clearly some sort of measuring device. He wasn't surprised when he took it back to the hole and found that it fitted the slot perfectly.

He took the tube with him to the bridge.

'Well?' asked Theodore impatiently.

'I think they're just for measuring the water height or something. We can check the two on the other side but I'd bet they're the same. There could be hundreds of them and I doubt any of them go into a bunker.'

'So now what?' demanded Thea, eyes hard in her angular

face.

'We need local information.' West held up the map. 'Twickstan isn't far.'

If not for the boy, they'd never have known what they were heading into. Now riding once more, they had passed several properties, all of which seemed unoccupied. This was nothing unusual in the Wasteland, except that they also saw several neat fields of crops that were obviously being cared for. Later they saw a work party on two carts but these people refused to communicate and fled towards Twickstan.

The town itself – a church spire and a water tower, at least – were already in view when they saw the boy. He walked out from behind a hedgerow and raised a hand. He couldn't have been more than fourteen-years-old and he took off a battered cap to reveal a mop of blonde hair. On his back was a heavy-looking pack.

As usual, Theodore was riding out front and he didn't stop.

West spoke up. 'Hey, he might be able to tell us something.'

'We're almost there,' replied the enforcer.

'There's something weird going on here. Can't we just hear what he has to say?'

Theodore rolled his eyes but wheeled his horse and trotted it back to join his sister, muttering in French.

'Hey there. I'm West. What's your name?'

The boy seemed glad that someone was being friendly to him. 'Avery. Mister West, can you tell me how far the next town is?'

'On the other side of the bridge? We passed a place called Dixon – that's about fifteen miles. Aren't you local?'

'Lived here all my life.'

Thea said something derogatory to her brother in French.

Avery continued his explanation. 'I want to leave. Had enough of her.'

West dismounted. Keeping hold of his reins, he approached the boy, trying to seem friendly.

'Enough of *who*?'

'You won't tell her?'

'I don't even know who you're talking about. Listen, we're strangers around here. We'd like some information. We can trade food for it.' West glanced at Theo, who sighed then nodded.

West walked back to June and reached into one of the saddlebags. The pork had been nabbed by the raiders but all the dried fruit was still there. West placed some in a little bag and gave it to Avery. 'I'll give you the same amount again if you answer our questions.'

'All right, Mister West. But you never saw me, right?'

'Right.'

The boy then shut his eyes, clasped his hands together and whispered to himself.

Thea again said something to her brother.

'So,' said West. 'Tell me about *her*.'

'Messenger. She's the boss around here. But I've had enough. Had enough of The Book, had enough of all the rules.'

'What book is that?'

Avery looked warily up and down the road, clearly concerned about being spotted.

'It's all about sins and sinners. If you do a lot of sin, Messenger will punish you. That's God's work, so she says.'

'Messenger is the boss in Twickstan?'

'Anyone that doesn't agree with her is a sinner. That's what she says, anyway. But my dad didn't like her so he left. Now I'm leaving too. Maybe I'll find him.'

'Avery, I'm interested in the area close to the bridge but there doesn't seem to be anyone living there.'

'Old Mrs. Burgess used to live there. Her family owned all that land. But Messenger makes everyone live in Twickstan – so she can watch us.'

'You've never been to Dixon?'

Avery brushed his unruly hair out of his eyes. 'No one's allowed to leave.'

'How many people are there in Twickstan?'

'About a hundred, I think.'

'And how does Messenger feel about strangers?'

'That depends on whether you're sinners or not. She'll take your guns – that's for sure. No guns are allowed in Twickstan.'

'No weapons?'

'Her people have weapons. But guns aren't allowed. She says guns are sinful.'

'Do you know where Mrs. Burgess lives now?'

'Messenger's got all the women living in the theatre. The men live in the town hall. That's how she likes it – everyone together.'

'Does Messenger ever make deals? If I gave her something, do you think she'd let me talk to Mrs. Burgess?'

Avery shrugged. 'Don't know. She's moody. If you catch her on the wrong day, she'll likely call you a sinner and go crazy on you.'

'Go crazy?'

'Get her people to beat you. That's what she does to sinners – helps them see the light, so she says. Robert Calder touched The Book last week without her permission. She had him beaten.'

'So, it's very precious to her?' said West, a thought already forming in his mind. This wasn't the first time he'd heard of The Book.

'Yes, sir. She said that God himself sent a rainbow to direct her to special place, a holy place. When she got there, she found The Book and that's where her path to the light began.'

'But there are other copies of the book?'

'No. Copying isn't allowed. The Book was given by the Lord to Messenger, not to anyone else.' Avery looked at the Cutters then back towards his home. 'You *definitely* won't tell her you found me, will you?'

'No. I promise.'

Avery took a deep, long breath. 'I guess I better keep moving. Someone will notice I'm gone before long.'

West returned to the saddlebag and retrieved the second half of the fruit. Avery took it with a grateful smile. 'Much obliged, Mr. West.'

West supposed he should have advised the boy to return to town but it sounded like he'd made up his mind. He also couldn't afford to compromise his own mission.

'Likewise, Avery. Be very careful.'

The lad put his cap back on, packed his newly-acquired food then set off towards the bridge.

'So, what now, West?' asked Thea.

'Can I suggest we get out of sight while we discuss it?'

The Cutters exchanged a few comments then silently guided their horses off the road. It was early evening and the sky was already darkening. West and Fetch followed the raiders down a slope and behind an old shack.

'They've got no guns,' said Thea. 'Let's go in, grab this Messenger, get the info we need and get out.'

Theo was evidently the smarter of the two. 'That won't work. There's a hundred of them, probably all loyal.'

'Not only that,' said West. 'We need to be on good terms. Even assuming I can get some information, I may need to search this area for several days.'

'You have an idea?' asked Theo.

'Going in with guns won't work. But I don't expect you two to leave your weapons here. I can go in alone tomorrow morning. Whatever happens, I'll come back before dusk, hopefully with what I need.'

'No chance,' said Theo. 'I'm not letting you out of our sight.'

'You can keep Fetch.'

'No. Thea stays with Fetch. I'll come in with you.' With a sly grin, Theodore withdrew his smallest blade from the sheathe on his vest. 'I don't need a gun.'

CHAPTER 8 - TWICKSTAN BRIDGE

◆ ◆ ◆

West and Theodore walked down the middle of the road and into Twickstan. West had seldom felt more nervous and he could feel sweat forming under his arms and trickling down his flanks. As if the unusual prospect of a town ruled by some religious dictator wasn't enough, he was accompanied by the murderous Cutter. At dawn, the four of them had moved up to an abandoned farmhouse on the edge of town where Thea and Fetch now waited with the mounts. West had spent a few moments looking around the house and had noted something interesting; something he reckoned he could use.

He wasn't surprised that the outskirts were unoccupied, given what he'd heard about how Messenger liked to keep control. The first locals they did see were gathered on two carts, more than twenty of them, some wielding farm tools. The driver of the first cart reined in at once and sent a young lad running back into town. He and several other men were armed with baseball bats held on straps over their shoulders and they insisted on waiting with the strangers. During this tense time, the workers observed the two but nothing was said.

Eventually three riders came out; two men and a woman, also armed with baseball bats. They weren't exactly welcoming but escorted West and Theodore into the centre of Twickstan. While the outer areas were largely neglected, the centre was clean and tidy, particularly the theatre and the town hall. Unlike most towns, there were no wrecks on the roads.

They came eventually to the church, where several crews were up on ladders and scaffolds, working on the tower. Across the arched entrance was a large wooden sign that read, '*WE ARE THE DIVINE'*.

'Is The Book kept in there?' asked West.

'Of course,' said the woman, before hurrying into the church.

The two men guided West and Theodore over to a bench. When one of them placed a hand on Theodore's shoulder, the raider shot him a glare. West tried to defuse the tension with a comment about the church but to no avail. They also then had to lie about Avery when one of the guards asked if they'd seen him. Thankfully, Messenger soon came out of the church to greet them.

'Have I sinners before me?' she asked, hands on hips as the new arrivals stood. She looked to be at least sixty years old, her greying hair so long that it almost reached her waist. Though heavily-lined, her face was somehow compelling, her eyes somehow young.

West had advised Theodore to let him do the talking and it seemed the enforcer at least had the sense to comply.

'From what I've heard about The Book, we are *all* sinners.'

'Quite so,' replied Messenger. 'Have you come to tell me your sins? For I will hear them as the representative of the Lord in this part of his world. I cannot forgive them – only He can – but I can help you find a righteous path. Do you wish to join the Divine?'

West smiled. 'That's a kind offer but we're here on other business. I'm looking for a place that I think might be close to the bridge. I would appreciate the opportunity to ask you and your people about it. In return, I can offer certain items, perhaps even money if it's of interest to you.' West knew that Reaper had given some to the Cutters for such purposes, along with batteries, medication, weapons and ammunition.

Messenger ran a finger and thumb down her chin and turned her attention to the raider. 'I expect those items include weapons. Where are yours?'

'We left them with our friends on the edge of town,' said Theodore. 'We didn't want to cause alarm.'

She turned to one of the guards. 'Search them.'

West had no idea where Theodore had concealed his knife but the guards checked them both thoroughly and found nothing.

'Guns are not permitted here,' said Messenger. 'As for pills, we trust in prayer and the Lord to protect us from illness and disease. Batteries are always useful. I suppose your friends have those too?'

'They do. If we obtain useful information here, we'll gladly give them in exchange.'

'I am rather busy this morning,' said Messenger before gesturing to those labouring at the church. 'As are we all. Idle hands are the devil's workshop.'

'My time is limited,' said West. He had made little progress so far and had only eight days before Reaper's deadline passed. 'It needn't take long.'

'I can give you a few minutes.' With that, she crossed the street. West and Theodore followed, the two guards beside them. Messenger entered what looked like a store but the interior was empty apart from a circle of chairs and an empty bookshelf. Messenger sat down and gestured for her guests to do so. West made sure he was close to her.

'This place you seek – what is it?'

'I believe it's underground. A facility built before the Cataclysm.'

Messenger cleared her throat and clasped her hands together in her lap. 'We reject the old world and everything associated with it. Ungodly debauchery is what caused the Cataclysm in the first place.'

West chose not to point out that this aversion apparently didn't extend to rejecting batteries.

'I understand. But it is of interest to our employer. None of your people need to know what we are doing. We won't be in the area for long.'

Messenger pursed her lips, as if she had made up her mind. 'I cannot be associated with sinful behaviour.'

West held up his hands. 'We have several different types of batteries. We are happy to-'

'-We have candles.'

'Food then,' said Theodore, his voice betraying his impatience. 'Just tell us what you want and we can have it here in a week.'

Messenger stared back at him. 'I believe you are a sinner. No one has met more than me and I know one when I see one.'

West's admiration for her acute judgment did not stop him pressing on with his plan. As their offers had been rejected, he had to take a risk.

'It's a shame you don't want to make a deal. It means I have to mention another matter.'

'Making threats is also a sin,' said one of the guards, slipping his baseball bat from his shoulder.

'Sins are always punished,' said the other, also brandishing his weapon.

'I made no threat,' replied West smoothly. 'There is simply something I would like to mention to Messenger. And I believe it would be in her best interest if we were to conduct that discussion in private.'

'Not a chance,' said one of the guards, a large man with a fierce glare.

West leaned forward and whispered to Messenger. 'It concerns The Book. Or rather the *books*.'

The flash of fear in her face told him his gamble had paid off.

'We will talk there.' She nodded to the rear of the room and stood up. 'Have no fear, brothers. I hear the Lord guiding me.'

Putting his hands in his pockets to reassure the guards,

West joined her at the rear wall.

Though she whispered, Messenger's eyes were angry. 'You do know that I can have you and your friends killed.'

'My employer is a raider by the name of Reaper. I daresay you've heard of him. I wouldn't want to have to tell him that you'd obstructed our mission here. What we're doing need not affect you at all but you must let me go about my business. For a start, there is a woman named Burgess I need to speak with.'

'You come in to Twickstan and give *me* orders?'

'I tried to make a fair deal and you weren't interested. I was, however, interested to hear that there is only copy of The Book? I've noticed there are a few empty shelves in this town so I'm guessing you got rid of all the others. And that's why no one is allowed out, right? In case they find their own copy at the bottom of the rainbow?'

Messenger glanced at her guards, as if afraid they might overhear.

'That would be awkward, wouldn't it?' continued West. 'Your story seems to have got you a long way but you know as well as I do how many copies of that book are out there in the world. What if I were to plant a few around Twickstan? I imagine that would make things rather difficult.'

He let that sink in before continuing: 'All I need is information.'

Messenger's expression had grown increasingly hostile but that now faded with improbable speed. She replaced it with a smile and gestured for West to return to the chairs.

'Brothers, this is no sinner but a friend to the Divine. We shall lend him our assistance.'

True to her word, Messenger asked the guards to escort West and Theodore to the theatre, where Mrs. Burgess could apparently be found. She also mentioned another man who had worked on the bridge and knew the area well.

On the way, Theodore quietly asked West what he'd said to her but West shook his head, knowing the guards might be listening in. He still wanted to get out of Twickstan as quickly as possible; with time to reflect, Messenger might decide to rid herself of this new danger entirely. Something told him that she was adept at removing threats.

The main area of the theatre had been transformed into a workshop. Some of the rows of seats had been removed but several elderly women sat in one of them, repairing clothing. An entire section of the theatre's front wall had been opened up to admit light. Mrs. Burgess wore spectacles and seemed very surprised that someone would wish to speak to her. Apparently as ordered by Messenger, the guards insisted that the discussion be carried out in the theatre's lobby, where it was quiet.

'Why yes,' she said when West had explained himself. 'That was Burgess property for four generations. I wish-' A glance at the guards stopped her from saying more.

'And that area borders the river?' asked West.

'That's right.'

'We're looking for an underground structure. Probably not built on your land but close by. It might be called a bunker.'

'Station,' she said confidently.

'What's that?'

'They were called stations. The military built them all over the country – to launch weapons and keep things going in case there was a war.'

Mrs. Burgess took her spectacles off. 'My father was interested in history, you see. Some of those stations were closed down but others were still being used at the time of the Cataclysm.'

'And this local station? You know where it is?'

'No. I mean, I know it's in the area but I don't know *exactly* where. The military were very secretive about these things. They would have built it on government land I'm sure. I guess it doesn't matter who owns what these days.'

'Do you know where that land is?' asked West.

'I don't. Sorry. Say, why are you interested in all this?'

'Don't worry about it, Mrs. Burgess,' said one of the

guards.

'Can you take me to the other man?' asked West.

With a begrudging nod, the elder of the two guards led the way towards the theatre doors. The four of them were almost there when Mrs. Burgess spoke up again.

'Hey!'

They all stopped and turned.

'You should talk to Kevin Mckinnon. He's got quite a collection of maps. Might be something there you can use.'

It turned out that Mckinnon was one of those currently tasked with church repairs. He seemed wary of the visitors but gladly retrieved a large metal box of his possessions from the public hall. Still evidently keen to keep disruption to a minimum, the guards insisted that West and Theodore examine them in a nearby empty room. It at least had a broad table, onto which West deposited ten maps, most of them kept in cylindrical cases. None of his three companions could help him but only Theodore seemed ashamed of not being able to read. The guards found some chairs and sat talking about their upcoming work assignments. Theodore leaned against the wall with his arms folded, his deep-set eyes fixed on West.

It seemed logical that the military would not openly share the location of their installations, particularly those underground. West therefore didn't take on the task with any great degree of hope, particularly when the first five maps proved utterly useless. The sixth, however – though tatty and worn – showed the town, the bridge, and a good portion of the river. While the map had been printed, pencil had been used to mark certain sections with names; and West even spotted the Burgess property. Other areas had been highlighted with red ink. One of them, which was almost at the top edge of the map, was marked by a label: PROPOSED SITE OF ROAD AND FACILITY. That road was denoted by a red dotted line that led off the map. Checking the key, West saw this map was '1 of 4' and had been produced in 1961, making it more than one-hundred-and fifty years old.

Rifling through the box, he located two more that went with the set of four. Fortunately, one was the map he needed. The red dotted line led to a wide, square area denoted by a green line. There was very little detail compared to the rest of the map. The area had been stamped: 'U.S. MILITARY'.

Messenger gave permission for West to take the map and – only two hours after they'd arrived – he and Theodore departed. As they walked away from the town hall, West glanced back towards the church. He saw Messenger standing alone, watching. He hoped that was the last he would see of her.

At last, he explained his gambit to Theodore, who responded with grudging approval. West felt he now had more of a measure of the man. He could feel his boredom and dissatisfaction at giving up control. West hypothesized that normal life held little interest for him, likely his sister too. They preferred mayhem and murder.

Once reunited with Thea and a clearly relieved Fetch, they rode back to the bridge then turned north, reaching the military area in early afternoon. The first they saw of it was the corner of a high, rusted fence. Here it was still standing but much of the rest had collapsed and was easily negotiated. After trudging across flat, dusty land, they reached a road. Following it towards the centre of the area, they passed a hollow full of plastic fuel cans and disturbed a family of foxes that fled at speed.

Eventually, they came to a surprisingly unimpressive collection of low buildings. Their approach disturbed a vulture, which flapped lazily into the sky before circling above.

'Not much here,' said Thea.

'I reckon that's a good sign,' replied West. 'Maybe most of it is underground.'

CHAPTER 9 -THE FIRST CLUE

◆ ◆ ◆

The four buildings were small. The first was little more than a wooden shack with two smashed windows. West was able to climb inside but found nothing. The second building was a circular, concrete structure topped by a collection of masts and aerials. The single metal door had already been forced open and all West discovered inside was a pile of mouldy blankets, a box of flares and two drums of fuel. The third structure was little more than a curved roof of corrugated iron that housed three vehicles. West had seen this type of vehicle before and knew they'd been used for construction. Though protected from rain, they had decayed beyond use.

The fourth building was no bigger than the wooden shack but constructed of concrete that looked extremely thick. There was only one steel door and no windows – only a tubular air vent on the roof.

'Could be for power,' suggested Thea. 'Seen 'em before. What did they call those things? Generators?'

'Or an armoury,' added her brother. He turned to West. 'If that station or bunker or whatever it is ain't here, that sure was a waste of a morning, wasn't it?' Theodore took his hat and off and ran a hand through his hair.

Fetch listened in silence. He just seemed happy not to be alone with Thea.

West still felt confident that this was the place. He approached the concrete box and examined the lock mechanism mounted beside it. He had seen these before: some sort of electronic panel that required a specific type of key. Even if he had one, it seemed unlikely that either it or the lock would still function.

'What, you don't have the key?' said Theodore, his mocking tone now becoming annoyingly familiar.

West strode back towards the tower. 'There's more than one way to open a door.'

*

Once they'd forced their way inside the circular structure, West and Fetch rolled the two fuel drums over to the fourth building. Tipping them onto their bases, West placed them as close to the door as he could, then retrieved the box of flares. A man had once tried to sell him a box so he knew how they worked.

He took one out and removed the cap, then struck the exposed end against the striking surface on the reverse of the cap. To his surprise, the flare instantly ignited. He expected it to create the burning light he'd seen previously but in fact this one produced smoke. It produced so much that West had to throw it down and kick sand to put it out. The Cutters found all this quite amusing.

'There are some of those at Spring Bay,' remarked Fetch.

'No good. We need something that burns.' After a moment's thought, West tore a long section off the cardboard box the flares had been placed in. He had already removed the caps of the fuel drums and now placed the end of the cardboard strip in one, leading the other end over the side.

'Can I borrow a match?'

Due to their cigar-smoking habit, both Cutters kept matches on them. West guessed that a gang as successful as Reaper's Boys had a lot more of such items than virtually anyone else. There was a lot to be said for being a raider.

With a weary roll of her eyes, Thea threw him her

matches. By this point, Fetch had sensibly led all the mounts behind the circular building and the Cutters now joined him. Looking at the two drums, West wondered if it wasn't too much. Both drums were at least half full. Then again, he didn't even know what the fuel was – or if it would ignite – and the steel door looked *very* strong.

He lit the match, then the makeshift fuse. Once satisfied that the cardboard would burn all the way, he retreated until the flames neared the open top of the drum. Then he turned and ran to the tower. Theodore and Thea had occupied the corner. Fetch was behind them and holding no less than five sets of reins.

West pointed at him. 'Make sure you've got a good hold of-'

He was safely around the corner but the deafening, air-splitting blast still blew his hat off. Theodore and Thea seemed to enjoy that but – unsurprisingly – the mounts did not. Fetch somehow kept four of them under control but Thea's horse pulled itself free and bolted away.

'You dumb bastard!' she yelled.

West looked over Theodore's shoulder and was pleased to see that the steel door had been entirely blown off its frame and into the building. The explosion had even made dents in the concrete and a little crater in the ground. Of the fuel drums, there was no sign.

Thea was still berating Fetch.

'I'll go and get it,' he replied quietly.

Shoving Fetch aside, Thea spoke to her brother, then climbed up onto his horse and rode after her mount.

Despite his keenness to get inside the building, West knew this was an opportunity; Theodore was temporarily outnumbered. The sharp raider was clearly aware of it too, however. For the first time in a while, he slipped his quick from his vest.

He aimed the gun at West. 'Come on then, hero. Let's go check out your handiwork.'

West walked past him to the ruined building. He saw now that the interior was very cramped, which demonstrated just how thick the concrete walls were. What remained of the door was on the far side of the structure, beyond what seemed to be its only real feature: a circular hatch painted green. It was mounted in a concrete surround about three feet off the floor.

'Well, well,' said Theodore.

West stepped inside and grabbed the little wheel at the top of the hatch. He tried to turn it clockwise but it wouldn't give. Then he used both hands, braced himself, and gave it all he had. The hatch moved an inch, then another, until he turned it through three revolutions and was able to lift it up. The hatch was so heavy that he lost grip as he lowered it and it struck the concrete surround with a loud clang.

West peered down into the shaft, which was quite wide and equipped with a ladder that descended into total darkness. He was struck by a flash of memory. He'd seen something like this before, he was sure.

Theo stepped in, blocking out the daylight. Already in his hand was a flashlight – another piece of equipment he kept on his vest.

The beam of light illuminated the entire shaft. It was hard to measure how deep it was but West guessed at least fifty feet. And at the bottom of it was a clearly visible section of metal grille.

'I guess that could be a bunker, or a station, or whatever.' Theodore passed West the flashlight. 'Go do your thing.'

STATION CHARLIE.

It was written in neat lettering on a metal panel not far from the base of the ladder. Directly was a set of lockers. To the left and behind the ladder were solid metal walls. Nearby was a poster clearly aimed at the bunker's inhabitants. It consisted of six words in large orange print on a black background: *BE SMART, BE SAFE, BE SECURE*. Close to the roof were exposed pipes covered with peeling yellow paint and several air vents latticed by cobwebs.

West was certain; he hadn't just *seen* one of these underground bunkers – he'd been inside. Beyond that, he could recall nothing.

To the right was the rest of the small entrance area and then a narrow corridor. West shone the light along it and saw that there was a door at the end, about twenty feet away. He had just shouted up to Theodore that it was safe and the raider had replied that he'd follow down soon. Though he knew it entirely illogical, West couldn't help worry that the murderous bastard might just seal the hatch and leave him there to die.

Before heading along the corridor, he began opening the lockers and soon discovered a few pieces of equipment. Some were familiar, others weren't: all looked useful. There were three more sturdy flashlights but, upon inspection, two proved to be fatally damaged by corroded batteries. West also pulled out an orange plastic suit designed to cover the whole body. Then he found several boxes containing masks which covered the mouth and nose and could be secured by a rubber strap. The mouthpiece was connected via a tube to a small, cylindrical air-tank. He had seen these before, including a variation of the design at Woodhaven.

West also discovered some well-preserved batteries and two cubic devices with a sensor attached to one side and a meter for measuring ...something. The next instrument he dug out was basically a long metal pole with a circular sensor at the bottom and another meter at the top. He had seen one of these before; the owner had been walking across a field with it, trying to locate a lost piece of equipment. The man had confided to West that such devices were very rare. They were called metal detectors. West whipped the panel off but found that the detector required an unusual type of battery.

After ripping the protective plastic off some batteries, he at least got one of the flashlights working. He moved his various finds aside to let Theodore, Fetch and Thea down the ladder.

'Let's make this quick,' snapped Thea. 'I don't like it down here.'

Theodore said something in French. From the way his

sister shook her head, West gathered she didn't agree. Theodore then jutted his chin towards the corridor and West hurried along it with his new flashlight, having returned Theodores'. The only thing West noticed in the corridor was a few small puddles of water and the sound of dripping in some unseen void.

The door was also opened by a wheel and as he did so, West saw just how thick it was – two inches at least. The door was set above the floor so they had to step over the base. Opening it released a flood of stale, musty air that caused all four of them to recoil and cough. But their curiosity soon got the better of them and they followed West into what seemed like some kind of command centre.

In the middle of the room was a broad table and under it were shelves containing dozens of plastic folders. On each side of the table were wall-mounted displays featuring no less than eight screens, just as West had seen on televisions and computers. (He had even seen a computer work once, though all it could do was show a page of writing – like a letter).

Below the screens was a series of keyboards connected by wires and other panels featuring a huge number of buttons and coloured lights.

'Wonder what they did down here,' said Fetch, running a finger across thick dust.

'Something important.' West reached under the table and pulled out one of the folders. When he opened it, he found page after page of stiff paper, each one packed with dense print. There were also many tables, diagrams and maps. He reached down and started retrieving all the folders, which were of the same design but in various colours.

'Don't tell me you're going to read all those?' said Thea, who was shining her own flashlight around.

West reckoned the documents might give him a clue about the other bunkers.

'Remember we're here for weapons,' added Thea.

West didn't share Reaper's interest in that regard. He was occupied by wider questions. 'So, start opening the lockers.'

'What lockers?'

'Under there.' West had only just noticed them but there seemed to be several beneath the screens on both sides.

'You two do that,' said Theodore to Fetch and his sister. 'I'll check through here. See how big this place is.'

At the far end of the room was another corridor which led past four open doorways – two on either side. West had already glimpsed some bunks there and didn't want to go further without checking the documents.

Thea clearly *was* desperate to get back to the surface for she worked with singular purpose, wrenching the lockers open and pulling out the contents. While Fetch hurried around to the other side of the room to do his share, West flicked through the first folder. His eyes picked up titles and phrases but he soon realised he had no real idea what he was looking for:

EMERGENCY PROCEDURES ...STANDARD DIAGNOSTIC CHECKLIST ...COMMUNICATION PROTOCOLS (CENTRAL COMMAND) ...LOGISTICAL & STRATEGIC PLANNING ...AUTONOMOUS SYSTEMS: CALIBRATION AND TESTING.

Unable to make head or tail out of it, he pushed the folder away and opened another one. This one was all text: different titles and language but similarly confusing. In frustration, he began randomly checking the folders, searching for any diagram or picture that might make sense.

He found one that showed Station Charlie itself, and he was surprised to see that the bunker was equipped with its own generator and an enormous tank that seemed to collect rainwater through the soil and funnel it downward. Everything he'd seen so far suggested that this place had been designed for people to live in for months, possibly even years.

Despite all he saw, nothing sparked any more specific memories.

He glanced back at Thea. She had pulled out more of the protective suits as well as mattresses and pillows, all the while cursing in French. Fetch had retrieved metal boxes that contained tins of food and what looked like medication.

The next folder West opened was marked on the first page: ***'MOST SECRET** (DO NOT REMOVE FROM INSTALLATION)'.*

The first few pages were taken up with more dense text. But about halfway in, West spied a map. In the centre of it, marked with a red dot, was Station Charlie. Also marked were Stations Alpha, Beta and Delta. Judging by the map, they were all at least a hundred miles away – but at least he had the locations. Excited by his discovery, West could see no compelling reason to share the information. Checking that Thea's attention was elsewhere, he removed the page, folded it and placed it in his pocket.

Hearing a metallic groan from the far end of the bunker, he decided to follow Theodore. As he'd expected, the four doorways led to basic sleeping facilities containing only eight bunkbeds. Beyond this was a larger, area equipped with kitchen facilities and what looked like a restroom.

The groaning noise was coming from another wheel like those on the door and the hatch. Theodore seemed determined to open it but this one belonged to a small, square hatch located half-way up the wall. Beside it was some white lettering that clearly meant nothing to the illiterate raider.

'Goddam hard going,' he breathed, still turning the wheel.

EMERGENCY ACCESS/RELEASE VALVE (MAIN TANK)

Tank, thought West. *The water tank. The enormous water tank.*

'Wait.'

'Maybe this is where the weapons are kept,' said Theodore, panting. 'Ah, there you go.'

The raider didn't need to open the hatch all the way: the force of the water did that. He was caught in the face with spray and sent sprawling backwards. By the time got to his feet, the water was already up to their ankles.

'Come on!' shouted West. 'We have to close it.'

But he quickly realised there was no chance. The water was coming out in such volume and at such a rate that he couldn't get near the hatch, let alone force it shut. Worse, there seemed to be nowhere for the water to go. It was visibly rising, already approaching his knees and flooding the corridor.

For once, Theodore lost his composure. His hat had fallen off and he now gazed downward at the water, mouth open. All West could think of was the diagram he'd just seen. The water tank dwarfed the rest of the structure, presumably designed to sustain the inhabitants for years. And it had had decades to fill up...

'Let's go! We have to get out!'

Without an acknowledgement, Theodore turned away, wading through the water back towards the others. As he followed, West glanced once more at the hatch, hoping that the flow might have lessened. It hadn't.

'Theo!' came the cry from Thea. Panic etched on their faces, she and Fetch stood helplessly as the other two struggled towards them. The water had already reached the other side of the command room and was now spilling over the rim of the door into the entrance area. The water was very cold and West could already feel himself shivering.

By the time he reached Fetch, it was up to his waist. He pulled his coat off and tucked the flashlight into his belt so that the light was shining upwards. Until that point, he'd thought they had time to reach the ladder. Now he wasn't so sure.

It seemed that the others had realised too because Fetch and the Cutters were now hauling themselves through the water towards the door. Fetch was clearly going to allow Thea through first, but that didn't stop her screaming at him and lashing out. Her fist caught him on the ear and he reeled back, arms flying up as his head hit the water.

West powered through as best he could, grabbing Fetch by the collar and pulling him upright. Using the open door for grip, he then moved himself and Fetch around and through it. The pair of them stumbled over the raised doorway. The Cutters were ten feet ahead, silent as they pushed their way onward, now close to the ladder. The water just kept coming and was now up to West's armpits.

Fetch was right behind him but was rapidly losing control

of himself: 'God save me, God save me, God save me.'

West only truly appreciated their situation when he felt his boots lift off the floor and his head near the ceiling. He was floating.

The Cutters had reached the ladder. Theodore shouted something inaudible and pushed his sister upward.

West realised two things in close succession. The first was that the entire bunker was going to flood, including the shaft. The second was that the water had rushed into the locker he had checked earlier, releasing the contents. The orange survival suit was floating nearby; and one of the cardboard boxes with the breathing masks.

West swam past the wild-eyed Fetch and grabbed the box. He reached out with his spare arm and hooked it around a support column to steady himself. Flipping open the box, he pulled out a mask, relieved to see that this one also had the tube and air tank attached. He put his mouth over the mouthpiece and began fiddling with the knob beside the tube. In seconds, he felt a flow of stale air and found that he could breathe.

'West! What do we do?' Fetch was pawing the roof, which was now only a foot above their heads.

West glimpsed Theodore's legs disappearing up the shaft. Perhaps they would make it after all. He and Fetch wouldn't.

'Here, take this. You can breathe through it.'

Keeping the apparatus – particularly the mouthpiece – out of the water, West waited for Fetch to swim over then gave it to him.

'There – just don't open your mouth fully until it's on. Hold the column there. This whole place will be under in seconds. I'll be back.'

Once Fetch had his mouth on it and was clearly breathing, West pushed himself off the column. Swimming towards the locker, his eyes scanned the water. Though he still had the flashlight tucked into his belt, the effect was reduced by the water. Bumping against a locker door, he forced himself to remain stationary and look around. If he didn't find a mask before the water reached the roof, he was a dead man.

'West!'

He hadn't expected to hear any more from Fetch. The man was only a dark shape now; a dark shape beside the dark column.

'Box here! Got another mask!'

'Put yours back on!'

'Okay!'

West knew Fetch wasn't the brightest and, if he was mistaken, this was the end. But he was out of time.

Thrashing his way back through the water, he grabbed the box Fetch pushed towards him and again steadied himself against the column. Fetch was not mistaken.

West's head touched the roof as he pulled the mask out of the box. He found the mouthpiece, then the knob, which he turned. He brought the mouth-piece close.

Nothing.

He turned the knob as far as it would go.

Nothing.

He moved his fingers down, felt the tube. It had somehow folded over on itself. Once he freed it, the air began to flow with a loud hiss. Shoving the mouthpiece between his lips, West bit down hard, feeling the musty air fill his lungs.

With one hand on the column, one steadying the mask, the water rose over his head. His eyes felt suddenly heavy, as if the water was trying to force its way in. All he could hear was his own breath. Everything else was quiet.

West had never been so terrified. Every time he inhaled, he feared that the air would run out or that the tube would snag or something else would happen.

An image forced itself into his mind: the two of them, lifeless and floating for ever in this black tomb.

He felt Fetch's hand brush his arm and it snapped him back into reality. They had to move. Though his eyes were fully open, West could see nothing. But he found Fetch's sleeve and tugged on it three times. When he could feel him moving, he kept hold and kicked with his legs, neck and back bumping along the roof of the bunker. It felt beyond strange that his boots were not touching the floor but he at least made progress.

In order to keep hold of Fetch, West pulled his shirt open and carefully pushed the apparatus down until it was wedged. Using his legs to move forward, he stretched out with his right hand to guide himself. Before long, that hand connected with something that bounced away. When it came back and he could touch it again, West decided it was one of the locker doors. This allowed him to orientate himself and he now turned to his left, hoping to find the ladder and the shaft.

When his forehead knocked heavily against something, he had to stop himself crying out. But his right hand told him it was another support column. He couldn't remember its position but grabbed Fetch's sleeve again and continued onward. He then brushed past something that his fingers soon identified as the ladder. For the first time in what seemed a long time, he felt a surge of hope.

He dragged Fetch closer so that he too would realise what it was. West hoped Fetch also understood the triple tug on the sleeve because he then transferred both hands to the ladder and began to climb. He had moved up several rungs when he realised there was a light above – a distant, circular glow. Then it disappeared. His first thought was that the Cutters were out and had shut the hatch on them. He was already cold and now felt a tremor of fear crackle up his spine.

But after climbing two more rungs he realised the light had appeared again. Now he was a little closer, he could see there was something in the shaft, blocking his way. And by the time he reached it, he knew what it is.

Theodore's inert body seemed to be stuck. Desperate to get out of the shaft, West pushed it aside and pulled himself past, careful with the breathing apparatus. The effort of the climb was making him inhale faster. He didn't know how long he and Fetch had and there was still some way to go. It seemed that the shaft was getting smaller; closing in on him.

Gradually, the light grew brighter until he could actually make out the rungs of the ladder and his pale hands in front of him. Though salvation was near, his strength seemed to be deserting him.

But now he could actually see the top of the hatch and the roof of the building. He guessed there was no more than twenty feet to go.

Then Fetch grabbed his ankle; and his grip was so hard – so desperate – that West knew something was badly wrong. He turned, looked down. Fetch was coming up towards him, pale face etched with panic. He had no mask on. He had no air.

Fetch was trying to get past but West doubted he'd make it. Instead, he took one deep breath himself then grabbed Fetch by the collar. He slid the mouthpiece out and, though he could feel water in his mouth, also pulled the apparatus from his shirt. Fighting the urge to climb, he passed everything to Fetch, who shoved the mouthpiece in. His face contorted momentarily but West could see he was breathing.

Now he *had* to climb. Telling himself to ignore the sour water sliding down his throat, he grabbed the next rung and hauled himself up the shaft. He felt five times heavier than he had when he started the climb but he pushed himself onward.

With a final heave, he pulled his head free and spat out the water before sucking in deep breaths of clean, sweet air. Feeling a tap on his left ankle, he realised he had to make way. He climbed two more rungs and collapsed onto the surround. His last reserves of strength gone, he rolled off and dropped heavily onto the floor.

CHAPTER 10 -FREE

West heard Fetch coughing and wheezing but he simply could not move. And now he began to cough too, then vomit; spewing up far more water than he thought he'd ingested. And when it was all out of him, he somehow felt even more exhausted. Gripping the surround, he pulled himself to his feet, a process not helped by his sodden clothes. He wiped vomit off his shirt, then watched Fetch climb out of the shaft. His face looked as pale as it had underwater and his eyes were bloodshot. He simply shook his head, looked at the water-filled shaft, then shook his head again.

'What happened?'

'Ran out of air,' said Fetch between panting breaths.

West lurched out into the daylight. He had just begun to enjoy the wonderful feeling of sunny warmth on his face when something smashed into his right shoulder and sent him flying.

He landed painfully on his side and looked up to see Thea snatch the largest blade from her vest. Her soaking hair was slick against her head and the deep-set eyes did not blink as she advanced.

'What are you doing?' yelled West. 'It wasn't my fault! Your brother-'

He stopped because he could see that she was beyond reason, beyond listening. She was alive but her beloved brother was dead. She didn't want explanations, she wanted blood. And as West knew well, Thea had killed for a lot less.

Scrambling backwards towards the circular building, he got up just in time to avoid the first slash of her blade. Her quick was still secure in her vest. It would be waterlogged – would it still work? It seemed that Thea preferred to have her way with the blade, which meant he at least had a chance.

The raider wiped wet strands of hair away from her eyes, teeth grinding as she stalked after West. He snatched a look over his shoulder. He was close to the building but not the door.

Where the hell is Fetch?

West realised how tired and dazed he was when he saw Thea lower the big blade and reach for one of her throwing knives. He'd forgotten about those.

Fortunately, his next thought was a bit sharper and it told him to run at her. It was pretty much his only choice: cut the distance and attack before she could throw.

Considering his condition, West did well, reaching her just as she drew her arm back to throw. But Thea was nimble. She simply spun away and West's flailing hands met nothing but air. It might have been his waterlogged clothes; it might have been some unseen hole or bump in the ground – or it might just have been total exhaustion – but he overbalanced and fell face-first onto the ground. As his head snapped around, he fully expected a blade to be flying at him.

He wasn't far wrong. Thea's right arm was back over her shoulder, the hilt of the throwing knife between finger and thumb. She started to smile...

That smile disappeared when the bullet hit her chest. She struck the ground with a thump and a stifled cry. She was still moving, palms turned towards the sky, fingers grasping.

West got up and walked over to Fetch, who seemed frozen in place.

'I'll take it.'

Fetch let go of the still-smoking rifle. West hurried back to Thea, whose mouth was working back and forth, producing only a strange hissing sound. All the hardness was gone from those small eyes; there was only fear now.

West put the second bullet into her heart. She moved no

more.

He let out a long breath and returned to Fetch, who was bent over, hands on his knees. West knew how he felt; he dropped the gun and sat down on his backside. Every single part of him ached.

'Is she dead?' asked Fetch.

'Yeah,' replied West. 'And I think maybe I am too.'

*

After a time, Fetch sat down with him, both of them silent under the warm sun.

'Idiot,' said West eventually.

'Who?' asked Fetch.

'Theodore. It was him. He opened another door except it wasn't a door – it was a hatch for the water tank. Who knows what else we might have found down there?'

Inadvertently reminding himself about the map, West reached into his pocket and pulled it out. Though it was soaked through, when he unfolded it, most of the features could be made out – including the locations of the other bunkers.

'*Another* map,' said Fetch.

'Yes, but this one is a lot more useful. It shows where there are other bunkers ...I guess I should call them stations now.'

'You want to go in *another* one?'

'Well, not right now, no.'

West then realised that he'd also lost the metal detector. If he was to spend time searching for subterranean bunkers and hatches, he couldn't think of a more useful item. Perhaps there would be another chance to get one somewhere.

He stood up. 'We should get out of these clothes.'

'What about...'

'I'll deal with her. You can lead the horses over there.' West nodded to the building with the curved roof. 'We'll fix ourselves up then get out of here.'

As Fetch gathered the five mounts and led them away,

West returned to Thea. He supposed it might be sensible to take one or more of her knives but he didn't want any reminders of the two killers. Gripping the vest, he dragged her over to the building. He lifted her body onto the surround then tipped her into the shaft. She landed with a splash.

'There you go,' West whispered bitterly. 'Together again.'

Fetch had tethered the mounts to the old vehicles and put out some water and feed for them. He had also removed the saddle from Theodore's horse but hadn't touched Thea's. Having undressed, he was now putting on some dry clothes. Like West, he possessed only the one set of spares.

West removed Thea's saddle and placed it with Theodore's. He then changed swiftly and went through their bags. Though he hadn't taken the blades, it would be madness not to claim the medication, money and batteries.

June and Sandy had been carrying the bulk of the provisions so there wasn't much reorganising to do. West also collected all the ammunition for the rifles but Fetch refused to take one of the weapons. West was minded to insist but decided he didn't need to force the issue right now.

'Sure you don't want one of the horses?' he asked.

Fetch shook his head.

West led the Cutters' mounts away a little, then removed their bridles and slapped their rumps, sending them galloping away. He could have sold them but both were marked with brands connecting them to Reaper. He had no desire to leave a trail for his enemy. When the ten days were up, the Boys would come looking, of that he had no doubt. He supposed one alternative was to return to Spring Bay and tell Reaper exactly what happened. West didn't much like that idea.

Clearly keen to leave, Fetch had already mounted up. West checked June's tether and took a moment to reassure the mule. He then climbed up onto the grey horse, placing his newly-acquired rifle where it was easily reachable.

'Which way?' asked Fetch.

West knew from the map that Station Alpha was the closest, though it was still a hundred and twenty miles away.

'North-east. I suggest we give Twickstan a wide berth.'

They set off, riding side by side.

'Thank you for what you did,' said West. 'I know ...it couldn't have been easy.'

'Had to,' said Fetch, brow furrowed.

Neither of them said anything for a while after that. As they approached the fallen fence, West glanced back at June, who was trotting along happily enough, as usual. At least he'd kept the mule. But once again, he'd lost his hat and coat.

'You know what, when you're fighting for your life, it's damn hard to stay well-attired.'

West only began to relax in late afternoon, when they were far away from Twickstan. Even so, he wanted to ride for as long as possible and didn't even think about stopping until the sky darkened and the sun disappeared behind a line of low, jagged mountains to the west. Due to its scale, the map showed only significant routes. West had tried to follow one of these earlier in the day but they'd found their path blocked by a section of road that had collapsed into the earth. He had no idea what might have caused this but they had to go a long way around and spent most of the day simply following a compass bearing. Though they passed the occasional patch of bright spring flowers, much of the land was colourless and lifeless. Only tough, hardy plants seemed to survive in this area, and they weren't much to look at.

The sky was clear, so West and Fetch agreed that rain was unlikely. They stopped within a stand of the ever-present ruined trees, their blackened trunks home to crawling insects that thankfully seemed to prefer the dark wood to the dark earth.

'What do you think about a fire?' suggested Fetch, his face bright for the first time that day.

'Why not? We've barely seen a soul.'

They had some firewood with them but, while Fetch

unsaddled the mounts, West grabbed a hatchet and gathered some more. Despite their condition, these old, dead trees burned reasonably well. West hacked big pieces out of them and made a pile beside the better wood. As the pair of them worked silently, the setting sun cast a pleasant pink glow into the narrow valley they had halted in.

Fetch suggested a meal of oatcakes and West was more than happy with the result. Fetch also added some dried sausage to one batch and some fruit to another, providing them with two courses.

'You're a damn good cook,' said West, sitting against a saddle facing the fire.

'Glad you like it. There's one more.'

West tapped his stomach. 'Don't have the space.'

'You don't look the same without your coat and hat.'

'Don't feel the same. First town we come across I'm going to get some replacements.'

Fetch had also brewed up some tea and West poured himself another mug full. He wasn't sure if the odd taste in his mouth and throat was from the water or the air-tank.

'I didn't really thank you,' said Fetch.

'You did. Three times.' West shook his head. 'We were lucky those mask things worked. It seems the military looked after all their gear.'

Fetch shuddered. 'That place. I'll be surprised if I don't have nightmares about it for the rest of my years.'

'I guess you're not enthusiastic about us going to find the next one?'

'Maybe I can just watch the horses this time.'

West grinned and drank his tea. The sun was long gone now and the flames the only source of light. Firewood was often scarce but West did love a fire, perhaps mainly because it meant hot food, not that he was a cook in Fetch's league.

'Why did they build these ...stations?'

West shrugged, wishing his brief flash of memory had sparked more detailed recollections. 'If I'd had longer with those documents, I might have worked it out. That deep underground, they'd be safe from attack. Which is why the structures survived the Cataclysm so well.'

'So, was it the army?'

'Not sure. Army or government. Or both.'

Fetch put down his mug and leant back against his saddle. 'I never really understood what a government is.'

'From what I've read, it was just the way they ran things. I guess the army worked for the leaders of the government.'

'Like Reaper and the Boys.'

'A little.'

'Do you think the weapons were there?' asked Fetch.

'Maybe. Maybe there'll be some at Station Alpha.'

'He'll come after us. Reaper.'

'He might. Perhaps he'll even follow our trail to Station Charlie. But then what?' West tapped the map, which he had laid out to dry near the fire. 'He doesn't have this.'

*

The night passed peacefully. They rose shortly after dawn, both still aching from their trials but well rested. It was another bright day and they made good progress north-east, tracking a minor but clear road that led them eventually to a place called Jacobstown. They agreed to spend some of the money: both were in dire need of a bath and a real bed – if only for one night. West had occasionally rewarded himself this way in the past and he reckoned his companion deserved it too. As they approached, he instructed Fetch not to use their real names. He would call himself Smith and Fetch would go by his real surname, Gibson.

Jacobstown was similar in size to Hexton and the population was listed on the town sign as two hundred and thirteen. On the way to main street, they passed a yard where a crew were re-working salvaged metal and wood into horse-drawn carts and carriages. The workers greeted the two travellers in a friendly fashion and this was repeated by the welcoming they received on main street. There seemed to be only one hotel but it was a big place with a broad sign rendered in yellow paint.

Outside *THE GOLDEN CHANCE* stood two people. The pretty girl with curly blonde hair and the lacy dress reminded West of the two women he'd seen at Reaper's place. The security man was rather less threatening than Rock, though he did have a shotgun hanging from a shoulder strap.

'Good day to you, gentleman,' said the girl. 'Welcome to The Golden Chance – where everybody gets lucky.'

'Good to know,' replied West. 'I could use a change in fortune. How much for a night? Us two and the mounts.'

'You got coin?'

'Guild standard.'

'That'll be one bit – you can pay inside. Only eight scraps if you're betting.'

'We're not betting,' said West. It wasn't a pastime he'd ever had much interest in; he'd already found enough ways to lose whatever he gained.

The young woman opened the door and whistled.

'What you carrying?' asked the man with the shotgun.

'Just what you see,' replied West honestly, nodding at the two rifles on his saddle.

'They go with you to your room and they stay there until you leave. You carry anywhere inside the hotel, you're out.'

'Understood.' West was glad they didn't have to surrender them, a policy followed by some establishments. He couldn't imagine that they were under any immediate danger but wanted a gun nearby even so.

He and Fetch took their bags from the saddles. Two lads had responded to the whistle and led the horse, pony and mule around to the back of the hotel. The woman opened the door and smiled as they entered.

Even though The Golden Chance looked large from outside, West was still surprised by the scale of the interior. To the right was a long bar that ran almost to the rear. The rest of the place contained tables of various sizes, thirty at least. Every single one was covered by a clean white sheet and gamers were seated at most, playing either cards or dice. Some were evidently rich because they wore nice suits, well-polished shoes and tall hats. They smoked cigars and cigarettes. Others looked like they might be down to their last stake.

'Good day, gents,' said an older woman behind the bar. She opened a notebook and picked up a plastic pen. 'Names?'

'Mr. Smith and Mr. Gibson. Do we pay now?'

She shook her head. 'When you leave. Are you playing?'

'No. Does every room have a bath?'

'The best ones do. Two scraps extra, each.'

West had his mind set on the idea now. 'No problem.'

'It takes a while to heat all the water but shouldn't be too long.'

'That's fine.'

'Are you eating with us tonight?'

West glanced at Fetch, who was clearly keen on the idea. 'I think we will.'

'Food's listed on the blackboard over there. Served from sundown. We'll put you in rooms three and five. Enjoy your stay.'

Just as they were about to pick up their bags, some music began. West hadn't noticed any musicians and the music he heard was unlike any he'd experienced before. It sounded very ... complicated. Opposite the counter, on the left side of the room, a middle-aged man had placed a cubic metal device on a table. It was connected by a wire to a heavy battery of a type West had seen a couple of times.

The woman sighed. 'It does sound pretty but that there is a waste of a battery.'

'What is this music?' asked West.

'I don't know. Best Walter can figure it, it's called Cassette.'

'Strange name.'

'Sure is.'

An hour later, the strange music was still playing. West could just about hear it through the walls of his room. He was lying in the bath: a nice, deep, long bath. The room wasn't bad: very clean with a comfortable-looking bed, an armchair and a wardrobe. West didn't have much to compare it to but he reckoned it was worth the money. He hadn't even bothered to clean himself yet; he just lay there, enjoying the warm water.

It was almost as if the last few days hadn't happened. His thoughts drifted back to the moment Silvera and the others had ridden out of those trees. Since then, the dangers had come thick and fast. But he'd survived, and he'd found himself a loyal, useful friend, and he had that map in his hands. West felt certain that if he could discover more about the stations, he would eventually uncover the one he remembered. Had he visited the place? Had he lived there?

The music stopped. Dragged out of his reverie, West imagined Reaper turning up with Rock and Silvera and a gang of men. The hotel suddenly seemed quiet. He heard heavy footsteps coming up the stairs, approaching his room. He wished he'd kept the rifle within reach. The door was locked but he was naked, defenceless. Why had he let his guard down? Why-

Whoever it was strode past his room and entered another. West let his head rest on the edge of the bath. Running his fingers through his hair, he felt dust and dirt. He submerged his head to clean his face but immediately brought it back up, his heart racing. Another memory had returned: the image of he and Fetch floating dead in the flooded bunker.

*

That night, the two travellers enjoyed a delicious meal of chicken and potatoes followed by apple pie. Afterwards, they drank some beer, and listened to Walter – the proprietor – explain how it was made. His father had read several manuals about brewing and passed on his knowledge. His brother now ran a brewery on the outskirts of town and apparently sold it far and wide. West had tasted a few types of beer and most was pretty rough. This stuff was smooth and strong, however, and he and Fetch downed four of them while watching the gamblers.

At one point there was a scuffle, which resulted in the

enforcer being called in. One of the combatants took exception at being asked to leave and threw a poorly-aimed punch. The enforcer knocked him out cold with the butt of his shotgun and dragged him outside, assisted by a couple of regulars.

Walter's wife – who had signed them in earlier in the day – was called Mabel and she recommended a tailor just down the street who would be able to supply West with a hat and coat.

Walter's music player wasn't used again but, late on, two fellows with guitars performed some tunes. They were accompanied by the young woman on the door and the owners' daughter. The locals seemed to know the tunes and Fetch joined in keenly with some clapping and hollering. West enjoyed the music but such closeness with other people was strange to him and he was glad he'd had a few drinks to ease his awkwardness.

All in all, though, it was a fine evening and he was glad to see Fetch forget his troubles. He didn't need to hear it from the man to know that shooting Thea had seriously affected him. West felt sure that he had not killed before.

The pair retired to bed around midnight and West fell asleep to the sound of the guitars playing a wistful song that reminded him of wide, open plains and even wider skies.

The coat was not exactly the same as his other one but it was black, knee-length and warm, which was good enough for West. The hat had a strong, wide brim and fitted well. While they were there at the tailors, West and Fetch also brought some underwear, socks and spare shirts. Even after these purchases, they still had over five crowns left from the Cutters' bribe money.

On their way out of Jacobstown, they passed a general store and called in to purchase some essentials. Fetch bought matches, candles, a lantern, tough metal crockery, tea and cooking oil. West asked about guns. The owner didn't keep them on display but pulled back a curtain to reveal five hanging from hooks. One was a heavy sixer with a handle embossed with silver. When he learned that the man also had two boxes of ammunition for it,

West decided to buy. He had the rifle but was unused to long-range weapons and wanted something he could pull out and fire quickly. The gun and the bullets set him back two crowns but the store-owner was so pleased at the sale that he threw in a holster.

As they rode out of town, Fetch cast a regretful look back at Jacobstown.

'I'm sort of sad to leave.'

West wasn't sad at all. He had a new coat, a new hat and a new sixer.

And a map.

CHAPTER 11 - BOOM

◆ ◆ ◆

For three days, they travelled north-east without incident. On the third day, they met a friendly husband and wife on the road who disclosed that they were now in the territory of the Harris Gang – another group of raiders. The two explained that they were not the worst of the worst and could generally be bought off, providing you had something to give. In the couple's case, this had involved handing over a third of their farm's produce, something they were no longer prepared to do. West also learned that the Harris Gang were based in a town called Fool's March. From the map, he knew that this was close to the location of Station Alpha. As he thanked the couple and rode on, he wondered about the contents of the bunker. Was there a stash of weapons or other valuables right under the noses of this Harris Gang?

That night, West and Fetch made camp halfway up a hill. It was a giant mound flanked by angular spurs of rock and narrow streams. From a distance, it seemed there was a pass between this hill and the one to its right but this area turned out to be a treacherous mass of sharp slopes and deep gullies. As West remarked, it looked as if a great hand had smashed the hills together to form this impassable barrier.

Where they'd stopped there was plenty of grass and the mounts soon set to grazing. Fetch wanted to light a fire but West was worried about the height and orientation of their position. He had no reason to think they were being pursued but anyone coming across the plain they'd earlier traversed would see the light. As it turned out, they faced a very different threat.

West and Fetch didn't generally keep watch at night. With only two of them, it meant a very short sleep after very long days of riding. West's horse wasn't particularly anxious but Sandy and June had a habit of shifting around if they sensed anything. When this had happened before, the cause had usually been a change in the wind or the cries of some bird or other animal.

The first West knew of it, he was being shaken awake by Fetch. The sky above him was full of stars and a cool wind was blowing across the hill.

'Something's out there.'

West threw his blanket aside. The sixer was in its holster beside him but he went to his saddle and retrieved the rifle. He and Fetch walked down the slope a few feet and looked out. Sandy and June were shuffling around and snorting. Even the horse was blowing and pulling on its tether.

Wishing he hadn't looked up at the bright stars, West scoured the dark slopes below. For several minutes, he and Fetch stood there, wind tugging at their hair. The mounts remained unsettled; West reckoned they had heard or smelled something that the humans simply couldn't.

'There,' said Fetch.

The starlight and moonlight were enough for West to see his pale hand and follow the direction of his arm. He saw it instantly, a dot of light, then another. Two eyes. When they disappeared, he continued scanning.

'There too. And another.'

Now they had revealed themselves, the interlopers began to move upward. The trio were well spread.

West put the rifle to his shoulder and looked along the sight. The longer he watched the central set of eyes, the more convinced he became that he was not watching a human. The head seemed low to the ground and moved with a smooth, patient grace.

'How far do you think?' whispered Fetch.

'Couple of hundred feet. The blinds you've seen – do their

eyes show up at night like normal animals?'

'Yes.'

West clicked off the safety and aimed at the central pair of eyes. The shot echoed out across the plain and was followed by a yelp. That pair of eyes disappeared and, over the next minute or so, the others retreated.

West and Fetch remained there for some time. Eventually, West turned and scoured the steeper slopes above them but he saw nothing. It was hard to measure time but he reckoned at least half an hour had passed since the shot when they heard the wolves howl. The creatures didn't sound defeated, or angry or vengeful. They sounded just like they always did.

While Fetch was packing the next morning, West ventured back down the slope. He found no body nor any blood but he did see some tracks in a patch of mud. He placed his hand against the paw-mark to get an idea of scale. The wolf's paw was far larger. West shook his head as he stood up. Normal wolves were quick and vicious enough; these things would be difficult to stop, even with a bullet.

Once back at the camp, he found that Fetch was just about ready to go.

'You saw the Eastern Glow?'

'I did,' replied West, who had observed the purple light in the sky just before he'd fallen asleep. 'I guess we've come some way towards it.'

Fetch mounted up and gave Sandy a reassuring pat. 'I heard it's like a rainbow. No matter how far east you go, you never get any closer to it.'

West gripped his saddle horn and launched himself up. 'I don't know about that. I once met a fellow who'd read up a lot about weather and geography and suchlike. Of course, everything he'd read came before the Cataclysm. He never saw one mention of the Eastern Glow. He reckoned it was something new.'

Fetch took a moment to absorb this, then nodded down

the slope. 'Did you see anything down there?'

'Wolf tracks. *Very* big.'

'Most likely blinds then?'

'Definitely.'

'A blind rat is one thing,' said Fetch, 'a blind wolf – that's something else.'

The wind that had begun as a breeze became a gale as they rounded the hill. With the heads of both riders and mounts bowed, they ploughed on. This was not the only difficulty: the slopes were part grass, part solid rock, part slippery shale. Wary of injuring their mounts, West and Fetch guided them carefully and both expressed relief when they were finally heading downward. The wind was much less powerful at ground level and they were able to move directly north-east for the entire morning.

After stopping briefly to water the horses, they pressed on into the afternoon across low, rolling hillocks dotted with outcrops of rock. At one stage, they saw a pair of riders galloping from east to west. But they were more than a mile away and showed no sign of either seeing West and Fetch or slowing down.

There wasn't much light left by the time they reached the location of Station Alpha. Given the large scale of the map, West had already estimated this area to be four or five miles across. They came to a stop at a crossroads in the middle of a valley. The land around them had clearly been used for farming because much of it was divided by ditches, hedgerows and fences. Two farmhouses were in view but both looked abandoned. West had mixed feelings about this. A local source of information would have been useful but did he want people to know of his interest in Station Alpha?

'Got to be in this valley, right?' said Fetch as they sat on their mounts.

'Got to be,' replied West. 'I don't see why they would build one on high ground.'

'Probably be fenced off, like Charlie.'

'Probably.'

Fetch pointed to a track that led off the road they were on. It ran to the south and into an area of unusually healthy-looking trees. 'There's got to be something at the end of that.'

West had hoped to apply some kind of method to the search – especially with the fading light – but there was no point standing around, wasting time.

'Let's go and find out.'

Though his horse was obviously tired, West urged it into a trot that poor June had to keep up with. Once through the trees, they came to another farm, the house accompanied by two large barns. Both were made of wood and half of one had collapsed. Their arrival disturbed a group of hens that scattered into the undergrowth.

'You want me to shoot one?' asked Fetch. 'They're nice and fat.'

West heard him but didn't reply. He was more interested in what he'd spotted behind the barns, a sight earlier obscured by the trees. He dismounted and threw his reins to Fetch. 'Won't be long.'

The grain silo was at least thirty feet high; circular with a conical top. The access ladder was surrounded by brambles so West had to pull a scythe out of the barn and hack his way through. But soon he was climbing upwards, unable to avoid memories of that terrible underwater ascent in Station Charlie. This journey was far more pleasant, though the crow that flew out of some nook gave him a nasty surprise.

From the top of the ladder, West was able to clamber up until he reached the peak of the silo. The view was as complete as he'd hoped. He scanned the surrounding countryside and saw no fenced square of land that reminded him of Station Charlie. He turned around and checked the territory behind him too but nothing immediately presented itself.

Then he saw the corner of a fence; the only corner that

hadn't been taken over by brambles and undergrowth and trees. And though the area it surrounded was quite small, in the centre of that area was a small, blocky building.

'See anything?' shouted Fetch.

West raised a thumb then slid down on his backside to the ladder.

When they reached it, West dropped down to the ground and jogged over to the fence. There were no collapsed sections here but he forced his way through yet more brambles and came to a latched door. It wasn't locked.

West grinned as he approached the building. It was concrete, identical in design to the one at Station Charlie, complete with the single, tubular air vent. Better still, there was no lock device on the door. All he had to do was twist the handle down and push it open. Once again there was the same concrete surround, the same green-painted hatch and the same wheel.

'Fetch, get in here! Bring the lantern.'

Just as he had before, West braced his feet, gripped the wheel and tried to turn it. The wheel didn't move an inch. He tried counter-clockwise, knowing that wouldn't work. It didn't.

'Damn it.' He was beginning to wish there was another building here – preferably one where he might find fuel drums and matches to light them.

Fetch arrived at the doorway.

'Here. Help me.'

Even with the two of them on the wheel, they couldn't shift it at all.

'I guess they didn't want anyone to get into this one,' said Fetch.

West's reply was short.

'Shit.'

That night, as they made camp in the grounds of one of the old farmhouses, West considered his options. He and Fetch had used the last of the daylight to search for something combustible but found nothing. West wasn't actually convinced that any old substance would do the job anyway; in fact, he reckoned he would need to purchase some explosive. Such materials made before the Cataclysm were notoriously unreliable and dangerous. There were, however, enterprising individuals who created their own because West knew it was used in mines. Fetch had heard it called 'blast powder' and 'boomer' while West knew of the terms 'blow dust' and 'dyna'.

'There are those silver mines south of Woodhaven,' he said, thinking aloud as Fetch refilled a pail of water for the thirsty mounts. 'But that's a hell of a long way away.'

'What about a fire?' suggested Fetch. 'We could cover the hatch with wood. If it got hot enough, it might melt through.'

'It might.'

Though glad of his reading ability, West found it frustrating that he knew so little of technical and mechanical matters. It was amazing to him that there were people smart enough to recreate – however crudely – some of the devices and items apparently lost to the world.

He sat against his saddle, still thinking. Fetch put some water on to boil and some tea-leaves in the pot. The flickering light from their fire illuminated the end wall of the nearby farmhouse. Like most in the Wasteland – raiders included – the pair preferred not to stay *inside* houses. West assumed that, like him, they had made so many unpleasant discoveries inside dwellings that they preferred to stay outside.

'I know what you're thinking,' said Fetch, now adjusting the firewood with a metal stake. 'Fool's March. The Harris Gang might have some boomer.'

For Fetch, this was pretty perceptive.

'They might. And they're close.'

'But?'

'But after recent experience, I'm not particularly keen on mixing with raiders.'

'Me neither,' said Fetch, with some feeling.

Within the glow of the fire, West glanced at his companion's swollen eye. 'What if I went alone? You can stay here with the gear and the mounts – guard that hatch for me.'

Fetch shrugged. 'Up to you.'

'We're partners now, aren't we? What do you think?'

Fetch smiled at this. 'I guess it makes sense if you really want to get through that hatch. But …well …you must be careful.'

'That couple did say the Harris Gang aren't the worst of the worst. How bad can they be?'

West set out just after dawn. Planning to return that day, he took only basic provisions along with his sixer, most of the money and the medication. He used the map to guide him to Fool's March, a journey of around three hours. Approaching via a well-used track, he reached the bottom of a shallow slope. Here, a pair of sentries leaned against an old wreck. Both picked up their rifles and kept them on him as he reined in.

The men wore hats with a white H sewn into the front. In the Wasteland, these were called English hats: they were black and circular with a turned-up edge. West could at least be sure that he had the right place; surely these were members of the Harris Gang.

He dismounted. 'Morning.'

'What's your business?' asked the elder of the pair. He had a long straggly beard that stretched halfway down his chest. West wasn't overly happy about the fact that he already had his finger on the rifle trigger.

'I'm here to trade.'

'Who with?'

'I'm looking for a very specific item. I have money and pills to swap so I'd appreciate a meeting with someone senior.'

'Is that right?' said the bearded man. 'And what makes you think *we're* not senior?'

'Probably the fact that you're on sentry duty. No offence.'

The younger man lowered his gun and chuckled at this. 'What do you say to that, Clancy?'

Clancy kept his eyes and rifle trained on West.

'This is Fool's March,' said the younger man, a chubby fellow with a nasty rash on his neck. 'You're free to trade with whoever you want. Just know that the Harris Gang is in charge here and everywhere else around these parts. You behave nice and you'll be just fine.'

'Understood.' West nodded towards the town. 'May I?'

Clancy came close. 'Watch your mouth and keep that sixer in the holster.'

'Thanks for the advice.'

Despite the hostile Clancy, West was surprised that his gun wasn't taken and reflected that perhaps the Harris Gang really weren't that bad. As he rode up the slope to the edge of the town, a young man who'd been sitting on a wooden rail came forward.

'Watch your horse for you, mister?'

As there were two horses and two ponies already tied up, West decided he'd risk it.

'How do I pay you?'

'Got any food?'

'No. How's this?' He took out a scrap and handed it to the lad.

'Guild money.' By the gleeful look in his eyes, the young man was clearly pleased with the deal.

West handed him the reins and headed along the muddy track that led into Fool's March. There wasn't really a main street to speak off, but dozens of criss-crossing paths that divided ramshackle buildings and tents composed of every colour and material imaginable. Those who dwelt in these tents looked dirt-poor and West spied dozens of grimy, barefoot children. It was also hard to tell which were dwellings and which were stores. Most people seemed to be selling something: from piles of timber and baskets of nails to bunches of flowers and cuts of meat.

West saw plenty more meat when he passed a slaughterhouse. The shriek of some animal meeting its doom sent a chill through him and he glimpsed a man with slick blood up to his elbows. Two similarly blood-stained women were outside, hanging fresh cuts on hooks beside a queue of customers.

The red barn at the centre of Fool's March was possibly the largest West had seen, the paint on the windows and timbers gleaming in the spring light. There seemed to be two levels below the sloped roof and it was accessed by open double doors. West was about to head inside when he spied a man clutching a handful of papers. It seemed to him that such a man might know more than most.

'Morning.'

The fellow stopped, as if surprised to see a fresh face.

West said, 'I'm here looking to trade.'

The man had a twitching right eye which he clearly could not control. 'Yes?'

'I don't suppose you know of anyone with access to explosive?'

After a calculating look at West, the man moved away from the doors behind a cart loaded with timber.

West followed him. 'Well?'

'I would have thought that information might be worth something?'

'I could just ask someone else,' said West.

'Fine.'

The man went to leave but West held up a hand.

'All right. Will you take Guild money? Two scraps.'

'Make it four.'

'Three. *After* you tell me.'

The eye was twitching even more now. 'You need to talk to Kelly.'

'Who's he?'

'*She*. Kelly Harris. Ward's youngest daughter. He trusts her to make sure nothing goes missing. Not easy when you run a raider gang.'

'Ward is the boss?'

'Ward Harris. Only son of Albert Harris. Albert started the

gang. His great-grandfather built this barn. Fool's March was just a farm back then.'

'Where would I find this Kelly?'

'Most likely in one in the warehouses.' The man pointed along the track that ran past the red barn. 'To the bridge then turn left. Now how about you pay up?'

The three warehouses backed onto the narrow stream that marked the northern limit of Fool's March. The water had been funnelled into an artificial channel here and a water-wheel constructed. Though currently inactive, the wooden wheel was connected to a complicated apparatus that led into a neighbouring structure. West had seen such a set-up once before and knew that the power of the water was harnessed to grind corn.

The warehouses were surrounded by a high brick wall with barbed wire at the top. The only way in was via a gate manned by no less than four members of the Harris Gang, all wearing the English hats. They were as tough-looking a bunch as West had seen in Fool's March, all armed with clubs and sixers.

He used his usual trick of putting his hands in his pockets as he approached.

Even so, one of the men – a hulking fellow with a hook nose – ordered him to stop before he even got close.

'Name's Caldwell. I don't know you. Men I don't know don't come in here. Matter of fact, they don't even try.'

'I'm looking for Kelly. To trade.'

'She know you? What's your name?'

'Smith. She doesn't know me. But I have coins and pills.'

Caldwell turned to one of the others and ordered him to go inside.

West's relief that he might actually get to meet Kelly Harris was tempered by Caldwell's advance. West was taller than most but this fellow had at least four inches on him.

'Where'd you come from?'

'South.'

'Who you with?'

West was beginning to tire of this man. 'When do *I* get to ask a question?'

Thankfully, Kelly Harris couldn't have been far away because she soon came through the gate with the man sent to fetch her. She regarded West coolly, hands tucked into a short green jacket. Her boots were black but with an extravagant heel and a red stripe down both sides. She was attractive, if rather masculine; strong-jawed with slicked-down black hair.

'I hear you have coin and pills.'

'I do.'

West reached into his pocket and held out the crowns and a packet of twenty pills. He knew from the brand name that these were strong painkillers. He also knew that they were often more expensive than weapons.

'That all of it?' asked Kelly.

West shook his head.

'And what do *you* want?' she added.

He would have preferred to conduct the conversation away from Caldwell and the other guards but he had to lay his cards on the table at some point.

'Explosive. I don't need much.'

'How much is not much?'

'What do you have?'

'It's probably easier if I show you. We don't let weapons through the gate. I assume you'll be okay with that?'

West pulled out his sixer and offered it. The guard placed it on a nearby barrel.

'We'll have to pat you down too,' said Kelly.

West grinned. 'Be my guest.'

She gave a trace of a smile but then strode back through the gate. Caldwell came forward and began checking him for concealed weapons.

West shrugged. 'What a pity.'

CHAPTER 12 -JUNK

◆ ◆ ◆

In front of the warehouses were two large tables covered by scaffolding and tarpaulins. The scene reminded West of Spring Bay but on a smaller scale; there were only nine people at work and none of them looked like slaves. One table was clearly dedicated to weapons and ammunition, while the other seemed to be more of a sorting area.

By the time West was waved through the gate, Kelly Harris had struck up a conversation with a woman, who was showing her some old book. Seeing West, she gestured for him to follow.

As they walked towards the middle of the three warehouses, she took a fob of large keys from her belt. 'Where have you come from?'

'South.'

'Any news?' she asked.

'Like what?'

'Any dealings or run-ins with the gangs down there? The Mountain Mob? Reaper's Boys?'

'I try to keep myself to myself.'

Kelly unlocked the enormous padlock that secured the warehouse door and led the way inside. It was a huge space, packed with shelving and illuminated by skylights within the sloped roof.

'Quite the operation you have here in Fool's March.'

'My family has always believed in getting ahead of the

competition.'

'You are raiders, though?'

'Some people call us that. But we don't rob people.'

'You do run protection rackets though, right? Tax people who live in your territory?'

Kelly halted and gave a him a sharp glare. 'How is that a "racket"? People need protection. Should we provide it for free?'

'Fair point.'

'Have you done a lot of trading, Mr. Smith? You don't seem to know a lot about getting on with your fellow traders.'

West held up his hands. 'I make no judgements. Just curious.'

They continued on to the back of the warehouse. Here, in the rear left corner, was a little room constructed entirely of metal. *'EXPLOSIVES. CAREFUL!'* had been written on the door in red paint.

'That says-'

'I know what it says, thanks,' said West.

Kelly seemed surprised. 'An educated man.'

'Not sure I'd go that far.'

She opened another padlock and ushered him inside. In the middle of the room was a table, against the walls were four metal cabinets. As West removed his hat, Kelly opened one of the cabinets. She took out two items and placed them on the table. Both were sticks of explosive fitted with fuses. One was wrapped in transparent plastic and looked very well made; the other was covered by paper, which was slightly torn. Kelly pointed to that one first.

'These are made by some guy up north. We bought two boxes – forty sticks. So far, I think we've used ten. Eight worked fine. One didn't work at all. One exploded early and killed a man.'

She relayed this fact without emotion and pointed to the wrapped explosive. 'Those are from a stash we pulled out of a military vehicle. Untouched. We've used eight. Five worked. Three didn't – we think they dried out or something. But these are *way* more powerful.'

'So, one's more reliable, but one's stronger.'

Kelly nodded.

'How much for one of each?'

She grimaced. 'I'm not all that interested in Guild coins. I know the use is spreading beyond Woodhaven but it hasn't spread this far.'

West took out all the tablets: forty of the strong painkillers and twenty of what they called antis. It was generally accepted that these could be used to counteract infections.

Kelly examined them. 'Seals look good. Let me check the brands.' She retrieved a notebook from the inside pocket of her jacket and studied one page in particular. 'All right, I think we can do this.'

West had one last pack of painkillers in his coat but he didn't mention those.

'Both sticks for the meds?' he confirmed.

'I'll even pack them up for you. Be very, very careful, and don't hang around in Fool's March with them.'

'I don't intend to.'

Kelly fished out a small metal tin, wrapped the explosive in more paper and placed it inside. West slid the pills across the table to her. He expected her to pass him the box. Instead, she made fists with her hands and planted them on the lid.

'What do you need this for?'

'No offense, but what do you care?'

'If something – or someone – gets blown up in Harris territory and I'm the one who supplied the explosive, I'm going to have some explaining to do.'

'No one is going to get blown up. The truth is I'm starting a mining venture but not in this area. You don't need to worry.'

West reckoned that at least one lie was better than two.

She cocked her head to one side. 'You got a tip on a site? What is it? Iron? Coal? They say there's gold around here too.'

'Like I said, it's a long way away.'

'My family is always looking for new business interests. We can help out with labour, transportation, security.'

'I'm working alone for the moment. But if-'

Someone shouted Kelly's name.

She ran to the door. 'Out!'

West grabbed his hat and the metal box and followed her through the door. Having swiftly locked it, Kelly ran down the central aisle at impressive speed. Clutching the box with both hands, West stayed close behind her. Once they were outside, he saw that the workers had gathered by the gate to see what was going on.

Caldwell and another man were waiting for Kelly.

'What is it?' she demanded.

'Some gang just rode in. Thirty at least.'

The expression on Caldwell's face told West everything he needed to know. If this guy was concerned, *he* was concerned.

'My gun, if you don't mind.'

Caldwell handed it to him and West holstered it. Tucking the precious box under his arm, he followed Kelly through the gate. Ignoring the workers still inside, she instructed Caldwell to close the doors and stay at his station. At her instruction, another of the guards reached inside his coat and handed her a quick with a fancy handle decorated with gems. Without so much as a glance at West, she ran towards the centre.

Though the red barn was obscured by other buildings, he could hear more shouting and dozens of horses on the move. He thought of his mount, still tied to that rail on the other side of town. Trying to look casual, he pulled the brim of his hat down and set off on a route that would take him around the centre, not through it. As he passed a dyeworks then a series of houses, townsfolk hurried towards the barn, all of them questioning each other, desperate to know what was going on.

West would have simply continued on his way if he hadn't passed the alleyway. Though the figure at the other end of it was a hundred feet away, he was unmistakable: sitting upright and alert in his saddle, hand on his holstered gun: Silvera.

West cursed again.

Moving to the corner so he wouldn't be seen, he hoped that

it was just Silvera and a few others. Then two more rode past. Reaper was speaking and gesticulating. His giant bodyguard, Rock, solemnly followed his boss.

West cursed some more.

Knowing he needed to see what exactly was going on, he also knew that his position was too exposed. He jogged past the alleyway and took the next left. Picking his way through an area of small shacks built almost on top of one another, he came up behind a group of about twenty who had gathered at a corner opposite the red barn.

At the barn itself, a force of armed locals now faced Reaper's Boys, who remained on their horses. The Harris Gang were being reinforced with every passing moment but Reaper and his followers didn't seem concerned. West was relieved to see that neither he nor his raiders had drawn their guns, though they had plenty of them.

'There's Ward,' blurted one of the onlookers. 'He'll put these bastards to rights.'

Several others weighed in, most of them insulting the interlopers.

Ward Harris was a well-attired man, with a long moustache the same snowy white as his hair. Despite his age, he clearly wasn't intimidated and approached the horsemen calmly. He hailed Reaper and soon the pair were talking, just too far away to be heard. The townsfolk were clearly desperate to know what was going on so they moved forward, even though it took them closer to Reaper's Boys, Silvera included.

West wasn't all that worried about what the two leaders were saying because he had little doubt about why Reaper was in Fool's March. What he was more concerned about was Kelly Harris. She had stopped to talk to some woman but was now striding towards her father. West couldn't be sure that their conversation would immediately place him in danger but – given what he'd just purchased – it seemed likely that Reaper would get to the truth before long. West's first thought was to retreat into the houses, find a good shooting position and take someone out – Silvera, maybe. Given the obvious tension between the two gangs, someone else would take a shot and, in all likelihood, the face-off would turn into a battle. During the ensuing chaos, he could make his escape.

The trouble with that plan was that not only the raiders would suffer. It seemed that just about everybody in Fool's March was present and West really didn't want all that blood on his hands. He also didn't want to see Kelly get hurt. Reaper might work out he'd been there but he didn't know where Station Alpha was and – if West could get in and out quick enough – he and Fetch could clear the area.

West sloped away from the crowd and, once in cover, found that he was virtually alone. Reaching the road that he'd come in on, he now had to cross it to reach his horse. The lad had obviously been drawn to the unfolding drama like everyone else, leaving his charges untended. Though there were a few people nearby, they were all watching the scene outside the red barn.

'You one of them?'

The voice came from behind him; a youthful voice.

West turned around and saw a boy of about fourteen. From beneath a floppy sun hat, the boy's eyes bored into him. In his hands was a single-barrelled shotgun.

'Easy now.'

'I asked you a question. You one of them?'

'No.'

'Then why are you sneaking around?'

'I'm not. I'm trying to get back to my horse so I can get out of here. I just don't want to get caught up in any trouble.'

West hoped that the truthfulness of that statement might make him more convincing.

The boy's hands were shaking. He cleared his throat before replying. 'How do I know that?'

'If I was one of them, I'd be *with* them, right? Did you get a good look at them, see the tattoos?'

The lad nodded.

'See any on me?' West removed his hat. 'I'm no raider. Just

going about my own business. What's your name, son?'

'Don't you worry about my name. What's yours?'

'Smith.'

West was now worried about someone else seeing this standoff; more attention coming his way.

'I'm going to go and get my horse. You should put that down.'

'What if I don't believe you?'

West had moved swiftly from feeling some sympathy for the young lad to wanting to grab the shotgun and crack him across the head with it.

'I'm going to get my horse,' repeated West.

The boy's fingers were still shaking.

West reckoned it took a lot of nerve to shoot a man in the back. He turned and strode across the road, without even glancing to his left. The grey horse tapped the ground with its hooves upon seeing him but thankfully kept quiet. As West calmly placed the metal box in a saddlebag, he saw the young man at last lower his shotgun and walk away. He'd been as sure as he could be but still felt a pang of relief.

Once in the saddle, West guided his horse through the empty shacks and tents, down the slope to the road. The sentry named Clancy and his compatriot were watching the town, clearly aware that something was up. When they asked what was going on, West told them. The duo clearly had orders not to leave their post because even mention of another raider gang in Fool's March didn't draw them away.

Once he was out of view, West urged the horse into a gallop. The more he thought about it, the more he realised that Reaper would quickly find out what he needed to know. Assuming the explosive did its job, he planned to be in and out of Alpha by nightfall. Then he and Fetch could slip away under cover of darkness, and escape once more.

The grey horse cantered or galloped most of the way, resting only once at a stream. He was so swift and sure-footed that

West even toyed with the idea of giving him a name. But that seemed like tempting fate, especially with Reaper's Boys so close.

West supposed that friends should probably be truthful with one another but when he finally reached the farmhouse and saw Fetch, he made no mention of the raiders. He simply dropped to the ground, tied the horse to a nearby tree and took out the metal box.

'How did you do?' asked Fetch.

West tapped the box. 'All good. You stay here. Leave it to me. Keep an eye out.'

'Why? Did something happen?'

'We have to be careful.'

'You're sure you want to go in there alone?' asked Fetch. 'Last time ...'

'This won't be like last time. I'll make sure of it.' West hurried over to his pack and emptied it. Then he placed the box inside along with the lantern and some matches.

'I'll be as quick as I can. And don't worry if you hear an extremely loud bang.'

The explosion blew the tubular air vent hundreds of feet into the air. West had shut the door to focus the blast and restrict the noise. Approaching the building from his hiding place behind a tree, he saw that the explosive had also blown the reinforced door off one hinge. He knew a better strategy would have been to dig out a hole in the concrete surround but he had neither the tools nor the time. In fact, he had simply placed the stick on the hatch, lit the fuse and hoped for the best.

Incredibly, one half of the hatch was still intact and West could now see that it had been sealed with some kind of substance from the inside. The hatch had split in two along a jagged edge and bits of metal shrapnel had embedded themselves in the concrete walls.

With no desire to lose another coat and hat, he removed both and placed them on the ruined door. With the pack on his back, he clamped the handle of the already-lit lantern in his mouth and clambered onto the surround. Carefully gripping the remains of the hatch, he lowered himself and swung his legs onto the ladder. From there, he could climb down.

After ten rungs, he stopped. He told himself it was because his teeth ached from gripping the lantern handle – but that wasn't really the reason. Wrapping his left arm around the ladder, he took the lantern from his mouth and held it below him. The glow didn't reach all that far but he could at least see that the way was clear. Even so, he couldn't avoid memories of that awful climb up an identical shaft, pushing a body aside before almost drowning. But once he'd reminded himself of what he might find, West got himself moving again.

Though he was soon stepping down onto the familiar metal grille and into a space identical in layout to Station Charlie, the similarity ended there. West held the lantern up, illuminating an area packed with junk that in some places reached three feet off the floor. There was, however, a narrow path that led to the corridor and the rest of the installation. Moving the lantern, West picked out a sign that read *STATION ALPHA*. Every other visible space upon the walls was covered in a multi-coloured scrawl of paint: letters, words, numbers, diagrams, poems … ramblings. Some was written in English; some was in a language – or languages – unknown to West.

And then he noticed something else, close to the ladder. A torch: not a flashlight but the thin, cylindrical instrument that produced a flame and could be used to melt metal and create a seal.

At Station Charlie, the military had closed off the bunker to keep everyone out. Somebody at Station Alpha had wanted to keep themselves *in*.

West drew his sixer and listened. If anyone was still down here, they would have heard the explosion and seen the damage to the hatch. He thought it unlikely that anyone was still alive but he couldn't be certain. He advanced towards the corridor, the lantern picking out the bizarre collation of objects. A yellow toy car. A metal traffic sign. Red shirts still on their hangers. Roof tiles. Trash cans. Post boxes. Fire extinguishers. Packets of spaghetti. Light bulbs.

On the far side of the room, the junk took on a different complexion. It was a jumble of cables, keyboards, plugs, screens and other devices. West stopped in front of it and lifted the lantern high. Some of what he saw was familiar, most was not. Before long, his eyes came to a rest on a circular shape attached to a metal pole. It was another metal detector, just like the one he had found – and lost – at Station Charlie.

Intending to retrieve it on his way out, West pressed forward into the corridor. Halfway along it, he stopped again and listened. The bunker was utterly silent; quiet in a way that the world above never was. Earlier, West had been struck by an unpleasant recollection – the escape from Station Charlie. But now, he experienced the wonder of this glimpse into the old times; a relic of the past hidden beneath the ground.

He almost felt as if – just by being here – that he was *in* the past, before the Cataclysm. But was it just familiarity? Because he had been in such a place before?

The door at the end of the corridor was slightly ajar. Lantern in his left hand, sixer in the right, West kicked it open, releasing a cloud of dust and cobwebs. Though the musty smell was the same, the interior was not. Laid out identically to the previous command centre, every single surface was covered in yet more junk. As he walked through it, his feet knocking assorted objects aside, West saw that one area of the table had been cleared. Neatly piled up here were some of the folders he'd found in Charlie but also newspapers and magazines and dozens of other documents. A packet of red pens sat atop one pile and red markings could be seen all over.

For some reason, West felt most afraid when he ventured towards the accommodation. As the lantern's weak light spilled across the walls and floor, he came to the first rooms. One was full of more junk; one contained water bottles, only a few of which were full. West moved on.

The next room on the left contained nothing but bunk

beds piled inside to make space. And in the last room, there was more space – around a single bunk bed in which a dead body lay. The piles of clothes nearby included pants and West somehow already knew that this was the dwelling of a man. A blanket covered everything but the skeleton's face. He somehow looked at peace.

When West moved, the lantern-light swept away from the bed and illuminated a book. It was a thick notebook and had fallen face down on the floor. Brushing away a spiderweb, West noted that another of the red pens was close by. He picked the book up and placed the lantern on the top bunk so he could read.

Flicking through the pages, he initially found little that was coherent. Most of the man's notes were only a word, or a sentence, or sometimes just a number. As well as the notes, numerous pieces of paper had been folded into the book. At first, it all seemed random, and West concluded that the contents were no more ordered than the junk-filled bunker. But then he began to notice certain key phrases that were repeated; some ruminations on the Cataclysm, some that seemed to focus on other underground and military facilities. Then West came across the exact same map he had retrieved from Station Charlie. This had evidently been important to its owner: it was well-preserved within a plastic wallet.

West realised now that he had found a kindred spirit; a man apparently even more devoted than him to solving the puzzle of these hidden places in order to answer broader questions. Suddenly, he was gripped by a desire to know this man's name. He looked at the start of the book but found nothing. Then he walked around the bed to a small bedside table. Here was a photograph in a dust-covered frame showing a young couple, embracing each other. West removed the back of the frame and saw writing on the reverse of the photo: *Maury and Jeanette, Florida, July 1999.*

Though keen to continue searching the bunker, time was short and West knew he was unlikely to find anything more useful. He took off his pack and placed the journal inside. With a last glance at the bed, he nodded at the bunker's only inhabitant.

Thanks, Maury.

The only thing he took on the way out was the metal detector. He couldn't avoid the feeling that somewhere in Station Alpha were the right batteries to operate the damn thing but he didn't have the time to look. He had just reached the ladder when the lantern gave out. There was, however, just about enough light in the shaft to see his way so he packed the lantern and set off.

Climbing out through the half-destroyed hatch, he was surprised to find that dusk was descending; he'd been down there longer than he'd realised. Knowing they'd have to depart immediately, West ran back to the farmhouse, now wearing his hat and coat once more. Approaching the camp, he was surprised to find the mounts alone. Fetch had bagged up all their gear but was nowhere to be seen. West dumped his pack and drew his sixer.

His first thought was to head for the grain silo. From there, he would be able to see what was going on. But that would take time. Was it even wise to leave the camp? Fetch might return while he was gone. West moved up to the corner of the house, hoping to see him.

He was still looking that way when he heard someone on the move. Spinning round, gun up, his eyes met the barrel of a rifle coming round the opposite corner of the house. Fortunately, Fetch was holding it. When he saw West, he placed a finger against his mouth, signalling quiet.

The two met beside the mounts, who seemed to sense their unease.

'Did you know they were here?' asked Fetch.

West nodded and brushed away a slight feeling of guilt. 'I saw them in Fool's March. How many?'

'Five. One of them's Silvera.'

'Least it's not *all* of them,' said West.

Fetch actually looked angry now. 'How many-'

'-Forget that. Where *exactly* are they?'

'Riding in from the north. I saw a flock of birds go up. Five minutes.'

The pair had been there long enough for West to memorise the surrounding territory. He had already made certain plans for certain eventualities. But he hadn't expected the raiders to arrive so quickly.

'My fault. Listen, we're not going to out-ride them. Best if you take the mounts and walk out of here. Head past the bunker until you reach the western side of the valley. I'll meet you at the cliff we saw yesterday.'

Fetch didn't seem all that convinced by this plan.

'Don't worry,' said West. 'They aren't going to get as far as you. I'll see to it.'

West quickly tethered June to Sandy and Sandy to the grey horse. He led them directly away from the house about fifty feet, halting behind a barn. He handed Fetch the reins then took the rifle from the saddle and pocketed two boxes of ammunition.

'Once you're on open ground, ride for the cliff. I'll find you.'

Fetch shook his head. 'You're going to fight *five* of them?'

West grinned. 'Surprise counts for a lot.'

CHAPTER 13 -GUNFIGHT

◆◆◆

Rifle over his shoulder, he hurried along the right side of the farmhouse then cut across the overgrown garden to a gate. Once through that, he darted to another barn with open doors. He positioned himself at the left corner, which offered a good view of the crossroads.

West was immediately glad that he'd moved quickly because the Boys were already there. Five, as Fetch had said, horses puffing hard as the men scanned in every direction. Silvera had removed his hat, revealing a determined expression on that lean, hard face.

West knew he had to hit them now, before they split up. This wasn't just to give Fetch more time; he didn't want to end up facing five foes in five different places. Just to the left of the barn was a low patch of undergrowth. West crawled to it then got up on one knee. He readied the rifle, butt tight against his shoulder, barrel poking between two branches.

West wasn't all that keen on killing men in cold blood. But he was heavily outnumbered and facing old enemies – his usual rules didn't apply. He reckoned it was some weird twist of luck or fate that had brought him together with Silvera once more. And now – with another such twist – the raider turned his horse, presenting an easier target.

West's shot took him high in the chest. Face frozen in shock, Silvera slid back off his saddle and fell to the ground. The four horses and the four men panicked. Two rode away; two almost rode into each other. West initially picked the closer of them for his next target but then the horse bolted.

Two have gone right. One's gone left.

The remaining man was still struggling with his bucking mount when West fired again. He missed the man but caught his horse. Shrieking, it threw the rider off and galloped away. He came down badly on his ankle. Struggling to his feet, he was reaching for his gun when the bullet tore into his gut. He hit the dirt only feet from Silvera.

Three to go. One went left. Two went right.

West crawled back to the barn, shouldered the rifle then hurried past the doors to the opposite corner. Peering around it, he saw a stretch of scrubby ground then the five-foot wall that ran parallel the road. Away to the right, the scrub gave way to an orchard. One riderless horse was milling around on the road so the raider was presumably down and looking for West. He couldn't see the other horse but could hear it cantering. He reckoned the rider was still on that one; hoping to stay out of trouble, maybe flank him or come up behind.

He scanned the wall, sure that at least one man was behind it. He noted the gate that connected the road to the orchard. The raider couldn't get over the wall without presenting an easy target. West didn't much like the idea of doing nothing. He had to take the initiative.

Crouching over as he ran, he made for the wall, wincing at the noise of his feet and legs striking the weeds. Halfway there, he glimpsed the barrel of a quick on the far side of the gate. It disappeared instantly but West wasn't about to miss this chance. He gently put the rifle down and drew his sixer. Walking forward, he examined the wall between he and the gate. There were several holes in the old brick, including one about five feet away. It was eighteen inches off the ground – just about right.

West carefully placed his left boot in it and stepped up. Left hand on the wall to steady himself, he looked over the top and to the right. The raider was crouching by the gate. Hearing West, he turned.

The bullet hit him in the face, colouring the air with a pink cloud of blood and flesh. His head rocked back, then forward, leaving him a crumpled mess hunched against the wall. West took the opportunity to turn left. He was glad to see the two others still on the ground, though one was moving.

His swift turn back to the right saved his life. A short, bearded raider was charging across the orchard, rifle in his hands.

West had already thrown himself upwards when the first bullet struck the wall. As he rolled over the top and came down in a heap, his first thought was that he'd been hit. His eyes stung with pain, as did the rest of his face. He put his hand to his cheek and felt something stuck in his flesh. When he pulled it out, it crumbled in his hand. Brick dust. Wiping his eyes on the sleeve of his coat, West readied himself, knowing the raider was coming.

Then he saw the two grenades hanging from the belt of the dead man. West took a brief glance over his left shoulder to check there was no danger in that direction then listened once more. If the man in the orchard was moving, he was doing so silently. West moved forward on his hands and knees and unhooked both grenades from the belt. The gate just ahead of the dead man was ajar, which helped West make up his mind.

He hooked one of the grenades to his own belt. Then he pulled the pin out of the other. Though he'd seen others use them, he wasn't about to take chances with the length of the fuse. He popped the grenade over the wall about ten feet ahead of him. As soon as it landed, he heard the raider scrambling away. Two seconds later, the grenade detonated. West stood, kicked the gate open and stepped into the orchard.

The man was on his back, lower legs shredded by the blast, looking down at his mutilated body in horror. West put him out of his misery with a bullet to his chest. As the shot rang out, an apple fell from a tree, now one of many blown to the ground by the grenade.

Four down. One to go.

And it seemed that the last man was keen to get into the fight. With a clattering of hooves, he rode out from behind the barn on the far side of the orchard. Evidently a skilled rider, he was able to guide his horse along the road without using the reins. He needed both hands for his assault rifle.

The burst of bullets cut across the orchard, sending more branches and apples to the ground. West briefly considered returning fire but the sheer volume of the onslaught sent him running. He did what he could by zig-zagging but bullets continued to rip up the grass and ping past him. Veering left, he threw himself over a bush, the sixer still in his hand.

Now finding himself close to the barn where the shootout had started, he heard the last man's horse slow as it reached the crossroads. The sensible choice might have been to take cover; wait for a chance. But West had got this far by taking the initiative and he wasn't about to stop now. This arrogant bastard might not expect the fight to come to him.

The horse accelerated into a gallop, having turned left and now riding parallel to the side of the barn. West positioned himself at the near corner. The sounds of the hammering hooves grew loud. Gun up, West watched it bolt past – without a rider.

Realising instantly that it was a distraction, he threw himself to the ground just as the assault rifle opened up. The raider had positioned himself at the far end of the barn and now held the trigger down. West was already rolling left, taking him behind the building as bullets tore up the ground.

Concluding that this last man might be the toughest of the lot, he got back to his feet, mind already working. He moved up to the barn's double doors and slipped through them. Due to the late hour, the interior was murky, but he could see areas of light where the old walls were damaged and holed. One of them was on the right side, close to the end where the last man had positioned himself.

West knew it was his best chance and he kept his eyes downward as he slipped across the barn, determined to avoid any obstacle that might give away his position. He listened too;

and he heard one of the horses, returning at a walk. He also heard one of the injured men, still whimpering.

Now he walked across slippery straw, holding out his left arm to retain his balance. His eyes had adjusted and he could see a clear path to the wall. He wasn't far away when a shaft of sunlight was momentarily blocked. Then came a click: the raider shoving in a new magazine.

The next hole in the wall was about two feet off the ground. West stopped, aimed. He heard the raider's footsteps; his calm, even breaths. He steadied himself, put his finger on the trigger. The light disappeared.

West fired his four remaining bullets, shifting his aim higher with every shot. As the echo of the last one reverberated around the barn, something heavy hit the ground. West took three paces forward and peered through the hole. He saw the raider's leg and his hand laying across it. He wasn't moving.

Having retrieved his rifle and reloaded the sixer, West left the assault rifle as there was little ammunition left. The last raider had been struck in the thigh and under the armpit. The leg shot must have hit something crucial because pints of blood had gushed out of him. When West saw that – and the youthful face of the raider who'd come closest to taking him out – he felt a pang of regret. With a tip of his hat, he walked out to the road.

Two of the horses were grazing nearby, apparently unconcerned by the demise of their masters. Like the last raider, West's second victim had lost a lot of blood, enough to create a puddle that had spread as far as Silvera. West's old enemy was now lying on his side, face ashen.

'You lucky son of a bitch.' With every word, blood leaked from his mouth and down his chin.

West didn't want to talk to the man.

Silvera bared his bloodied teeth. 'I hope you-'

West put the second bullet into his heart. The raider exhaled then tipped slowly onto his back.

West stood there a while, weighed down by guns that felt

even heavier than usual. Though he now felt the faint warm glow that came with victory – with *survival* – he wished the raiders hadn't found this place. He wished he and Fetch had got away clean. Because the Boys would find their dead compatriots and Reaper's desire for revenge would only grow. West knew it was inevitable now; a leader couldn't possibly let another affront like this go unpunished.

He took one last look at Silvera. 'Why couldn't you have just left me alone?'

By the time he reached the cliff, night had come. The moon and the stars were obscured by a thick layer of cloud, meaning that he had to call out to Fetch to locate him. West was desperate for a drink and the first thing he did was empty a bottle of water.

'I heard the shots,' Fetch said as West sat down, the tiredness now setting in. 'There were lots of them.'

'Yep.'

'Silvera? Did you-'

'I'm still alive aren't, I?' snapped West. 'Which means they aren't.'

He wasn't entirely sure why he replied so angrily. He just knew that he was in no mood to tell Fetch the tale: if the man was that interested in fights and killing, maybe he should do some of it himself. Shocked into silence, Fetch took the two rifles and placed them on a saddle. West just sat there on the cold, hard ground, hands clasped together.

Not for the first time, he wondered how he did these things. It couldn't all be instinct. Fighting seemed to be what he did best and he didn't think anyone got good at anything without either experience or training; or both. At least he'd escaped the raiders again; at least he could keep searching for answers.

'You're shivering,' said Fetch after a time.

West stood up. 'I'm all right. We should keep moving. Can't run into too much trouble if we stick to the middle of the valley.'

'Where we headed?'

'I'll decide tomorrow. For now, we just need to get away from here.'

'Got it. We riding?'

'Sure. Those mounts have had enough of a break.'

West let out a long sigh and buttoned up his coat, unsure why he hadn't already done so.

Fetch soon returned with the grey horse and offered him the reins.

Once up in the saddle, West nudged his mount forward and they started away. He looked back to where the dead men lay and was glad to see only darkness.

The next light they saw was The Eastern Glow. Slumped in his saddle, West had almost dozed off when he first saw the distant, paler patch of sky that soon pulsed with reds and purples. The mounts were initially disturbed but West and Fetch pressed them forward, even as distant forks of lightning cracked the sky open and struck the earth. Unlike a typical storm, there was no thunder, though West did wonder if they were simply too far away to hear it. They watched the storm, using it to guide their way along the valley until it finally ceased. When dawn came, the cloud thickened and dumped heavy rain. For a time, day was darker than night.

*

To the north and east lay a bleak plain broken up only by the occasional scattering of low scrub or cactus. They halted at a shallow river, where Fetch replenished their water supplies, even though they couldn't build a fire to heat it yet. Here, West also cleaned his face, picking out the last fragments of brick stuck in his skin. Thankfully, the rain had eased off and he promptly fell asleep before Fetch could prepare any food.

When he awoke, there was a plate in front of him. Suddenly struck by hunger, he wolfed the food down and drank a little of the remaining clean water.

'I guess I should have bought some provisions at Fool's March.'

'Not what you were there for,' replied Fetch, who was sitting on his saddle at the top of the river bank, gazing back towards the valley.

West looked up at the sky. Enough of the cloud had burned away for him to pinpoint the sun and he saw that it was midmorning.

'We should keep moving.'

'Where to?'

West wasn't sure about that but the very thought of Reaper made him nervous of inaction. Then again, it would be stupid to travel too far without some kind of plan.

'Rain will have washed away our tracks,' pointed out Fetch.

West was so dozy that he hadn't even considered that. He decided they could spare an hour.

'I'll have a look at this journal, see if I can work something out.'

West worked methodically this time, starting at page one and reading everything. There were two problems, however. The first was that old Maury didn't seem to have employed much of a method. He had written note upon note, scratched out as much as he had written, and arranged those notes in various, confusing forms. The second problem was his handwriting, which was always messy and often indecipherable. After ten pages of getting nowhere, West took out all the folded-up papers, including the map identical to his own.

The first page was a typed list of names, including ranks and numbers – some sort of military document. Maury had made notations all over it with his red pen but West couldn't find anything that made much sense to him. The next document was another directory of some type, and it seemed to relate to military installations. West examined it but found no mention of the underground stations. The third document was actually a collection of photos held together by a clip. The pictures showed military structures, vehicles and weapons. The photos appeared to have been torn out of magazines and papers. West had seen such images before. The photos included land vehicles and ships equipped with huge guns. West found it almost impossible to believe that such things had ever existed. The fourth document was another collection, this one of technical diagrams – again, mainly structures and vehicles. Flicking through them, West came across one installation that was denoted, '*REGIONAL COMMAND HUB, AREA 14*'.

He soon realised that it was an underground structure very similar to the stations but on a much larger scale. It was also deeper below the surface and contained more than a dozen different sections. West spent a long time examining the page but found nothing that might give him a clue to the installation's location. As this was by far the most interesting discovery, he then searched through the journal, seeking further references to the command hub. There were none.

Hearing Fetch move, West turned and looked up the bank. The former raider was on his feet, shading his eyes as he surveyed the valley.

'What is it?'

'Nothing. Just wild ponies. A dozen or more. Not coming our way.'

Even though there was no danger, West couldn't avoid the feeling that he shouldn't use up any more time on the journal; not for now, anyway. He took a last look at the schematic of the hub then placed it inside the journal.

'Let's go.'

Watered and fed, the horse, pony and mule seemed in good heart, even though they had to cross the river. The water never got beyond their knees but West had seen horses put to fright by a lot less. Once up the steep far bank, they continued travelling east. West reckoned this was as good a direction as any; it took them further from danger and into territory neither of them knew. It seemed logical that he could find out more by discovering new areas and perhaps through meeting new people.

They spent the day riding across low, marshy ground, occasionally having to retrace their steps to avoid the worst of the boggy terrain. West reckoned it was worth it because he was aiming for a line of low hills; he was sure they'd both feel safer on the other side of them. Fetch didn't say much and West felt a little guilty for his harsh words after the gun battle. There didn't seem much sense in criticising the man for what he wasn't and what he would never be.

'That's the trouble with the warmer weather,' remarked Fetch, wafting away some insects. 'These damned critters start showing up.'

'I hope there aren't any blind *insects*,' replied West, glad of the distraction.

Fetch whistled. 'Don't. You'll give me nightmares.'

West felt he should at least explain what had occurred at Fool's March, though he had no desire to recount the bloody shoot-out with Silvera and his crew. Fetch listened carefully, and was particularly interested in the town and Kelly Harris' warehouse. Thinking of her, West just hoped that there had been no confrontation between the Harris Gang and Reaper's Boys. The quick appearance of Silvera's crew suggested that Reaper had despatched his raiders in various directions.

'He sure caught up to us quickly,' said Fetch. 'I thought we had longer.'

'Me too.'

'He won't find us again,' said West, trying to sound more confident than he felt.

An hour before the sun went down, he noticed its dying rays sparking off something metallic. He and Fetch took a southerly diversion and eventually came across an incredible sight.

Half-submerged in the marshy ground were the remains of a vast airplane. It seemed to have sustained a great impact because it had broken in two, exposing metal bodywork that reminded West of a dead horse's ribcage. There had evidently been a fire at some point because the rear half was blackened and holed. Despite the hour of the day, they agreed this was a find worthy of investigation.

With the lantern to guide their way, they entered the front section of the aircraft, passing rows of unoccupied seats before reaching the cockpit. Strangely, there were no bodies here either. West did, however, find a spare uniform which identified the aircraft as military. There was also a large compass which would have been useful but was too heavy and well-fixed to remove. Fetch located some flares but was even more pleased when he pulled a first aid kit out of a locker.

'Worth it just for this!' he exclaimed, showing West the white box with a red cross on top.

West had conducted his own search and his only real find was a set of maps held within a long tube. He had no idea what they showed but – as with the journal – he'd have time to study them later.

'Shall we search the back?' asked Fetch.

West peered out of window and saw that the sun was close to the horizon. 'Let's get over those hills. Find some dry ground.'

For once, it was Fetch who seemed reluctant to leave. 'At one time, this thing was in the sky, flying like a great big metal bird. They were so lucky, the people back then.'

West tucked the maps under his arm and led the way out. 'I don't know about that ...but they were definitely luckier than us.'

CHAPTER 14 - WOLVES

◆ ◆ ◆

West rose with the sun and went for a walk, the journal in his hand. Though the site where they'd camped was not as wet as the marshy plain, there was no real shelter to be found. A gusty wind unsettled them for the first half of the night, a light rain for the remainder. Fetch did have a shelter he could put up but the rain was never quite heavy enough to persuade either of them to leave their blankets. Now it had stopped entirely. They agreed not to light a fire and to get moving as soon as possible. But where to?

West could find nowhere dry but sat down anyway – one of the advantages of a long coat. He had stayed within sight of the camp, and now gazed out at the lifeless plain to the east. The earth he was sitting on was almost like sand and he could see that the plain was of an even lighter shade. Many months ago, he'd heard that there were great dunes of sand in the east, though few had actually seen them.

West hoped that a clear mind and a new day might bring a breakthrough with his examination of Maury's journal but he was soon cursing, floundering once again in a bewildering fog of names, lists, ruminations and even poems. The man seemed to have spent much of his time considering what had caused the Cataclysm. But West had heard all these theories before; he wanted to know if Maury had discovered anything more substantial.

He unfolded the schematic of the Hub. Maury had at least

learned of its existence, but that wasn't much use without some clue to its location. West returned to the journal but now realised that – especially in the second half – Maury seemed to be looking backwards upon his own life, mentioning significant experiences and family members more often.

There were, however, three other names that recurred. Deciding that he wasn't getting anywhere on his own, West walked back across the slope of the hill to the camp. Fetch handed him a plate of breakfast. West wasn't hungry but he ate it nonetheless, knowing he faced another long day. Fetch had already started packing up.

'Tell me if these names mean anything to you: Maria Flores, Carl Steven Maggs, General Blackridge.'

Fetch stopped what he was doing. 'Can you repeat them?'

West did so. Fetch looked up at sky for a moment then shook his head. 'Sorry, don't know 'em. They all in the book?'

West brushed a hand across his empty plate to clean it off. 'Yep. Flores four times, the others twice.'

'*General* Blackridge. Sounds like maybe he was in the army.'

Though he knew that no adult listed on a document from before the Cataclysm could still be alive, West retrieved the list of military personnel from the journal. As expected, he found no mention of any Blackridge, though there were two generals.

'Ah, shit. I have no idea where to go. Or what to do.' West felt suddenly devoid of energy, as if all the trials of recent days and weeks had caught up with him.

Fetch ambled over to West's saddlebag and took out the long tube recovered from the airplane. Removing the cap, he tipped out the maps inside.

'Did you check these yet?' he asked, flattening out the first of the maps on the saddlebag.

'No. A map's only useful if you know what you're looking for.'

West could see from where he was sitting that none of the place names were familiar. 'That's not even this part of the country. Best leave it to me, Fetch. You can't read.'

Without a reply, Fetch moved on to the next map, then another.

Letting out a long sigh, West lay back on the ground, again not caring about getting wet.

'Two and five,' said Fetch after a minute. 'Twenty-five. That's the name of the road. Not so far away.'

He at least had that right. All the roads in the country were assigned numbers and some maps showed them.

West lay there, watching a bird circle high above them in the clear blue sky. It was so high that he couldn't even guess at its size; it might have been an eagle, it might have been a crow.

'What was that name?' asked Fetch. 'Black something?'

'Blackridge. But you can't read, right?'

'I know black. I know colours and a few other words.' Fetch pointed at the map. 'Is that Blackridge?'

West stood up, walked over and checked the name. 'Yes.'

Fetch beamed. 'Maybe that's it.'

'But it was a name, not a place.' West grabbed the journal and found the first reference. General Blackridge had been etched in pencil and when he looked closely, he saw there was a faint comma between the words. The second reference didn't feature a comma but, below it, Maury had written two questions: *Go there? Find out what he has?*

It seemed that Maury had never done so but it was the only lead West had.

'So maybe there's a general *at* Blackridge.'

He grabbed the map and made some calculations. 'About eighty miles north. Two or three days. Still takes us away from Reaper.'

West turned to his companion, who was still beaming. 'Good work, Fetch. Real good work.'

Only when that day had ended and another began did West really begin to feel some sense of relief. Though there were few landmarks, they passed two roads marked on the map and headed directly north whenever possible. They hadn't encountered anyone since the shoot-out and knew the intermittent rain must have covered their tracks.

Even if they were being pursued, they would certainly see their enemies coming. For mile after mile, West and Fetch rode across plains that were as easy on the riders as they were on the mounts. In a few areas, there was lush, green grass and even a handful of flowers but most of the ground was dark, hard earth. Worse than that, in places an odd orange fungus had covered ground and vegetation; it appeared to kill off plants and emitted a bitter smell.

At first, the open territory made West feel vulnerable but by that second evening, he was accustomed to it. Even so, the pair agreed to forgo a fire yet again. West spent much of the evening cleaning and oiling their weapons. He recruited Fetch to help but noted the man's lack of enthusiasm for the task. He reckoned his companion would be quite happy to never pick up a gun again.

That night, the Eastern Glow returned and they had to comfort June and Sandy when the great shards of lightning blasted the earth. The grey horse seemed unperturbed. He was so steady and tough that West decided he now deserved a name. He and Fetch came up with a very long list before West eventually settled on Ranger. He hoped to keep this horse longer than the others.

The Eastern Glow wasn't all that disturbed them that night. An hour before dawn they heard the heavy thrum of many hooves. Thankfully, the moonlight illuminated only another herd of wild ponies that galloped westward without passing close to the camp.

But that was not their last encounter with the ponies of the plain. In the afternoon of the following day, they negotiated the first of a series of low, rounded hills. And it was while crossing a flat section between two of these hills that they also crossed paths with the herd.

They heard them before they saw them; the familiar beat of their hooves that seemed to transmit itself through the ground like a warning. West and Fetch agreed that this sounded like a lot of animals but neither of them could believe the sight that greeted them from the east. Scores of ponies were on the move; and they were not cantering but galloping, as if running for their lives.

West and Fetch urged their own mounts into a gallop, desperate to clear the narrow valley and avoid the stampede. As the herd thundered towards them, West knew nothing would stop it. With seconds to spare, he and Fetch at last reached a slope, struggled up a few yards and sought refuge behind an outcrop of rock. The first of the ponies charged past, wild eyes bulging, kicking up clouds of dust.

'Hundreds!' West shouted as they dismounted. 'Maybe more.'

'Did you see that?' replied Fetch. 'Two near the front just went down. The others just kept going over the top of them!'

Though protected by the outcrop, they were only yards from the stampeding herd and both men had to hold the reins tight to keep Ranger, Sandy and June in check. By the time the rear of the herd came into view, West reckoned there were five or six hundred at least. He'd heard tell of such large groupings of horses and ponies but had no idea they could grow to such a size. It was only when the last of them galloped by that he saw why they were fleeing with such desperate haste.

'That was close,' said Fetch, oblivious to what West had observed.

'Wolves!'

West handed Ranger's reins to Fetch and reached for the rifle on his saddle. He wrenched it clear, clicked off the safety and lifted it to his shoulder.

There were three. Tall, lanky beasts with pale, scarred bodies just like the blind rats. Two were some distance away, pursuing a trio of younger ponies left behind by the herd. Of more immediate concern was the third wolf, which had given up chasing the main herd and halted in the disturbed earth left behind. Snout to the air, it turned towards the men. The ears quivered and it loped towards them. One hundred feet swiftly became fifty.

'Go,' breathed West, already training the rifle sights on the wolf.

A wide-eyed Fetch scrambled away up the slope, leading horse, pony and mule.

The wolf was accelerating, snout still high. As it got closer, West was able to grasp its true size. The blind was at least five foot at the shoulder, seven or eight long. When it stopped at the base of the slope, he couldn't drag his gaze from those white, sightless eyes. But he forced himself to check on the other two creatures. One was still pursuing the ponies; the other was still.

Baring its teeth, the wolf leaped up the slope. West reckoned it was about twenty feet away when he fired the first shot. The creature yelped with pain but stopped only momentarily before charging upwards once more.

Don't run. Don't run.

If he hadn't told himself that, West would have fled what was undoubtedly the most terrifying thing he'd ever seen.

Somehow his second shot went high. By the time he pulled the trigger again, the animal was less than ten feet away. This shot caught it in the chest, dead centre. The wolf shrieked, stopped, seemed to catch scent of him again. When West hit it for the third time, it was already leaping once more.

The impact seemed to slow the wolf in the air and it came down just short of him, claws raking the toe of his right boot. As the jaws snapped blindly, West fired again. The fourth bullet tore in between its eyes. Only then did the head drop forward and the beast stop moving.

'West!'

He didn't need to reply to know why Fetch was shouting. The second wolf was coming his way, already at the base of the slope. His rifle had only one bullet left so he dropped it. West was about to reach for his sixer when Fetch's rifle landed on the ground just to his left. Even as he reached down and grabbed it, West knew he had made an error. He was out of time.

With a great roar, the wolf bounded upward and launched itself at him. Still trying to get his fingers on the trigger, West somehow stumbled and landed on his backside. Blotting out the sun, the wolf came down on top of him.

Fully convinced that this was the end, West closed his eyes. He only opened them again when he realised that he hadn't been bitten or clawed. The wolf had somehow impaled its throat on the barrel of the rifle, the butt of the weapon stuck firmly into the ground. Though blood was leaking from the wound, the wolf was still thrashing around.

As it fought on, one great white paw thumped down onto West, pinning him. He reached for the rifle, hoping to fire straight into the wolf's throat but its movement wrenched the weapon away. Spluttering and growling, it continued to blindly flail around, despite the hunk of metal stuck in its throat.

West's right arm was wedged under him but his left was free. He reached past the huge paw and hooked the trigged guard of his sixer. Blood spilled onto him and the thick, bestial scent of the wolf filled his nostrils. As the great snout came towards his face, he wrenched his left arm out and stuck the sixer barrel in the wolf's mouth. This time, one shot was enough.

As the beast fell away, the paw was at last off West's chest and he could draw in a full breath. He could hardly believe he was still alive.

'You okay?' asked Fetch eventually.

'Er ...been better.'

*

With the third wolf still out there, they made their escape quickly, not stopping until they reached a shallow stream that meandered across the plain. West removed his coat and tried to clean off the worst of the drool and the blood.

'I can still smell those horrible things.'

Fetch retrieved some soap from his saddlebag and took

over the cleaning. 'I guess I could have taken a shot myself but I don't think I would have hit it.'

'I never saw an animal move so fast.' West squatted down and cleaned his face.

The peaceful, idyllic scene was hard to reconcile with what he'd endured only a couple of hours earlier.

'And I was starting to like it out here too.'

'We can still make Blackridge by nightfall,' replied Fetch. He rubbed soap into the coat's thick fabric then scrubbed at it with a cloth.

'I hope so.'

West walked away through the stream, belatedly realising that anger was building inside him. He kicked at the water. 'Maybe I could just have one day – *one* day! – where nobody – giant wolves included – tries to kill me. *One day*! Is that so much to ask?'

Sandy the pony chose that particular moment to release a large turd that landed on the pebbles with a wet thud.

West turned to Fetch; smiles became chuckles and then full-throated laughs.

In late afternoon they reached another body of water, but this one was very different to the stream. Around six miles south of Blackridge, the trail they were following cut through short, steep hills. The ground was uneven, peppered with rocks and pebbles, so West and Fetch dismounted. They heard the river long before they saw it, halting when the trail passed a cliff high above the roaring, churning waters.

'Wouldn't want to fall in there,' remarked Fetch.

'Wouldn't last long,' agreed West.

The river seemed to smash its way through the narrow, steep rocky walls, creating choppy waves, froth and spray. West watched a branch careening along, pulled and pushed and spun by invisible eddies and currents.

'Come on. I'd rather not arrive in the dark.'

The trail ran parallel to the river for a while before descending to a wooden bridge. The structure was about twenty feet long and looked solid enough but the waters were high, striking its underside, sending spray into the air. On the far side, the trail ascended up past a shadowy cave that faced the river.

'What does that say?' asked Fetch.

West hadn't noticed the writing on a nearby rock face: several phrases detailed neatly in white paint.

RAIDERS, THIEVES, RUSTLERS AND RAPERS BEWARE!

YOU ARE ENTERING TERRITORY OF THE LAST REGIMENT.

When West spoke it aloud, Fetch gazed thoughtfully at the sky. 'Last Regiment. I've heard of it. Can't say I know what it is though.'

'Me neither. Lucky we're not planning any raiding, thieving, rustling or raping. Not at the moment, anyway.'

West shortened the tether that attached June to Ranger then towed the horse on to the bridge. The noise and the closeness of the water clearly unsettled them but, with a bit of coaxing, they allowed West to lead them across to the other side. He waited there for Fetch, who was so desperate to cross quickly that he tripped twice.

With some encouraging words for Ranger and June, West set off up the stony path. He was almost past the cave when he realised there were people inside it. The four of them stepped forward, all holding guns. West would have reached for his sixer if he hadn't been so totally and obviously outnumbered.

There were two men and two women, all wearing dark blue clothing and black boots. Each had their surname written in small, neat white lettering on their chests. Three also wore blue caps and the fourth a metal helmet. They were very well-equipped, their belts holding flashlights, ammo pouches and grenades. Two were holding assault rifles, two had quicks.

'Afternoon,' said West.

One of the men advanced. He was no older than twenty-five: a tall, lean fellow with short, spiky hair. Around his neck was a yellow handkerchief. According to his uniform, his name was Lovitz.

'You're on Regiment territory. You're under arrest.'

'What is the Regiment?'

'You'll find out.'

'And what gives you the right to arrest us?'

'Raiders aren't welcome here.'

'We're not raiders.'

'Then what the hell is that on your friend's neck?'

West had always suspected that Fetch's tattoos would get them into trouble sooner or later.

'All right, he *used* to be a raider.'

'Oh yeah?' replied Lovitz with a cynical sneer. 'Reformed character, is he?'

'Listen, we just want to get to Blackridge.'

'Good, because that's where we're taking you. Blackridge *Fort* to be exact.'

At a nod from their leader, two of the others moved out of the cave and down the trail to cover Fetch.

'We'll have to take your weapons.'

West gestured to his sixer and allowed Lovitz to pull it out of the holster.

'Will we get them back?'

'That depends on what General Dawson decides to do with you. When it comes to raiders, he often goes for imprisonment. Or execution.'

His attempt to scare West was entirely wasted.

'Did you say *general*?'

CHAPTER 15 -BLACKRIDGE

◆ ◆ ◆

When they reached Blackridge Fort, there was still enough light for West to realise that it was a unique place. Before the main settlement, they passed two patrols and three sets of guards. It seemed like a town that might have been prosperous before the Cataclysm: spacious, well-built houses each with their own garden. West had tried to ask their captors about what exactly the Last Regiment was but had been told to keep his mouth shut. What he could see was that there were scores, possibly even hundreds of them, all well-armed and wearing the same blue uniform. There also seemed to be another group of non-soldiers who wore only blue shirts and were all engaged in some sort of work. Every shirt had an emblem sewn into the right sleeve that featured a yellow bird and a lightning icon.

A team of these 'non-soldiers' was making repairs to some kind of power line that ran along one of the central streets. West and Fetch had earlier passed a series of four windmills and a long structure of black and grey panels that could be moved using a system of wheels, pulleys and arms. West had no idea what it was though he had seen windmills before. They also passed a number of stores, though most were now closing up for the day. In the centre of Blackridge were three large, brick-built houses that had evidently been taken over by the regiment. Their blue banner flew above the entrance to all three, again featuring the yellow emblem.

Between two of the buildings was a smaller structure, the

roof of which was topped by barbed wire. Two soldiers stood on either side of a metal door. Having greeted the guards, Lovitz ordered his team to take the prisoner's gear off the horses.

'What happens now?' asked West.

Ignoring him, Lovitz instead spoke to the guards. 'Two trespassers caught in the south eastern-sector. Suspected raiders.'

'I told you we're not raiders,' insisted West.

Lovitz pointed to Fetch. 'Evidence suggests otherwise.'

West nodded at the door. 'Evidence suggests this is a prison. You can't lock us up for no reason.'

One of the guards was a fierce-looking woman with a shaven head named Cale. Despite her tough appearance, she at least explained what was going on:

'We'll make a decision after you've been interrogated. Standing order from the general is to capture any suspected raiders in our territory. We've been hit three times in the last month, lost five people.'

'Sorry to hear that,' said West. 'But I'd like to meet the general. I believe we might be able to exchange information.'

Lovitz smirked when he heard this.

'He's a very busy man,' said Cale. 'We'll see how you get on with Captain Bull – he's in charge of interrogations.'

At a nod from Lovitz, his subordinates led Ranger, Sandy and June away.

'They belong to us,' said West.

Cale answered again: 'And if the captain decides you're no threat, they'll be returned to you.'

Lovitz grinned at West. 'Hope you have a good night. There are all sorts of colourful characters in there.'

The second guard, who was male, tapped the handle of his holstered quick. 'I'd prefer not to have to use this.'

West knew there was no point trying to resist any further. At least Cale seemed reasonable and he could make his case to this Captain Bull. Then again, he didn't much like the thought of being put behind bars.

Cale opened the metal door. Lovitz took his rifle off his shoulder and aimed it at the captives.

'Get in there. Now.'

Cale gave him a sharp look but said nothing.

'What about our gear?' asked West.

'You'll get that back too,' said the other guard, now waving West and Fetch inside.

West gave a nod to Fetch and the pair of them walked through the open doorway.

Lovitz couldn't resist one last jibe: 'You boys have fun now!'

The pair followed Cale through a narrow corridor to a room where a third guard sat at a desk, a steaming mug in front of him. He yawned, picked up at a pencil and dragged over a notebook.

'Names?'

'Smith,' said West with a glance at Fetch, who followed his lead.

'Gibson.'

Cale added, 'Suspected raiders, picked up by Lovitz' squad. South-east.'

The guard made some notes then pointed his pencil at a corridor to the left.

'They can go in two.'

'What about this Captain Bull?' asked West.

'Captain's gone home for the day,' explained the man. 'He'll see you in the morning.'

West glanced at Cale, who shrugged.

'Dobbs! Freley!'

Two more guards strode around a corner, along the corridor and into the room. They carried no guns, only long, wooden clubs that hung from their belts.

'Coats and hats off,' instructed the guard at the desk.

West glowered at Cale.

'You could be hiding anything in there,' said the guard. 'Off – now!'

Fetch had only his camouflage jacket but he removed it and placed it on the desk with West's coat and hat. West never liked taking either off when he was around other people. It made him felt vulnerable.

'Put 'em in.'

West shrugged off one of the guard's hands but set off along the corridor. He wasn't surprised to see Fetch chewing the inside of his mouth.

Around the corner, they came to two large cells, both secured with iron bars that ran from floor to ceiling. The cell to the left contained only one man while the cell to the right contained seven. They had been sitting on two benches but now all stood to observe the new arrivals.

'Back from the door,' ordered Dobbs, club in hand.

One of the prisoners muttered and another stuck a finger up but they did withdraw. Freley unlocked the narrow door, opened it and ushered West and Fetch inside. As the door was locked behind them, West was already beginning to wonder if his interest in the general had clouded his judgment. He and Fetch had been free men only hours ago. Now here they were; stuck in this hole with what looked like seven raiders. The only good thing was that he didn't recognise any of them.

While three of the prisoners simply watched the new arrivals curiously, four others came close, surrounding them.

'Play nice now, Muller,' said Freley.

'I always do.' Muller was not all that big but he was wearing a grimy vest that displayed a tanned, muscular body. He had only a little hair on his head but a thick beard. He had formed fists with his hands and was now bumping them together in an excited manner. Judging by his eyes, West guessed he would be, at best, unpredictable, at worst – dangerous.

He decided to defuse the tension by sitting on the nearby bench. Not daring meet the gaze of the prisoners, Fetch joined him. West now noted that all four men had the same scar etched on both cheeks: a triangle. He had no idea what that signified.

'Who you with?' asked Muller.

West glanced at his compatriots. All three looked tough but only one was bigger than West. Not that it really mattered; he and Fetch couldn't match four of them. While he considered his response, one of the other prisoners asked the guards where their dinner was. Freley told him to shut up. He and Dobbs had just sat down at a small table in the corner, where they had a card game going.

'We're not with anyone,' said West. 'You?'

Muller pointed at his cheek. 'Don't you know what this means, boy?'

'Can't say I do. We're not from around here.'

'We're the Blades. And sooner or later, the rest of our gang is going to get us out of here and burn this place to the ground. What's your name, boy?'

'Smith.'

'What about you?'

Fetch gulped visibly as he looked up. 'Gibson.'

Muller snorted. 'Oh my, I do believe he's shaking. Are you two boyfriends?'

West crossed his arms and decided to distract Muller. He nodded across the corridor at the lone prisoner, who had now come to the front of his cell. West hadn't noticed before that he had a black eye and a bruised cheek.

'Why's he over there on his own?'

Muller grinned.

Another of his men spoke up: 'That there is Ainsworth. He likes men. Can't help himself. Muller gave him a good beating so he's over there alone now. "For his own protection", so they say.'

West was disappointed to see that Muller's attention had returned to Fetch. 'Are you like Ainsworth, boy? You like men too? Because if you do, we're going to have a serious disagreement.'

Muller walked to Fetch and stood over him. 'Well?'

West had hoped the guards might intervene but they hadn't even looked up from their card game.

'Step back,' he told Muller, holding his gaze.

'Or what?'

West was tempted to stand up and crack this idiot across the face. But if that was a solution, it wasn't a long-term one. There was another obvious strategy:

'So, you're Blades? We're Reaper's Boys. Gibson, here, he ain't one for fights. But he is the cousin of Reaper himself. I can see from your reaction that you know his name. I suggest you leave him – and me – alone. We don't want any trouble.'

'Suppose I don't give a shit about Reaper,' snapped Muller. 'Far as I know, he don't come this far north.'

'That's a big gang though,' said one of the other men. 'One of the biggest.'

Muller turned around. 'You know what, Otis, I've had about enough of you piping up. I'm boss of this crew. If you don't like it, maybe you want to replace me?'

Otis was the largest of the four – far larger than Muller – but he put his hands up and moved away.

Now Muller stood over West, their boots almost touching. 'What about you, Smith? You want to take a shot?'

'I've had a long day. I'm not looking for a fight.'

'But what if a fight's looking for you?'

West felt sweat drip from his armpits as his anger grew. He didn't like this bastard getting in his face. And though a fight was probably best avoided, maybe this was the only way. If he could take Muller down quickly, it might deter the others.

'Huh?'

The tap of the raider's boot against his shin was light, but it drew West to his feet and before he knew it, he had pushed Muller away.

At that, the other three closed in and West's plan for a swift win swiftly disappeared.

'All right, you lot!' bellowed Dobbs, hurrying over and rattling his club along the cell's bars. 'Any more of that and you'll *all* be getting a beating. And if we have to call the captain, you'll get plenty worse.'

Freley came over to support his fellow guard. 'You've

caused enough trouble already, Muller. These men have nothing to do with you. Take a seat and calm down.'

Muller was breathing hard, sweat glistening on his brow.

'I didn't start it,' said West, taking deep breaths to calm himself down. 'Like I said, I'm not looking for a fight.'

Another of the Blades put a hand on Muller's shoulder. 'Not worth it, man.'

This time, he actually seemed to listen. But as he walked away and sat down on a bench, he didn't take his eyes off West.

'I know you.'

West had been so preoccupied with Muller that he hadn't even noticed the young woman enter. She wore the blue Regiment shirt and was carrying a tray of food which she now put down on the table. She was pretty, her blonde hair tied back, her bright green eyes now moving from West to Fetch and back.

'I know you. It *was* you two, wasn't it?'

'Er...' West turned to Fetch, who shrugged.

'You're West,' she added. 'You two helped me escape from the slavers. Do you remember? Do you remember my name?'

'I do now,' said West. 'Isobel.'

It took a while, but after a long conversation with the guards and a visit from Captain Bull, West and Fetch were freed. Isobel had passionately defended them and pleaded that they be released. West thought it wise at that point to explain why they'd used different names; to avoid being tracked by raiders, which was in fact the truth. Their belongings were returned but their weapons were not. It was agreed that the captain would question them further in the morning and decide if they'd be permitted to stay in Blackridge.

And so, barely an hour after entering, West and Fetch found themselves back outside the jail with their saddles and gear. The female soldier, Cale, and her compatriot had been replaced by another pair of guards.

'Thanks again, Miss Isobel,' said Fetch. 'I can't say I much liked the idea of spending the night in there.'

'Glad to help,' she replied. 'The Blades are a small gang but that Muller is a nasty piece of work. They say he's killed plenty in his time.'

West's mind was on something else: 'It was dark when we set you free. How did you recognise us?'

'Just your voice,' said Isobel. 'Maybe it was because it was dark that I remembered it so clearly. Believe me, if you'd been in my situation, you would remember whoever got you out of it.'

'Thanks for returning the favour.'

'How did you end up here, Miss?' asked Fetch.

'That's a long story. How about we find you two a bed, then we can get some hot food?'

'Sounds good to me,' said West.

He and Fetch hoisted their saddles onto their shoulders. Isobel helped out with the bags and led the way.

'Where are we going?' asked West.

'The fort.'

It was only a couple of streets away; a large, blocky building that loomed out of the darkness. As they got closer, West saw that it was surrounded by a ten-foot wall. Lights could be seen behind various small windows and a brazier illuminated the entrance. Two soldiers stood close to the flames, warming their hands.

'It was a jail,' explained Isobel. 'Good choice by the general, if you ask me.'

She took out a blue coloured card with writing on it and a brief note provided by Captain Bull.

'These two are with me,' she said, showing the documents to the guards.

The elder of the men nodded and waved them through.

Once past the gate, they crossed a broad courtyard where West spied two more men on patrol. All the guards wore armoured vests and helmets and were armed with heavy assault rifles. Yet another pair were stationed at the entrance to the building.

Inside, they soon came to a broad, busy corridor, illuminated by lamps hung from the wall. West had rarely seen so many people in one place. Everyone was clad in either the full blue of the soldiers or the blue shirt of those like Isobel; and everyone moved purposefully, as if they all had a job to do.

'This is some place,' remarked Fetch.

Isobel led them to the right, along the corridor. 'I think it's 108 we need – to get a room for you two. Sorry, it's all still pretty new to me.'

The door to room 108 was open. Isobel spoke to a middle-aged man who took a key from a large rack and gave it to her.

'There's two beds in there. You need bedding, go see Supplies.'

'We don't need that,' said West, feeling that Isobel had already done more than enough.

'Up the stairs,' she said on the way out, leading them along the corridor and up one level. They came out in what was clearly the main part of the jail, an open space with three levels of cells all connected by metal stairways and gantries.

'It's better than it looks,' said Isobel.

The room was on the first level. Though as small as West expected a cell to be, it was furnished with a bunkbed, an armchair, a lamp and even a full bookshelf.

'Phew!' said Fetch, dumping his saddle. 'That was getting heavy.'

'Not bad, eh?' said Isobel, putting down the bags she had carried.

West grinned. 'Compared to the last place – pretty damn good.'

Half an hour later, he was looking down at a fine plate of food: mutton stew, mashed potatoes and greens. Fetch had already tucked into his dinner and Isobel had just returned with a tray of drinks. She handed out three glasses of a pink liquid.

'Fruit juice and water,' she explained. 'Really good.'

The place where the soldiers ate was called the canteen, and though the cooks were packing up, there were still about twenty people eating. Judging by the food counter, the number of tables, and what West could see of the kitchen, the place could handle plenty more than that.

'I like it here,' said Fetch between mouthfuls of potato.

'Do you ever take your hat off?' Isobel asked West.

'Don't spend all that much time indoors. Certainly not in a place like this.'

'Honestly, I don't think there is anywhere else like this.'

'How long you been here?' asked Fetch.

'Don't answer that,' said West. 'Give us the whole story after the night we met.'

'You're really that interested?' she asked.

'Of course. Plus, while you're talking, we can enjoy our dinner.'

Isobel smiled but her face darkened as she began her story.

'That night, I just kept running. Thankfully, I never saw the slavers again. But I had nothing. Nowhere to go.'

West felt rather guilty at hearing that; and he wondered how the slavers had captured her in the first place. That was another story.

'I had good fortune and bad,' Isobel continued, hands clasped together. 'I came across a farmhouse run by an old couple. It was out of the way and they said they never had much trouble with raiders. They gave me a bed and food in return for work. They had pigs and sheep. I worked just about every hour of the day but it was worth it. The woman even gave me some shoes.' Isobel gave a wry grin but that faded too. 'Her husband … old bastard must have been seventy but he tried it on with me. I had to leave. I went before dawn, took enough food for a few days. I headed north and almost walked straight into a raider camp. I don't know which gang it was but there was a lot of them. Took me three days and nights to get clear.'

West saw that Fetch was as engrossed as he was in Isobel's story. He supposed just about everyone in the Wasteland had been through something similar at some point: a journey where danger could come from any direction.

'Then things started to go better. I stopped at a well and met a woman. She was a traveller-trader; sold herbs, trinkets and such like. She had come from the far north – up here – and heard about the Regiment. She said that you didn't need to bring anything at all. As long as you followed the rules and did your job, they'd take you on. I liked the sound of that and it's not like I had many other choices. It took me a while to walk all the way up here but as soon as I came across a patrol, I told them I wanted to join. That was three weeks ago.'

'So, you're one of them now?' said Fetch, who had almost finished his meal.'

'Not exactly. I'm what they call a "halfie". When you join up you get the blue shirt but not the full outfit unless you become a soldier. If I pass selection, I can start training in six months. Some people work on a crew instead but I want to be out there.'

West sat back in his chair. 'What exactly do they do – out there?'

'Order and Progress. It's written on the emblem and that's why the general started the Regiment. He wants to make the Wasteland safer, help people lead better lives. You saw the windmills, the solar panels?'

'The *what* panels?' asked Fetch.

'So that's what they are,' added West.

'They take power from the sun,' explained Isobel, 'just as the mills use the wind. There are engineers here: they can make electric, just like in the old days. Early stages right now but it's more than anyone else can do.'

Isobel's green eyes sparkled. 'The Regiment is the Wasteland's best hope. Maybe even the only hope.'

She walked them back to their room, explaining that she shared quarters with three other women on the ground floor. As Fetch began unpacking, West stood with her in the doorway. Isobel adjusted the belt on the jeans she was wearing. West thought she had a fine figure; athletic and strong but womanly.

'I'll be along first thing in the morning,' she said, 'to take you to the captain.'

'Thanks. Do you think there's any chance I might get to see the general?'

'I've only seen him a couple of times myself, only spoken to him once. He likes to meet all the new recruits. Why do you want to see him?'

'I have some information I'd like to exchange.'

'About what?'

West liked and admired Isobel but he'd known her for a grand total of a few hours. This wasn't the time to disclose everything. 'It's complicated.'

'Okay. Well, I'll leave you to it. You've had a long day, I guess. Night, Fetch.'

'Night, Miss Isobel. And thanks again.'

'No problem.' She turned to West and looked up at his head. He at last taken his hat off as they left the canteen.

'Do you mind if I do something?'

'Sure.'

Isobel reached up and made some adjustments to his hair. 'Wearing a hat all day is no good for it. There, that's a lot better.'

West felt himself blushing. 'Thanks.'

'Do you have a first name?'

'Not that I use.'

'All right then. Night, West.'

'Night, Isobel.'

She walked away along the gantry.

When West turned back into the room, he saw Fetch grinning.

'What?'

CHAPTER 16 - REMNANT

◆ ◆ ◆

The interview with Captain Bull went well. He was an imposing figure but Isobel was allowed to attend and Bull listened carefully as she described her rescue. West had earlier decided that they would simply tell the truth but also play down the likelihood of Reaper pursuing them as far as Blackridge. He didn't go into detail regarding the bunkers but suggested to the captain that it would be in the general's interest for them to share information. Bull seemed slightly annoyed by this but did promise to put the proposition to his commander. He then turned his attention to Fetch, who was able to answer honestly about his years with the Boys. Bull was eventually satisfied that neither he nor West represented a threat to the Regiment. However, the captain was in charge of security and therefore imposed two limitations upon them.

Firstly, they were not to move around Blackridge without Isobel or another escort. Secondly, while they could use their mounts if they wished, their weapons would remain confiscated until further notice. West readily agreed.

'I like it here,' announced Fetch, when the three of them later walked down main street. As usual, there were several armed soldiers in view, but there were also scores of locals. The stores were open and they even passed a school where students could be seen attending class.

'Feels safe,' added Fetch.

'I know what you mean,' said Isobel as they stopped outside a food store. West had seldom seen such a variety of vegetables and they had already passed a butcher and baker.

'Where does all this come from?'

'Mostly South Warren,' replied Isobel. 'An area of land west of Blackridge. Fed by a deep underground spring so it's better quality for farming than most. Some people say it's just as important to Blackridge as the fort or the regiment. Without it, we wouldn't be able to support so many.'

'How many are here?' asked West.

'More than six hundred. It changes all the time with different units stationed in different areas. The general's always sending them off here and there.' She pointed to a pair of soldiers on horseback. 'That will be me in a year's time.'

Fetch had wandered over to another store. In the window were numerous garments, a lot of them military, including plenty of camouflage.

West joined him at the window. 'You do need a new jacket. Here, we might as well spend it while we have it.' He took about half the Guild coins out of his pocket before realising they might be useless.

'Will they take this?' he asked Isobel.

'No but the place down there will change it. Blackridge has its own currency.' She pointed to a store some way down the street. Unsurprisingly, the sign hanging outside it showed a collection of coins.

'While Fetch is doing that, perhaps we can take a walk,' she suggested.

'Sure,' said West, only then realising how much he wanted to spend some time alone with her. 'You don't have to work today?'

'This afternoon. I swapped shifts for this morning.'

'Okay with you, Fetch?'

'Sure,' he answered. 'You want anything?'

'A new hat?' suggested Isobel.

'No chance,' said West. 'We can back here in an hour. Don't lose that money'

Fetch was already through the door.

Isobel wanted to show him South Warren so they headed out that way. Though Blackridge was far busier than most towns, there were in fact some unoccupied properties beyond the centre, many of which had been cannibalised for building materials. They passed only a pair of patrolling soldiers but West saw more on horseback when they reached South Warren. The fields were quite small but there were many of them and dozens of locals at work. Another crew was putting up a building attached to an existing settlement of barns and silos. According to Isobel this was The Farm, where all the produce was collected and stored. Once she'd shown West that, she took him to a little pond, where they found themselves alone.

It was a sunny, cloudless day, so West removed his coat and laid it down for them to sit on. As they did so, he also took off his hat. He did his best with his hair then turned to Isobel. 'How's that?'

'Not bad.' Even so, she made a couple of adjustments. 'You're handsome when you don't scowl.'

'I don't scowl.'

'Trust me – you scowl.'

'I guess I should just be happy with the compliment.'

'You should.'

West wanted to tell Isobel how pretty she was, how much he liked and admired her. But he'd not felt this relaxed in months and he didn't want to ruin the moment. He wasn't used to spending time alone with a woman. He reckoned she was also quite a bit younger than him.

'How old are you?'

'Twenty-three. You?'

'Er ...mid-thirties.'

'That sounds about right,' she said. 'There's only a few grey hairs in your beard.'

'Actually, I need a shave.'

'You can get a good one in town.'

'I might just do that.'

They were silent for a moment. West watched spindly insects skitter across the pond. Along the edge of the water were thick banks of vivid green reeds.

'I've never seen anywhere like this. I guess this is what it was like before.'

'Maybe,' said Isobel, plucking a piece of grass and rolling it between her fingers. 'I've been out here a couple of times. I like the peace and quiet.'

'How did you end up with the slavers?'

She didn't respond immediately, instead gazing out across the water as if lost in thought.

'You don't have to tell-'

'-No, it's ...I should. It's not good to keep everything in.' She took a long, deep breath before continuing. 'I come from the south, the far south. They say it's only a hundred miles from there to the sea but I don't know if that's true. It was just me, my mother and my father. Where we lived there were no big raider gangs but lots of smaller ones – always fighting – and we got caught in the middle of it. When I was just a little girl, Father moved us north. I can still remember the journey. They'd take turns to ride with me on the pony while the other one walked. Everything we had was in those bags. We moved around for months.

'But eventually we moved into the hut – that's what they called it because it was so small. Father went to work in a mine. He used to come home every night covered in white dust. It was very hard work but he brought in enough to keep us going. And whoever ran the mine made sure there was no trouble with raiders. But every day he'd come home coughing. Then he began to get these terrible headaches – so bad that he'd scream and Mother would take me for walks until it was over. Then he was coughing up blood. They said it was because of the mine but nobody really knew. He died when I was eleven.'

West wondered if he should say something but Isobel pressed on with her story.

'Mother did her best. She moved us from one town to another. She tried to hide it from me but I knew what she was doing. You know, to make money.'

West nodded. Many in the Wasteland had suffered but it seemed Isobel had endured far more than most.

'She used to leave me in the evenings. One night she never came back. There was talk that some man had taken her away. Or killed her. I don't know.'

For the first time, Isobel's eyes filled with tears. West wasn't sure what to do but he knew he had to do something. He put his hand on hers.

'How old were you then?'

'Fifteen. I didn't have much. And when I look back on it now, I think that was a good thing. Because I had to work hard, keep busy, keep moving to find the work. I think it's good that I was young too. When you're young you don't think so much. I think more now.'

'You did find work then?'

'There was no land like this but there were farms. I must have worked at twenty places, maybe more. And everywhere I went I learned something: what to feed a new born lamb, how to plant seed, how to cut wheat. I must have planted and picked every vegetable or fruit or crop there is.'

'I'm surprised they don't have you working down here.'

'I didn't tell them,' said Isobel with a slightly guilty smile. 'I've done enough time in fields and barns. I like the town and the fort. I like being around the soldiers. And they don't mind if you're a woman – not at all.'

'I noticed that.'

She looked down at West's hand on hers. He took it away, unsure if that was what she wanted.

'I guess I should finish. There was a group of women. *Just* women. They had a bit of land with mountains on three sides. Quiet place. Safe, so we thought. Started off barely a dozen of us. A couple of us knew a bit about farming. The land was wild and the soil wasn't much good but we gave it everything we had. By the time it all ended, there must have been thirty of us or more.

'It was hard. I spent three winters there and those were the hardest times of all. We really did think we were safe but somehow the slavers heard about us. They came in one day, scores of them, those jail-carts all ready. They sold most of us pretty quickly. I made trouble. Fought back. Swore. Spat. They beat me for it but I made sure no one bought me. Then you came along.'

West just shook his head. 'I don't know what to say.'

'I told you my sorry tale. What about yours?

Even while he'd been engrossed in Isobel's story, West had known this moment would come. He felt her eyes on him.

How could he explain that – the last two years aside – his past was nothing but an impenetrable black hole?

'It…well…it's difficult. The truth is I've been on my own for a long time. Just making my way. I wish I could say it had all been peaceful but trouble has a way of finding me. It turns out what I'm best at is fighting and killing. I don't know what to make of that.'

'I heard what you told the captain. You're not a raider. Unless you were lying.'

'I'm not a raider. It's just. The past …'

'It's all right,' said Isobel with a smile. 'You don't have to tell me everything.'

'You did. It's not fair.'

'Life isn't fair,' she said. 'We both know that.'

Of all the things West admired about Isobel, the greatest was that she hadn't allowed bitterness to sour her. It would have been impossible to guess that she'd been through so much when she maintained such a hopeful outlook.

Maybe you'll tell me more when you're ready.'

'I will,' said West.

She looked up at the sky. 'Time's getting on. If you're going to kiss me, you better do it soon.'

West thought of little else as they walked back into Blackridge. The kiss had started hesitantly but ended passionately and the intense feeling it had sparked was still with him.

They didn't say much during the walk though Isobel briefly gripped his hand just before they reached main street.

They found Fetch sitting on a bench, still admiring his purchase: a dark green army coat and a pair of riding gloves.

'Very nice,' said Isobel.

'Fits like a glove,' replied Fetch, patting the coat.

'What about the gloves?' remarked West, drawing smiles from the others.

'I should get going,' said Isobel. 'What about you two?'

'We have to stay with you, right?'

'Right. Come on. I'll drop you off at your room.'

As it turned out, West never got that far. The three of them had just entered the fort when Cale approached. The female soldier pointed at West.

'Smith? Or West, is it now?'

'West.'

Cale raised an eyebrow and ran a hand across her hairless head.

'General Dawson has a minute. If he decides you're worth his time, you might get more.' Cale turned to Isobel. 'I'll take him back to his room after.'

'Thank you, corporal.' It was clear from Isobel's deferential manner that Cale was someone she respected. Still, she managed an encouraging smile as the soldier led West away, past the canteen and along the corridor. He had put his coat back on but was holding his hat as they strode past several rooms where he saw "halfies" doing paperwork and a quartet of officers poring over a map.

General Dawson's office was at the end of the corridor, guarded by a sturdy male soldier who eyed West as they halted.

Cale knocked on the door.

'Come!'

Cale opened the door half way but held onto West's arm.

General Dawson was sitting in an armchair in a corner, a pile of papers in his lap. He was smoking a cigar, the smoke from which was drifting up and away through an open window. He looked to be at least sixty, his grey hair cut short and neat. His blue uniform was immaculate and his black boots gleamed.

'Got something to tell me, young man?' he asked, eyes keen through the cigar smoke.

Though he had told Bull pretty much the truth, West knew he needed to embellish a bit to get some time with the general.

'Pleased to meet you, sir. Over the last few weeks, I've gained access to two underground military facilities and have information on others. I believe some may have considerable supplies of weapons, possibly still usable.'

The general sniffed then nodded. 'I'll give you five minutes.'

'You can leave your coat out here,' said Cale.

'All right but I'll need this.' West reached into the inside pocket and retrieved the journal. Cale took the coat while the guard patted him down. Once that was done, West was ushered inside. The guard followed him in and shut the door. While the soldier took up a position beside the general's chair, Dawson pointed his cigar at West.

'Five minutes. Use them wisely.'

'As you may know, my friend and I were captured by the raider who calls himself Reaper. He is very interested in locating and exploring these underground facilities. He sent me to investigate them along with two of his people. I found two bunkers and learned that they were called Station Alpha and Station Charlie by the people that built them. I got inside Station Charlie first. When it flooded, the two raiders sent to watch us were killed. All I was able to retrieve was a map, but that showed the location of other bunkers, including Alpha. From there I retrieved this.'

West held up the journal. 'It was written by a man who lived there.' He pulled out the schematic. 'This document shows an even larger underground structure called the Hub.'

General Dawson held out his spare hand so West handed him the diagram. The old soldier inspected it for a while.

'Go on.'

'The journal also mentioned yourself and Blackridge. The man who wrote it, Maury, seemed to think that you might also know about this Hub.'

'What's your interest in all this?'

'I'm curious. I think if we find this Hub, we might find out more about the past; about what caused the Cataclysm.'

'That's not what I call it,' said Dawson, taking a long puff on his cigar.

'I call it The War. I know there were other conflicts before but I think it deserves the title. We've all seen the pictures, how the world was. I can't believe there was a war worse than the last one.'

'Sir, *do* you have any more information?'

'These weapons. What did you find?'

'In Alpha, nothing, but the whole place was covered in junk and I didn't have much time. In Charlie there were several large crates. There were mines and rocket launchers.'

West had heard of these weapons from an arms trader. He had only a basic understanding of what they were.

'The weapons were in Charlie,' said Dawson, a calculating look in his eye. 'The bunker that flooded. So, I can't corroborate what you tell me. Convenient.'

'The weapons were there, general. There are other stations but I think the Hub is the key.'

'Maybe the weapons are there, maybe they aren't.' Dawson took a long puff and breathed out, watching the cigar smoke curl away.

'I came here in good faith,' said West. 'Offered what information I have. I think it's only fair that-'

'I'm old, Mr. West,' said the general, his tone deep, his voice steady. 'Seventy next year. I have over six hundred men and women under my command. Raiders coming at me from the north and the west. My health isn't all that good. If it was better, I'd be out riding like I used to.' He gazed at his cigar. 'My doctor says I should give these up and I daresay he's right. What I'm saying to you is that I may not have that long. And in all my years, one thing has never changed. Like you, like this Maury fellow, I want to know *why*. The truth is, if I don't find out soon, I may never know.'

Dawson tapped the schematic. 'Maybe this place can give us some answers. 'I started the Regiment twenty years ago. We've taken over many sites, explored far and wide – even as far as the Eastern Sea. We've picked up a good deal of paperwork in that time. I presume you can read?'

'I can.'

'Good. I hope you'll get along with Samuel. He has his problems but he's as smart as they come. Amongst other things, he looks after the archive for me. You show him that journal; he'll show you what we have. Between you, maybe you can find this place.'

'I appreciate that very much, general. I'll do my best.'

'Good. But let's be clear, Mr. West. You're now my partner. You working with me, with the Regiment. You don't go off on your own. You think raiders hold a grudge? Believe me, that's nothing. The last thing you want to do is cross me.'

A minute later, West was being escorted along another corridor to a quiet quarter of the fort. Cale knocked on a door which was opened by a man of about thirty with wavy, red hair. He wore the blue regiment shirt with a pair of long, baggy shorts and some odd-looking shoes.

'Hey, Cale.'

There was also something odd about his voice.

'Samuel is deaf,' explained Cale. 'But he reads lips – so as long as he can see you, he can understand you. And he reads letters and numbers better than anyone else in the fort.'

'Ah. Good to meet you.' Knowing a decent relationship with this man was essential, West shook hands with Samuel.

'I'll come back in an hour,' said Cale. 'General says you can get to know each other then start work properly tomorrow.'

'Fine.'

Carrying his coat and hat, West entered the room.

Samuel bolted the door behind him. 'Sorry. Security is important for what we have in here.'

'Looks like you have a lot.'

The office was divided in two by a glass partition and both halves contained a large table surrounded by four chairs. The walls were lined with metal cabinets, shelves and desks. There were dozens of piles of paper, countless pens and pencils and three stained mugs but, overall, the impression was of an orderly place.

'What do you do in here?'

Samuel sat down. 'Depends what the general needs. I look after his maps and some of his logistics. Whenever I have spare time, I go through everything in there.' He pointed to the second area, beyond the glass partition. 'That's the archive. I must say, you don't look like someone who spends a lot of time studying.'

West shrugged. 'Jack of all trades, I guess.'

'Cale didn't say much about what I'm to help you with.'

West sat down and placed the journal on the table between them. 'I'd appreciate it if you didn't share this with anyone.'

'Not including the general, I presume?'

West nodded. 'With the help of this journal and a couple of maps, I've located two underground bunkers and I'm looking for a third: a much larger one. I believe there might be weapons there; and even information to help us understand the Cataclysm.'

'I call that the Great Question,' replied Samuel with a wry grin. 'I wish I had more time to try and answer it. If you'd like to make a start, I can show you how the archive is organised.'

'Good idea. What the hell is that?'

West's attention had been seized by a diagram plastered across one side of a large cabinet. It showed what appeared to be a military vehicle that moved upon a track and was topped by two machine guns.'

'One of the rollers. That's not what they were called in the past but it's what we call them. We have two.'

'Two? They work?'

'They do. We have a couple of very smart scientists here and they were able to create fuel to run the engines. I helped with the design. Impressive, eh? I've been out a couple of times. It's an amazing feeling, driving along on top of those things. If we had more fuel and three more rollers, we'd never have to worry about raiders again.'

'Guess not.'

Samuel stood up. 'Come through. I'll show you-'

He was interrupted by a knock on the door. When he unbolted and opened it, a middle-aged male officer was standing there.

'Can you get maps 113 through 117?'

'Sure. What's going on?'

'Big raid up in the north-east sector,' said the officer gravely. 'Twelve of ours dead.'

'Twelve?'

'It's getting worse. *Much* worse.'

CHAPTER 17 -CROSSROADS

◆ ◆ ◆

That evening, the talk in the fort was of little else. West, Fetch and Isobel ate dinner together again and the canteen was busy with soldiers wolfing down food. Apparently, they were part of a detachment General Dawson was sending to reinforce the north-east sector. According to Isobel, Captain Bull was to lead the force. As well as being in charge of security, he was also one of the general's most valued field officers. The faces of the male and female troops betrayed a mix of excitement and fear. They spoke in hushed, urgent tones, many of them with large backpacks and weapons; they were eager and ready to leave.

The air of tension somehow spread to West and his companions. No one said much and he already felt distanced from Isobel after their time together earlier in the day. She pushed her food around the plate and didn't finish it.

'You all right, Miss Isobel?' asked Fetch.

'Not really. I ...I wish I was going with them.'

'Better to be trained first,' said West. 'You'll get your chance.'

She forced a smile. All three of them watched as a junior officer came in and told the soldiers to gather in the yard. They quickly finished up any remaining food, grabbed their gear and filed out of the canteen. The staff who worked there watched them leave.

'I heard this raider gang has been causing problems for a while,' said West.

Isobel nodded. 'They say the north-east sector used to be quiet. Not anymore. They're growing quickly and when they move into an area, they don't just raid it. They take it over and make it theirs. They call themselves The Merciless.'

West snorted derisively. 'Where do these assholes come up with these names?'

'It's not funny,' replied Isobel. 'They've killed scores of people and dozens of ours.'

West was a little taken aback by her reproach. 'I know. It's just ...these men.' He glanced at Fetch. 'Men like Reaper. They just can't leave other people alone. They have to be in control. They have to *rule*.'

'Actually, the Merciless are led by a woman,' said Isobel. 'But no one knows her name.'

'Like the Divine,' said Fetch as he finished his dinner. 'They were led by a woman.'

'Who?' asked Isobel.

'A group we ran into,' explained West.

'Raiders?'

'No.'

'The Merciless are different,' said Isobel. 'Most of the raiders steer clear of the Regiment. They know we're more than a match for them. But it seems like the Merciless want to take us on: take our territory – Blackridge, everything.'

Having finished his food, West sipped some water. 'If it's to be a war, you're lucky to have the general in charge.'

'Can I help you tomorrow?' Fetch asked West. 'With this library thing?'

'The archive? No, it'll mostly be reading and I think one stranger is probably enough for Samuel. Maybe you can go check on the mounts?'

'Sure.'

'What exactly are you looking for?' asked Isobel.

'Like I said, just some information. The general seemed to agree that it's in our interest to work together.'

'So, you'll tell *him* but not *me*?'

West reckoned it *was* time that he told her, if only to ensure he didn't lose her trust. But his hesitation stopped him getting that chance.

'Guess not,' said Isobel, standing and taking her tray with her.

'Isobel.'

'Goodnight, Fetch.' With that she marched over to the counter, dumped her tray and hurried away.

West did not sleep well that night, and was glad to have a task to occupy him when morning came. He didn't want to ask for Isobel's help so called out to the passing Corporal Cale to escort him down to the archive. Once there, he sat at a table, waiting while Samuel assembled the documents that he thought might be of use.

West knew he could have told Isobel about the bunkers earlier on but he didn't really see why she cared so much. Then again, if it would regain her trust, perhaps the gesture was worth it. There was no great risk in telling her; he just felt that the less people who knew, the better.

He was surprised by how much the whole thing had affected him; surprised by how much he cared. Then he told himself it didn't matter; he'd likely be on the move again soon and Isobel would be forgotten just as she had before. And yet he wondered; would it be so easy to forget her this time?

Samuel had already created four piles of paper when there was a knock on the door. The officer standing outside handed him a folder. West couldn't hear all of the conversation but it was obviously an urgent matter. Once the door was shut, Samuel hurried back to West.

'I need to get on with this now so I'll just go through what we have here. After you told me about this bunker, I tried to find anything that might be related.'

He tapped the first pile of documents. 'This contains stuff we took from a government building. There are maps of this and nearby regions; charts showing administrative structures; and some material on different agencies and procedures for emergencies. Might be something there.'

Samuel tapped the second pile. 'This is all military. Mostly personnel lists, dispositions, logistics and so on but there's also some material on structures, so who knows?'

Samuel tapped the third pile. 'This came from several sites but it's all geographical: mining surveys, topographical information, climate data, soil samples etc. Probably a longshot but anyone building a bunker might need a lot of that info, correct?'

Not waiting for an answer, the young man tapped the fourth, and last, pile. 'All this here comes from power companies. It occurred to me that this Hub place would need electricity from somewhere.'

Perhaps reading the look on West's face, Samuel patted down his red quiff and shrugged. 'I mean it's all a longshot, I guess.'

'Time will tell.'

Samuel hurried into the other section and turned his attention to the contents of the folder.

West had already decided which pile he would check first. He reached over and hauled the military documents across the table.

Three hours passed and he learned a great deal about chains of command, emergency protocols and communication networks but nothing even vaguely connected to the bunkers and certainly not the Hub. Samuel received several more visitors and, from what West gathered, the situation in the north had worsened, with Captain Bull's force being reinforced with one of the roller vehicles. West was interested to see this great machine on the move but forced himself to continue his work.

He now switched his attention to the government documents but had still made no progress by midday, when a light meal was delivered by the canteen. Wondering what Fetch and Isobel were doing, West persisted through the afternoon, churning through sheet after sheet of paper, much of it discoloured or damaged in some way. Anything that seemed useful, he placed in a pile to his left. By the time Samuel announced that he was closing the office, that pile was still pitifully small.

'Can I take these with me?' he asked.

'Sorry. Nothing leaves here.'

West cursed under his breath. He felt as if he had wasted the day.

They couldn't find Isobel. West eventually saw Cale again and she took he and Fetch down to eat. After much persuasion from West, the helpful corporal also went to Isobel's quarters only to report that she was "busy". West and Fetch ate alone in the canteen, where there was now only one man on duty. He seemed annoyed to be stuck serving food while there was fighting to do and came to sit with them.

He disclosed that the Regiment force battling the Merciless had been virtually wiped out. Captain Bull's reinforcements had already left and a second force would depart at dawn. The cook wouldn't comment on the roller but Fetch reckoned he had heard its engines earlier in the day. There were also rumours of raider activity to the south and the cook seemed hopeful that the likes of him would be called to fight. West just hoped that Isobel was left safely in Blackridge.

It seemed strange to be reading through documents with the fort in uproar around him but he was back in the archive at first light. Samuel admitted that one of the rollers had been deployed but wouldn't say much more. West had seen no more of General Dawson but the whole building was now suffused with a palpable tension. Samuel did comment that the veteran leader was facing one of his sternest tests.

West began sorting through the documents with renewed energy. He didn't like what he was hearing and couldn't avoid the feeling that he needed to make a breakthrough quickly. Having kept count, he knew that he'd already looked at over two thousand pages.

Before long, he thought he'd made progress with some of the geographical data. Documents showed that a company had been excavating sites in an area north of Blackridge and correspondence suggested the job had been commissioned by the military. West spent an hour looking into it further before realising that it was all about quarrying materials for an army base – to be built on the surface.

But he was getting used to this process now and his eyes were quicker to pick out relevant words and phrases. He stuck with the pile of geographical data and found some material from another company that also seemed to be taking orders from the military. In this case, the firm had collected soil samples from a very large area east of Fool's March. West found every other document produced by the company – Kilcline Surveying – and a few other sheets that related to the soil samples, which had been collected over a hundred years earlier. A letter from a military logistics officer to a representative of Kilcline suggested that they were trying to identify 'feasible sites for the facility'. Much of the rest of the letter didn't make sense to West but it also mentioned "difficulties associated with the larger structure when compared to the other stations". Maybe this "larger structure" was the Hub.

Now West began to get really interested; especially when he found the list of potential sites attached to the letter. A few had names but most were simply described by a list of numbers. Two of those were circled by faded blue ink.

'Hey, Samuel. Can you help me with this?'

'Sure.' The young man hurried into the second section.

'Do you know what these are?' West pointed to the numbers.

'I do. Map coordinates.'

'Map *what*?'

'It's a kind of code. A sequence of numbers that denotes a certain location.'

West was still bemused. 'So, can you show me where these are – the two circled in blue?'

'If you'll give me a moment, yes.' Samuel crossed to a shelf and took down a heavy book with a stain upon the cover. He found a page that showed a map overlaid with a grid and then turned to another page. West had seen such maps before – with numbers written at the edges – but he'd never been able to match them up before. Samuel did just that.

'Here's the first of them. This point is north-east of us here. About seventy miles away. But-'

'But what?' demanded West, swiftly becoming impatient again.

Samuel grabbed another map book, this one also full of papers. He turned to a page, pulled out a sheet and consulted the diagrams and illustrations upon it.

'My predecessor was mapping all the craters within the Wasteland. This first location is in the middle of one. If the bunker was built there, it would have been destroyed along with everything else in that area.'

'Shit.'

'We can still check the second one.'

West did not feel confident so he was surprised when Samuel turned to another page then looked at him and grinned. 'This could be it. It's out in the Eastern Sea – a hundred and ten miles east of here.'

'How can you be sure?'

'I can't. But General Dawson sent an expeditionary party out into the sea about five years ago. I read the report. He wanted to learn more about the lands beyond and the cause of the Eastern Glow. They never made it beyond the Sea but they reported a sighting of a man. When they got to his position he'd disappeared.'

'Could have gone underground.'

'Exactly.' Samuel pointed to the map. 'I remember the name of the place. The sighting was very close to these coordinates, near this place Whiterock.'

'Are you sure?' Fetch had just got up from the bed, an old

newspaper in his hand.

'As sure as I can be. It's quite a distance away though and ...well, it's in the Eastern Sea.'

Fetch let out a long breath and anxiously rubbed the back of his neck. 'You mean to go there, I expect.'

'I do. But not alone.'

'Don't worry. I'll come.'

'I was kind of assuming that. I mean with some of the Regiment. General Dawson is busy but Samuel has promised to explain to him what we've found. I know it's a difficult time but I'm hoping he'll provide a team to come with us, maybe even some equipment. Have you been reading?' West pointed at the newspaper.

Fetch shrugged. 'It's not easy.'

'I can try to teach you a bit. When there's time.'

'Much obliged.' Fetch folded the newspaper up and walked to the front of the cell. 'Quiet in here today. Cale looked in about an hour ago. She asked if we'd consider joining up. I told her I wasn't much good in a fight but she sure made it sound like something worth doing.'

'Maybe it is.'

'But you got your mind set on that bunker.'

'I guess I have,' admitted West.

'Wonder what Miss Isobel will have to say.'

'Who knows? Seems like she's staying out of the way. Well, mine at least.'

'No, I mean she's coming up now,' added Fetch, putting down the newspaper and doing up the shirt buttons he had left open.

West smoothed down his hair and tried to look relaxed as Isobel entered the cell. She was a little out of breath and her expression was anxious. 'You have to go. You have to get out of here.'

'What is it?' asked West.

'These raiders to the south. They're close. It's Reaper's Boys.'

*

A few minutes later, the three of them walked out of the fortress. It was not a difficult decision. Despite his feelings for Isobel and his admiration for General Dawson and the Last Regiment, West knew that by staying he was endangering them as well as he and Fetch. All Isobel knew was that a patrol had fought a brief skirmish with one of Reaper's scouting parties about ten miles to the south. They had killed a man and seen the telltale tattoos on his body. West could imagine no other reason for their presence. If it had been a more local gang, the move might have made sense; striking while Dawson was preoccupied with the Merciless. But Reaper was a long way from home. West was once again shocked that his nemesis had been able to track them this far. He clearly wasn't one to leave a score unsettled.

'Where will you go?' asked Isobel as they hurried past the guards and onto the darkened streets of Blackridge. The men each carried their saddle while Isobel hauled a couple of bags. Though he and Fetch had saved her once, West now reflected that she had returned the favour twice.

'I'm not sure,' he said, glad that Fetch remained quiet.

'Probably best that I don't know. Listen, there's one other thing I have to ask you about. Cale told me that we've received reports about some group of soldiers. It's said that they only travel at night, in small groups, that they have weapons and gear like no one's ever seen. People are calling them "wraiths". You two have travelled a long way. Do you know anything about them?'

'No. I've not even heard that name. Fetch?'

He shook his head.

'As if we don't have enough enemies,' said Isobel.

'Might not be enemies,' countered West.

Fetch said, 'Will you get in trouble for helping us, Miss Isobel?'

'I doubt it. I think we have bigger problems. Did you make any progress in the archive?' she asked as they passed a trotting patrol of four soldiers.

'Some.' West knew he couldn't avoid Dawson finding out about Whiterock but surely it would be a while before he could turn his attention to it.

'Isobel, if you do speak to the general, please tell him I'm sorry we had to leave but it's for the best.'

'I will if I get the chance.'

They soon reached the stables and it was so busy that no one seemed concerned by their presence. More than a dozen horses were being saddled and as many troops had just arrived with their weapons and equipment. All staying quiet, Isobel, Fetch and West hurried past them to the rear of the stables where they found Ranger, Sandy and June. West and Fetch led them out and began saddling the horse and the pony while Isobel dug out a sack of feed for them. Just as they were finishing up, some officer arrived at the front and started barking orders.

'We can get out this way,' said Isobel, calmly opening the rear doors and leading them out onto a quiet street.

West tethered June to his horse while Fetch made some adjustments to the mule's load.

'Listen,' said Isobel, grabbing West by the arm. 'There shouldn't be too many patrols around but be careful. They might take you for raiders – shoot first and ask questions later. I suggest heading out to the east or west.'

'East, I think,' he replied, eager to make what progress they could towards Whiterock. They still had a number of maps and he just hoped it was marked on one of them.

'All ready,' said Fetch. Joining the other two, he let out a sad sigh. 'Here we are again – saying farewell in the dark. Thank you, Miss Isobel. I shall miss this place. You too, of course.'

'Goodbye, Fetch. I'm sure we'll meet again.' She kissed him before he walked over to Sandy and mounted up.

West leaned in close and whispered. 'I'm sorry. Really. I wish things could have been different. I wish there was more time. You'll be here, won't you? You'll stay with the Regiment?'

'I'm not going anywhere, West. I'll see you.' She kissed him on the mouth, then briefly touched his face before hurrying away along the street.

CHAPTER 18 -DECISIONS

◆ ◆ ◆

West wasn't sure what frightened him more; going up against Reaper's Boys again or being the cause of them attacking the Last Regiment. At least the former would concern only he and Fetch; the latter would be more a question of guilt. But he knew he could not have persuaded Isobel to leave, even if he'd thought it for the best.

In any case, it seemed his companion was equally preoccupied because neither of them said much as they rode away from Blackridge. Close to the edge of the town they sighted a four-man foot-patrol but – after hiding in a shadowy warehouse – they avoided the soldiers and pressed on. The sun had set a while ago and now they rode through the darkness, following the bank of a narrow river. The moonlight on the black water helped them see their way and West was minded not to stop until they had to.

At what he guessed to be around midnight, they came to a path that led easily down to the river. With West leading the way, they guided Ranger and Sandy to the shore. June was obviously thirsty too because she instantly trotted forward. West took off his hat and used it to fan himself. The night wasn't warm but they hadn't stopped in hours.

'I feel kinda bad,' said Fetch after a while. 'Leaving Miss Isobel and Cale and all the others. Of all the places we've been, seems to me maybe at Blackridge they're doing it right.'

'I know. All we can hope is that by leaving, we draw Reaper away. That's our fight. Not theirs.'

'And their fight?' said Fetch. 'Is that ours?'

'Not right now,' replied West. 'But maybe it could be. Is that what you want to do? Fight with them?'

'I don't know.' Fetch looked along the river for a while. 'No. We should see this through together, for better or worse.'

After a couple of miles, the river bore away to the north. They therefore lost the reflected light but navigation was easy across the flat, open territory, the mounts plodding through low grass. West was determined to keep moving, only halting close to dawn when they came to a stretch of young, spindly trees. As always, he was glad to see a part of the Wasteland that had somehow renewed itself. Tying the mounts to these trees, he and Fetch laid out, determined to take only a couple of hours rest.

Judging by the position of the sun when he woke, West knew it had in fact been longer. But he swiftly climbed up the sturdiest of the trees and saw no signs of pursuit. To the east was a sight that both excited and frightened him.

Here were the great dunes he'd heard of. Untouched by vegetation or the decay so common elsewhere, they were composed of pale brown sand that had been carved by the elements into sweeping arcs and ridges. Faces illuminated by the sun appeared almost golden while those in the shade were an inky black. The dunes extended as far to the east as West could see. He had observed nothing like this landscape in the Wasteland and it seemed almost impossible that it might exist here. And yet he couldn't shake the feeling that he'd seen it before.

With Fetch still sleeping and the horses munching what little plant-life there was at the base of the trees, he retrieved the journal and the cylinder containing the maps they'd recovered from the airplane. Laying them out on a blanket, he began searching for Whiterock.

As time went on, the rising sun warmed the air. He removed his coat and rolled up his shirt sleeves. Eventually he found his destination, on one of the larger maps from the cylinder. It was impossible to tell whether there was – or had ever been – any kind of settlement, or if it was just the rock formation illustrated on the map. The area around it was exceptionally barren, with only a few points of reference to the west that they might use to navigate. One of them was a place called Little Blanca, close to where the dunes became the plain now known as the Eastern Sea. This he found on another map that also included Blackridge and he soon had a reasonable idea of where they were.

When Fetch woke up, West explained what he'd learned.

'How far is this Whiterock?'

'About another ninety miles. I guess we might do it in three days.'

They had filled up all their water-skins and bottles in Blackridge but West was already wondering how long they might last in the bleak dunes. Fetch had been unable to take his eyes off them since he had stood up.

'Ain't gonna be any rivers in there.'

'We'll have to ration our water carefully. Three days to get out of there too. What we have will need to last us a week.'

'Don't look like there's going to be a lot of shelter out there either.'

'Agreed. But it's spring, not summer. We should be all right.' West nodded back towards the map. It might be just as quick to get out to the north, which might suit us anyway.'

'I guess we should get going then.'

'I guess we should.'

'I really thought Reaper would get tired of us eventually. I thought he'd give up.'

'One way or another, I've killed a lot of his people. I don't think he can.'

They rode for only an hour. Though the sand wasn't as thick as West had feared, progress was very slow and there was no point tiring the animals for minimal gain. The few clouds present in the morning had disappeared by the afternoon. Having rolled their sleeves up earlier due to the heat, West and

Fetch rolled them down again to avoid getting burned. None of the dunes were higher than a hundred feet but climbing up them was agonisingly slow and the descents weren't a great deal quicker. The mounts were clearly not enjoying themselves and by mid-afternoon their coats shone with sweat and their tongues hung from their mouths. West and Fetch gave them only what water they felt they could afford.

Though the temperature wasn't too high, the relentless sun heated the sand which eventually became warm to the touch. Both men were drenched in sweat and West began to wish he'd invested in some lighter clothing. As they trudged up yet another dune, he decided that a conversation might distract them from the discomfort.

'The general was an impressive character. A shame you didn't meet him.'

'I would have liked to,' answered Fetch. 'We need more like him. Less like Reaper.'

West didn't want to pursuit that subject. 'All those documents I read. All those people. There were tens of thousands of people just in the army. Maybe more.'

'Do you think they needed a lot of soldiers because there were so many wars?'

'Maybe. But there were way more people in general before the Cataclysm.'

'I heard that,' said Fetch. 'What's a million again?'

'A thousand thousands,' replied West.'

'I don't think I ever saw a thousand thousand of anything,' said Fetch. 'I can't imagine that many people. I saw a show once – music, dancing girls and all that. That was a hell of a crowd. Someone said there was five hundred.'

'How about a million grains of sand?' said West, scooping a handful and throwing it at Fetch's feet.

'I guess you're right.'

Nothing more was said until they were over the dune and heading down the other side.

'Do you think about Isobel?' asked Fetch suddenly.

'I do,' admitted West with a sheepish grin.

'I guess you haven't ever stayed in one place too long. Me neither except for Spring Bay and that ain't the type of place anyone wants to settle. I think it would be nice to be with a woman, maybe have some kids, build a house. Seems like maybe that was what most people did in the old days. Otherwise, why would there be all those nice houses? All those cars to drive around in? Seems like it's a lot harder to do now.'

'Sounds about right. Life's not easy here. Not many people get what they want.'

'There was a woman I knew at Spring Bay,' added Fetch. 'Don't know if she's still with them or if even if she's still alive. She could read better than anyone. She'd read everything she could lay her hands on. She said that back in history – before and *way* before – life got better for people as the years passed. They worked less, enjoyed themselves more. All through history, so she said. She couldn't stop thinking about how it could all go *backwards*.'

Fetch halted for a moment and wiped his sleeve across his clammy brow. 'She was a smart woman. It's a damn good point to make.'

It was good to see something man-made. After hours of struggling across the unforgiving sand, West felt like he might never see a settlement again. But as they crested a particularly large dune, they looked down upon a house and a big shack situated next to a small pool glittering beneath the sun. The traces of a road could also be seen. It ran perpendicular to their path but most of it had been swallowed up by the sand.

'Shade!' exclaimed Fetch. 'And water!'

West was relieved too; with no sign of the sun relenting, they would need a break before tackling the dunes once again. According to the map, Little Blanca was at the edge of the sandy area and from there the ground flattened out to become the Eastern Sea. He hoped to reach it the following day.

Halfway down the dune, Fetch let go of Sandy's rope. The

pony had obviously seen the water because he summoned the energy to trot down the slope to the pool. By the time the others approached the farmhouse, Sandy was already slurping water. June was too obedient to protest but Ranger was tugging at his reins. West relented and soon horse and mule were heading after the pony.

Fetch ducked into the shadowy interior of the shack. To the left of the building was an open space packed with rusted equipment and then the house. Most of the roof tiles had fallen through, leaving only a skeleton of bleached, holed wood. There was not a window left intact and the door was missing. West saw a spider the size of his hand crawling up a wall. He could not imagine what could have persuaded anyone to settle here, even before the Cataclysm.

Fanning himself with his hat, he entered the shack. Close to the entrance was a half-full barrel of water and, as he passed it, West caught a whiff of something metallic. When he leaned over the barrel and sniffed it, the strong smell almost made him gag.

'Horses!'

Before Fetch even moved, West was out of the shack and running to the pool. Ranger and June were closer so he pulled them away from the water first. Chucking the reins at Fetch as he arrived, West bolted over to Sandy, who was still gulping it down. Once he'd pulled the pony away, West knelt down at the side of the pool. He smelled the same metallic tang, though it wasn't as strong as the barrel. Spoiled water was common in the Wasteland and smell was usually the best method of detecting it.

'Shit!'

'Damn it, I should have checked,' said Fetch.

'We both should have. Too worried about ourselves, I guess.'

'Horses don't usually drink if it's bad.'

'They will if they're thirsty.' West kicked the ground in frustration. They had been lucky so far with the mounts and now they'd risked them through sheer stupidity.

'Should we give them some of the good water?' suggested Fetch.

'No, no. It should have refreshed them, at least. Now we have to wait and see if it *poisoned* them.'

West was too hot to be hungry but he ate a little along with Fetch and they both drank. He could have easily downed the whole flask but knew they'd have to be disciplined if they were going to make it through the dunes and the Eastern Sea. Then again, it wouldn't make much difference if the mounts perished.

They didn't tarry long; and for an hour or so West convinced himself that they'd dodged a bullet. Ranger, Sandy and June matched their masters' pace for pace and, when they entered an area of lower dunes, progress improved. Better still, a layer of cloud slid in from the west, making the sun hazy and lowering the temperature.

They were crossing a relatively flat area when Sandy began to slow. It wasn't unusual for him to make the odd protest but a few words from Fetch was generally enough to get him moving again. Not this time.

A bubbly froth had appeared around the pony's mouth and within seconds he had dropped onto his knees. His breathing accelerated and he began to toss his head, eyes rolling.

'Never did that before,' murmured Fetch.

West was very doubtful that Sandy would ever get up again and was already more concerned about Ranger and June. Without the mounts, their journey into the Eastern Sea was effectively over. They simply couldn't carry all that water and food and make good time on foot.

Fetch knelt by the pony. When he placed his hand on his neck, Sandy at first shied away but then accepted it.

'There are plants,' said Fetch. 'Plants that make them throw up what's poisoned them. But I don't know-'

'-I don't either,' said West. 'No plants here anyway.'

Within a quarter of an hour, Sandy was lying on his side; and then West knew it really was over. The poor pony's condition was disturbing Ranger and June but, so far, they seemed all right. Fetch was now sitting in the sand beside Sandy, hand still on his neck. Judging by his shuddering shoulders, he was sobbing. West knew he'd had the pony for several years but they were wasting valuable daylight.

'That's it, Fetch. He's not going to get up. We have to keep moving.'

'I ...I don't want to leave him alone.'

'We can't do any more for him. Unless you want me to finish him off?'

Fetch shot a glance at West with glassy, bloodshot eyes.

West felt for the man but he had no intention of waiting any longer.

'You can catch up then.'

With that he set off across the plains, towing Ranger and June behind him.

West did not look back. His attention was occupied by horse and mule but both plodded on and he gradually became convinced that they would not succumb to the same fate as the pony. He reckoned both were younger and he was sure they hadn't drunk half as much.

At one point, they passed a patch of low scrub that suggested to West that they might be nearer to the far edge of the dunes. Hearing something behind him, he turned to see Fetch jogging up, having covered the distance in quick time. Glancing back at the plain, West could still see the fallen pony.

'He's gone,' said Fetch. 'I had to stay with him.'

With a nod, West continued on his way, though they soon had cause to halt once more.

They both saw it: a trail of paw-marks running across the dunes. The sand made identification difficult but West reckoned the tracks were most likely that of a wolf, and a damn big one at that. They were currently ascending a slight slope and both men now looked around in every direction.

'Just what we need,' remarked Fetch.

They saw nothing but West knew from bitter experience how quickly the creatures could move. Worse still, the trail hadn't been disturbed by wind or rain; it couldn't have been more than a few days' old.

'Let's keep moving.'

Despite the fear and tension caused by the events of the day, the beauty of twilight over the dunes was inescapable. As the sun dipped towards the horizon, its fading light coloured the thin layer of cloud a deep orange red. In no time at all, the tracts of sand facing the sun appeared the same colour; the rest was an impenetrable black.

West and Fetch didn't have much to time to appreciate the sight as they were now forcing themselves towards the peak of the highest dune they'd encountered. The sand was loose and seemed to slip away underneath them with every step. Yet as they – and Ranger and June – reached that crest, their effort was rewarded. At the base of the slope was a stand of skeletal trees where they would find a little shelter. And, in the distance, were the angular shapes of a settlement that West felt sure was Little Blanco. After reaching it the following morning, they could press on into the Eastern Sea.

With a grim nod, Fetch set off down the crest. In the last hour, he had taken over leading Ranger and June; West guessed that it made him feel a little better about Sandy.

When the Eastern Glow returned, it came with a vengeance. The two companions had just settled down under their blankets when the colour of the sky above began to change, the darkness imbued with streaks of purple and dark red. The sun was long gone; this was something else. The clouds that had disappeared after dusk were replaced by others that were not brought in on a breeze but seemed to gather out of nothing. These clouds first appeared benign but from within them came a clap of thunder so loud that West felt his ears ring.

Terrified, Ranger and June bolted, pulling their tethers easily off the branches they were wrapped around. Fortunately, Ranger's path took him directly past Fetch who got up in time to wave his hands, slow the horse and grab the reins. June, meanwhile, was already on her way but – with a despairing dive – West flung out a hand and caught her reins. Once on his feet, he dragged her back towards the trees.

'You hold on to him!' he yelled to Fetch. 'I'll hobble them. It's the only way.'

Plucking a length of rope from his pack, West steadied June then used it to tie her two front legs together. She didn't like it much but by the time it was on, there wasn't much she could do. West used two more lines to tether her to the trees and hoped that was sufficient. None of this was easy in darkness, though the coloured light above was of some use.

By this point, Fetch was engaged in a full-on fight with Ranger that he looked set to lose. West grabbed some more rope and clamped one hand onto the horse's bridle. The next clap of thunder was as loud as the first and Ranger almost burst free. But they kept control of him and now West worked quickly, thankful that Fetch spoke calming words to the horse while he bound its legs. Once that was done, he tied no less than three lines from its bridle to the trees.

'Nice going,' he said to Fetch, breathing hard as the horse continued to neigh and buck.

'Can't afford to lose 'em!' said Fetch, cringing as another clap of thunder was unleashed. This one was followed by a bolt of lightning that struck so close that both men fell to the ground out of pure shock. When the light cleared from West's eyes, he saw light of a different sort: a lone tree around thirty feet from his position was on fire. Fetch stared at it, open-mouthed.

Though they feared the thunder and lightning, the mounts were driven to new levels of terror by the flaming tree. West claimed the hatchet they used for firewood, ran to the tree and set at the trunk. Ash and flaming twigs rained down upon him but he was determined to hack through the wood. Once he was halfway through, two well-aimed kicks at last knocked the tree over. There were only a few areas still alight and these he put out with more kicks that covered the flames with sand.

This at least allowed the horses to calm down. There was more thunder and more bolts of lightning but none struck nearby. And then West had a real chance to look at the sky.

It was if another fire was alight behind the clouds: a broiling, seething tumult of purple and red. From a distance, the Eastern Glow was a beautiful curiosity; viewed up close it was a devastating display of light, noise and fury.

Yet it came as swiftly as it went and by midnight the horses were calm, the two men beneath their blankets once more. But, as ever in the Wasteland, West could not relax. He thought of the tracks, of the wolves he had faced before. When he finally found sleep, his finger was still curled around the trigger of his sixer.

CHAPTER 19 - DONT STOP NOW

◆◆◆

On the approach to Little Blanco, they saw a sight that in turns scared, confused and intrigued them. Sticking up six feet out of the sand was a tubular shape that sparkled in the morning sun. First fearing it was some kind of creature, West and Fetch approached warily. But as they came closer, West realised that – whatever it was – it was not alive. The structure bent over into the shape of an r and seemed to be composed of hundreds of tiny glass balls. Where it emerged out of the ground, the surrounding sand also appeared crystalline.

'What the hell?' said Fetch. 'Who could have made this? And why? Damn thing's got me spooked.'

West felt exactly the same until he looked carefully at the ground.

'Actually, I don't think it was made by a person. Glass is made from sand.'

'What?'

'It's true. A craftsman told me. If you heat it, sand turns to glass.'

'Are you kidding me?'

'No word of a lie,' said West. 'Strange as it sounds, I reckon this was caused by the lightning. It hit the sand, heated it up – made that.'

Yet even as he said it, he wasn't sure. The structure really did look like some glass snake that had burst out of the ground. As if their experiences since coming east hadn't been bad enough, this was a bizarre turn. But West didn't plan on letting it distract him.

'Let's keep moving. Can't be more than an hour or so to Little Blanco.'

They made good time and the flat territory beyond the abandoned town was also a welcome sight. West didn't want to ever see another dune in his life.

Walking into the town, they discovered that the buildings of Little Blanco were blanketed by sand that had blown in through doors and windows and broken rooves. There was little breeze on this day, however, and the whole place was eerily quiet. Ranger and June started at the sight of a scorpion scuttling towards them but West saw it off with his boot. On they walked, through a place that seemed like it might soon be totally enveloped by sand and wiped from existence.

Nearing the edge of town, they spied a circle of bricks that didn't seem as old as the rest of the place. Once closer they could see it was a well, and one fitted with a rope and a pail. West heard the pail splashing against water when he tried the rope so he let it sink a bit then hauled it up. He placed the pail on the ground and both men sniffed the water.

'Smells pretty pure to me,' said Fetch.

West agreed and licked a drop off his finger. Initial signs were good so he scooped some out and tasted it.

'That's damn good water. Let's fill up.'

This was not to be the only gift that Little Blanco had to offer. West was keen to take on as much water as possible so he went looking for another receptacle. It was difficult to get through the piles of sand and inside the buildings but he eventually came across a big plastic water can – the kind with a handle built in and a twist-on lid. These were prized across the Wasteland because they were solid, easy to carry and easy to clean. On his way back to the well, he spotted an abandoned cart in the middle of a street. Running over to it, he found two skeletons nearby, the bones as bleached and dry as the roof timbers all around. The pair seemed to have been ambushed while raiding a nearby house because the door was open and the cart half-full.

Though he'd not drawn his sixer yet in Little Blanco, something told West to do so as he dropped the water can and headed inside. Brushing cobwebs away, he entered the home and looked around. The kitchen had clearly been emptied but there was also an open door and a set of stairs leading down into a cellar. It was common for useful items like tinned food and flashlights to be stored in such places so West elected to take the risk.

There was just about enough light to see but he proceeded carefully down the rickety wooden steps. At the bottom of them was a metal cabinet, the door fully open. The men with the cart evidently hadn't got as far as emptying it. Every single part of every shelf was occupied by a different pack of batteries, most of them sealed with plastic wrapping.

West smiled.

'You're not going to believe this,' he said when he returned, water can in one hand, five packs of batteries under his other arm.

'I think these will fit the metal detector and I've got more for the flashlight. I like this town.'

Fetch didn't seem all that interested in the good news. He'd been very quiet since losing Sandy.

'You all right?'

Fetch pointed to a stretch of ground between two nearby houses. 'There are more tracks over there. Fresh. Looks like wolves again. Three or four.'

It was easy to see why it had become known as the Eastern Sea. The sand was the same pale brown as the dunes and the terrain was remarkably level, with no trace of any plant-life. Having consulted the map, West knew they had around sixty miles to go, heading in a direction between east and north-east.

With the new supply of fresh water and the remaining mounts apparently healthy, he felt confident they could make it. The batteries did indeed fit the metal detector, which would surely give him a far better chance of finding the bunker. All this meant that he left Little Blanco in high spirits, though the same was evidently not true for Fetch.

All things considered, West was glad of their friendship. Sure, Fetch annoyed him at times and West wished he was a better fighter but the man was honest, loyal and dependable. These qualities were not all that common in the Wasteland. So, if he was going to drag the man – without his pony – across another desert, West reckoned he ought to offer him some encouragement.

'Once we're there, I'll give it a day or two but no longer.'

Fetch picked up his head and nodded.

'We can't afford to stay in one place for too long,' continued West. 'Not if Reaper's still on our tail. I reckon we head north and keep riding. He can't follow us for ever. It even occurred to me that we might somehow let him believe we're dead. Maybe spread some rumours or something.'

'Sure ain't nice having to look over your shoulder all the time,' said Fetch as he did just that. 'For men or for wolves.'

As Ranger and June seemed well enough, they spent the afternoon in the saddle. West went with June because she wasn't used to being ridden and knew him the best. Ranger protested a little when Fetch got up on him but soon both animals were striding along happily enough.

In mid-afternoon, a gusty wind rose, strong enough to blow sand into the air. The men pulled their hats low and tied handkerchiefs around their necks to cover their noses and mouths. Navigation would have been difficult but by then they had gone far enough for the rock structures to be visible in the distance. West hoped one of them was Whiterock.

They decided to walk as the going was tougher for the animals too. West soon found himself thinking of Isobel; hoping that Reaper would get nowhere near Blackridge and nowhere near her. Even with his forces stretched, surely General Dawson had enough to deal with the raider.

For so long, finding the truth about the bunkers and the Catclysm and his past had seemed like the only matters worth his time. But though they had spent just hours together, Isobel had affected him like no other. He hoped she would be all right and he hoped he would see her again.

They came like hunters. Four of them, approaching from the south, forming a half-circle as they advanced towards their prey. When the pair first sighted them, West cursed bitterly while Fetch simply bowed his head. The walk of the wolves became a lope and they were soon only two hundred yards away.

West already had his rifle in his hands. 'Get the saddle-bags and the other gear off.'

'What do you-'

'-No time to talk, Fetch. Just do it.'

West clicked the safety off and now positioned himself slightly away from Fetch, June and Ranger so that he could have a clear line of sight to the wolves. They were padding forward in unison, heads low to the ground. He wondered how long they'd been tracking them, not that it mattered now. It occurred to him suddenly that flames might see them off but there wasn't enough time to pursue that idea.

'I'll take her,' he said as Fetch finished removing the bags from June's saddle. Like Ranger, she was already puffing, aware they were in trouble whether she'd seen the wolves or not. By the time Fetch had the rest of the bags off the horse, the wolves were only two hundred feet away. Fetch kept hold of Ranger with one hand but had enough sense to take out his rifle.

West aimed at one of the wolves and fired. The shot seemed to echo out across the entire plain. He reckoned he hadn't missed by much but it made no difference to the four animals, who pressed onward, intent on attack. Remembering his previous encounter, West thought it likely that they might charge at any moment, possibly together.

'You know what we have to do, don't you?' he said, head and gaze shifting constantly.

'I do,' said Fetch. 'Which one first?'

'This one. I'll do it. Might upset Ranger so keep a tight hold of him.'

'I will.'

Briefly shouldering his rifle, West patted June on the cheek. 'Sorry, girl. I hope it's over quick.'

He led her away a little so her head was aiming to the south-east. He whacked her on the rump with his hand but that wasn't enough so he used the butt of his rifle. June shot off, her stubby legs already kicking up sand. This drew one wolf away and it soon accelerated, great strides powering it across the plain. But June was running for her life and it looked like she'd be some way away before she was caught.

One of the other wolves emitted a growl that rolled across the flat ground and seemed just as loud as the gunshot. West thought it might be a signal for a charge but the blinds simply continued their relentless march. He moved closer to Fetch.

'Hundred and fifty feet. They'll cover that in no time if they want to.'

He couldn't decide what to do about Ranger. If they sent him away, the horse would draw off another one, possibly two. In the end, he didn't have to make the decision.

The three wolves sprang into a full run, teeth bared as they bounded across the sand. Ranger reared, pulling the reins out of Fetch's hands, then bolted directly away from the wolves. The one closest to him moved smoothly into a pursuit.

'Yours right, mine left,' said West, rifle at his shoulder.

His wolf was closer than a hundred feet when he fired. This time he got lucky, hitting the blind in the face. With a yelp, it lost its footing and fell headfirst into the sand. West was already shifting his aim right when Fetch fired his first round. He missed. West caught the second wolf low but didn't even slow it down.

Fetch cried out as the wolf bore down on them then flung itself into the air. His panicked second shot caught it in the belly but by then the creature was already on him, one great swipe sending him flying into the sand.

West had sufficient time to spin to his right and put one into the wolf's side. It flinched for a moment but was by then already pawing at the prone Fetch and about to sink its teeth into his leg. West's fourth shot went in above its ear. The wolf toppled over almost instantly.

'Look out!' cried Fetch.

Blood flowing from its face, the first wolf was up and moving again. Knowing he was down to one bullet in the rifle, West dropped it and plucked the sixer from its holster.

Red drool dripping onto the sand, the wolf didn't have the strength to get up beyond a limping lope. West waited until it was close enough to be sure. The first sixer bullet struck between its white eyes. The creature took one more step, then collapsed onto its front paws.

Fetch was still on his back, watching.

West felt angry; angry that again his companion had been of little help. But that anger was nothing compared to the rage caused by what he saw next:

Poor Ranger was backing up, trying to pull away with all his might. The wolf was up on its hind legs, jaws clamped on the horse's snout, paws on its neck.

West stalked across the sand towards the battling creatures, wishing he couldn't hear the agonised shrieks of the horse that had served him so well. Even when he was within twenty feet of it, the blind wolf didn't notice him, so fixated was it on bringing down its prey.

West shot it twice in the neck at close range, sending fur and flesh flying. The beast fell, head thumping onto the sand. As Ranger reeled away, the enraged West kicked the wolf in the head, causing one white eye to spin in its socket. His third shot killed it.

Spluttering and puffing and groaning, Ranger simply

stood there, blood flowing from several awful punctures in his head. He tottered as West walked over. West wanted to calm him but his touch caused Ranger to shy away, whimpering.

West put the bullet in behind his eye, turning away before the horse hit the ground. Though the sixer had saved him, he flung it at the ground and unleashed a long, hateful, shout that burned in his throat.

Blood and killing and death had found him once again.

They saw nothing more of June or the last wolf. Other than a bruised arm for Fetch, the pair had at least suffered no injury. But West couldn't bear to look at either the dead wolves or Ranger and he wanted to keep moving.

They couldn't do so quickly, however, because they had to rationalise their gear. With no need for horse feed, they could at least take most of their provisions. In terms of water, they had lost the big container but still had several flasks Ranger had been carrying. Other than that, West made sure that he had the map, the flashlight, the metal detector, his guns and ammunition. His rifle and the metal detector went over his shoulder, the rest went into the saddlebags, which he and Fetch tied together and placed over their backs. It was not comfortable.

*

As the hours and the miles passed, it seemed that neither of them had anything to say. But, like Fetch, West would often glance to the south, hopeful for some sight of June. West reckoned he was getting soft; they were only animals after all. But when he thought of how he'd acquired them, all the places they'd been, and the fate they'd suffered, he felt almost tearful. He reflected that life had been a lot easier before he'd met Fetch and Isobel. The trouble with friends was that they made you care; and once you cared about other people, before long you cared about dumb animals.

In late afternoon, he became so annoyed with the saddlebag straps cutting into his neck that he pulled the arrangement off and flung it to the ground. Fetch took his off more gently but was clearly no happier. The silent companions drank a little water before putting the bags around their necks once more and trudging eastward.

With the setting sun warm on their backs, West kept his eye on what he hoped was Whiterock, though it seemed to get no closer. The tower of rock and the others to the north were literally the only point of reference in view. There was no shelter, no water – just sand and more sand. Only when the sun had finally disappeared and the last of the red light faded from the sky did West call a halt.

He simply dumped his bags and sat down.

'Fire might raise our spirits,' said Fetch, 'but we ain't got no wood.'

'Why mention it then?'

Fetch said nothing to that and nothing as they both drank and ate a little food – some dried fruit and beef jerky. West couldn't even be bothered to tidy his gear or get undressed. He simply dragged out his blanket and lay on it with one of the bags for a pillow. He placed the rifle next to him and kept his sixer in his hand.

'I hope that last wolf does come,' he said quietly. 'Nothing would give me more joy than blowing its goddamned head off.'

Contrary to expectations, he slept well that night and awoke with only dim memories of red and purple clouds drifting above. Fetch was already awake and he'd just set a mug down on the edge of West's blanket.

'There's some fruit cordial in that. I bought it in Blackridge. Real tasty.'

'Thanks.'

'I did a circuit,' added Fetch. 'Went out quite wide. Didn't see any tracks.'

West nodded then started the fruit-flavoured water, soon downing half of it. 'That is good.'

'Not much of a storm last night,' said Fetch, glancing up at the sky. 'Suits me fine.'

He then pointed towards Whiterock. 'Do you think we'll make it today?'

'We have to. I don't like being stuck out here on foot. Anyone on a horse is going to see us easy and run us down. Like I said, we'll look for a day, then get out of here. We're sitting ducks right now.'

With a rueful grin, Fetch gestured to the green camouflaged jacket he'd purchased in Blackridge. 'Guess this ain't a lot of use out here.'

As usual, West found that his annoyance with Fetch soon faded. True, the man was not a fighter – and apparently could not shoot straight – but he had done his best. Fetch was at least not one to complain and, as the day unfolded, he once again demonstrated his fortitude and resolve.

Stringy cloud gave them the odd moment of relief from the sun but it was windless and hot; and West felt as if he was drowning in heat and light. They simply had to drink to keep going and he knew that the water wouldn't last long in these conditions. But Fetch matched him pace for pace and this in turn drove West on. His feet ached and his calves ached but he did his best to ignore it. Later, they cut up a towel to make the saddlebag straps more bearable.

Unlike the previous day, Whiterock seemed to get nearer with every hour. As their third day in the Eastern Sea drew to a close, they were within a couple of miles. West double-checked the map but he was sure they were headed for the right place. Assuming the planned military facility was indeed The Hub, it was positioned just south of Whiterock. Though he knew he'd have to cover a good deal of ground, West thought he had a decent chance of finding the old station with the metal detector.

'You know what?' said Fetch, interrupting his train of thought. 'The ground is darker here and I've seen a few little plants dotted around. Could be water somewhere close.'

Spying another plant, Fetch stopped and knelt beside it.

'Here's one.'

'Forget it,' said West as he pressed on, 'let's keep going so that we can-'

Suddenly, his left foot went from under him. He stumbled forward and then his right disappeared too. Before he knew it, West was up to his waist in sand. And he was sinking.

'What the hell!'

Casting the heavy saddlebags off, he scrabbled to find grip but could already feel the wetness and liquidity in the sand beneath the surface.

'Quicksand,' said Fetch, rather unnecessarily. He dropped his bags and began opening them.

'Forget it!' ordered West. 'The rope was on the mule. Clothes – tie them together!'

Fetch pulled out his spare shirt, which he twisted up and tied to a pair of pants. As he removed his jacket, West stretched his arms out wide to halt his downward progress. Unfortunately, this movement led to him being sucked down even further until his chin was touching the treacherous sand. It seemed so relentlessly malign that he felt like was being attacked by some subterranean creature.

But Fetch had done his work swiftly. Keeping his jacket in his hands, he swung the makeshift rope to West, who grabbed the shirt sleeve at the first attempt.

'Slow and steady,' he said. 'Those clothes aren't all that strong.'

Fetch did as he was asked, leaning back but pulling hand over hand until West began to move up. They both winced when the sleeve tore but – by gripping the body of the shirt – West was soon being pulled clear. He had grabbed his saddlebags on the way past and, by spreading hands and feet wide, he was able to manoeuvre his way to Fetch. Once safe, he rolled onto his back.

It took him a while to catch his breath but the first thing he did was clap a hand on his friend's knee. 'Thanks, man.'

Fetch raised a thumb then shook his head. 'You know what, I used to think drowning in water was the worst way to go

– now I'm not so sure.'

The patch of quicksand turned out to be far larger than West could have imagined. They had already set about extending Fetch's makeshift rope and were now discussing adding a weight to help them find their way. But then West realised that there was a simpler method of navigating around it.

'Hold on,' he said, walking back and then to his left, surveying the ground ahead. 'Like you said, darker soil. And those little plants seem only to grow within it.'

As he moved further, West could make out the curved limit of the quicksand extending to the east. 'I think we can find our way around without too much trouble.'

For once his prediction turned out to be correct and they were soon moving again, keeping a safe distance from the dangerous ground. It was quite huge – at least a mile across – and at one point the fading sunlight illuminated a white bone sticking up. Some poor animal had suffered the fate that West had narrowly escaped. There was truly something to be said for not travelling alone.

The far eastern edge of the quicksand was not far from the towering Whiterock. There was actually quite a bit of hardy vegetation on the ground here and the rocky outcrops seemed to spring up from nowhere. Away to the north, a low ridge was visible which seemed to mark the boundary of the Eastern Sea.

Whiterock was the highest and most slender of the dozen or so rock formations, reaching at least three or four hundred feet into the sky. It wasn't actually white and neither were any of the others. The rock was a pale brown and striated by rust-coloured layers that, to West, matched the tone of the innumerable wrecked cars of the Wasteland. As they came to a halt, they spied a dark bird flap out of some hollow and circle the tower before coming to a rest on top.

'Nice to see a bit of life,' remarked Fetch as he put down his bags.

West had turned his attention to the ground to the south. As well a bit of low, scrubby brush, there were even a few cacti here, some as tall as a man. With night approaching, West had no intention of starting his search for the Hub yet but, like the rest of the Sea, the territory looked so bleak; so empty.

'At least we're here now,' said Fetch.

'I'll start at sun up,' replied West. 'The towers will give us some shade.'

He had also dumped his bags and was still gazing at the land to the south, where he'd thought the Hub might be.

'You all right?' asked Fetch.

'I don't know. We left Blackridge. We lost the mounts. I just almost died. And all for an educated guess. Maybe this is all there is. Maybe there's nothing here.'

CHAPTER 20 - TROUBLE

◆ ◆ ◆

The Eastern Glow once again became a storm. While it lacked the ferocity of what they'd earlier faced, West and Fetch were concerned enough to move away from Whiterock in case a lightning strike hit the formation above. Though he'd seen the display before, West found himself transfixed by the hypnotic patterns of light that daubed the sky. The shapes and colours were in a constant state of flux and, once again, disappeared as quickly as they arrived.

West woke at dawn and let Fetch sleep on. During the night, he had recalled the state of Little Blanco; how much of it was covered by sand. For all he knew, the same fate might have befallen the hatch that led to the Hub; there might even have been enough to cover a small building. According to the coordinates he had discovered, the proposed location was half a mile directly south of Whiterock. Having tested the metal detector, he set out, measuring the distance with his paces.

Though he passed some cacti, when he reached half a mile, he found himself in an area that consisted entirely of sand. There wasn't even a pebble, let alone a sign of anything man-made. Keen to start anyway, West activated the metal detector and tried it out by aiming the wide, circular sensor at his sixer. The device answered with a high-pitched whine. He had no idea how far down it could reach but it was still his best chance. Marking his location with his coat, he began walking around it in increasingly wide circles, keeping the sensor close to the ground.

After an hour or so, he was quite a way from his coat. So far, all he had located were a couple of shell casings. These he showed to Fetch when he came out with a bit of breakfast.

'Want me to take over?' he asked as West tucked into the last of the beef jerky.

'Thanks, but I'll stick with it for now. I just realized we don't have much to dig with.'

'I'll take a look round,' replied Fetch. 'Got some nails. If I can find some wood, we might be able to put something together. Like you said, the towers are the only shade for miles. Maybe some other people stopped there.'

'Maybe.'

Fetch turned to the west, his expression contemplative. 'I never knew there were places like this. Don't think many other people do neither. Makes me think about *other* places. The rest of the world. I sure would like to see the ocean one day.'

'I know what you mean.'

As midday approached, West gave serious thought to letting Fetch take over. He was also beginning to believe that this whole mission into the Eastern Sea was for nothing. Now a *long* way from his coat, he continued to walk in ever-widening circles. All he had found was a few more casings, a coin and a screw. It was at least easy to expand the search in a precise manner: he simply followed his last set of footsteps. He had purposefully left his water flask behind so that he didn't drink too much but was now very thirsty.

West was about to head back towards Whiterock when the detector began to whine. He moved forward a foot: the pitch of the whine decreased. He moved back and to the right: the pitch went higher. He took another step to the right and the dial shot up to near maximum. West knelt down and began scooping sand away. It was pretty inefficient without some kind of tool but Fetch hadn't returned yet so was presumably still looking for materials.

West worked harder and harder, soon reaching sand that was colder and more solid than that on the surface. He glimpsed something metallic – at least he thought he did – but then the sand slipped down. Digging with renewed vigour, West belatedly realised that the detector was still whining. Not wanting to wear down the battery, he switched it off.

That was when he heard Fetch shouting. And then he saw him. The man was running at full speed, a rifle in each hand. And now West realised that he could hear something else.

A great slab of metal shot out from behind Whiterock. The tracks were propelling the huge vehicle along at impressive speed and, from the rear, dark smoke puffed into the air. It was painted light brown and the top half was composed of a smaller section fronted by the remnants of a large gun. Upon this section were at least four visible figures, one of whom now pointed towards Fetch. Shortly afterward, the vehicle changed direction and rumbled onward.

West swiftly realised that his wish to see one of the Last Regiment's rollers had been granted. He struggled to make sense of what he was seeing. General Dawson had at least two important threats to deal with; why expend energy and resources chasing down West? Perhaps he had underestimated the general's interest in the Hub and the mysteries of the cataclysm.

Leaving the detector where it was, West strode towards Fetch, who was sprinting at top speed, his face twisted into a fearful grimace. West was already beginning to adjust his perception of exactly what he was seeing when Fetch shouted to him.

'It's Reaper! Reaper!'

West's eyes switched back to the roller. He could see one man in the vehicle's turret with that tell-tale V of hair. A large figure had just appeared beside him: it had to be Rock. Ahead of them, another man was in a sitting position, manning what looked like a pair of mounted machine guns.

Fetch threw West his rifle. Just as West caught it, the machine guns opened up. They both ducked down as bullets whizzed overhead. Then the firing abruptly stopped. As the roller closed to around a hundred yards, the sound of the rattling tracks halted. Though the vehicle stopped, the engine could still be heard.

Reaper lifted himself up and sat on the rear of the turret. He removed his glasses and shouted above the din.

'I suggest you drop the guns, gentlemen! Those pea-shooters aren't going to do much damage to this thing anyway.'

'That depends what we hit!' replied West, not keen to give up the only weapons they had.

'Very true.' Reaper gave an order.

West saw movement and only then did he notice the head of what had to be the driver – poking up not far from the machine-gunner. Both raiders were wearing helmets and goggles.

The tracks whirred into life again and the roller quickly gathered speed. West put his rifle to his shoulder and aimed at Reaper. Beside the leader of the raiders, Rock was holding what looked like a very large assault rifle.

West wasn't sure why the raiders hadn't continued firing but that soon became clear: Reaper called a halt, with the tank no more than thirty yards away. Rock seemed to bend down and when he straightened up, another person had appeared in the turret. A woman. With blonde hair.

'I believe you two are acquainted!' shouted Reaper. 'We wouldn't want this pretty little face to get hit by stray gunfire, would we, West? I told you to put those guns down.'

The hollow that had just formed in West's stomach now felt like a ball of lead.

'Oh no,' said Fetch. 'Not Miss Isobel.'

Again, this was a development that West was struggling to understand. But he had to act quickly.

'Do it.'

They both dropped their rifles on to the sand.

'And the sixer!' said Reaper.

West did as he was told. He couldn't currently see any way out of this so he decided to try and keep his enemy talking.

'How'd you find us, Reaper?'

'I guess you could say we got lucky – and it's about goddam time! We ran into a patrol of those soldier boys south of their town. Killed three of them. The fourth was real scared, so he told us everything we wanted to know. We were especially interested to hear about you and your little friend here. And this.'

Reaper slapped the metallic hull of the vehicle. 'Ain't it the greatest goddam thing you ever saw? Young Isobel here was really quite noble. I threatened to burn a few locals if she didn't show herself, and out she came! I guess this General Dawson don't realise he's not the only one with his own little army. Well, he'll get quite the shock when he heads home.'

'Big mistake, Reaper!' countered West. 'Bad idea to make him your enemy.'

'Maybe, maybe not. After all, I've got me this thing now.'

'Where are the rest of your men?'

'Enough talk, West! I hold all the cards. You two walk over here and get down on your knees.'

West took his first few steps. Fetch matched his slow pace.

West whispered. 'If we give up, we're dead.'

'I know,' replied Fetch as they walked past their guns.

'That machine gun fire won't be very accurate when the roller's moving. The quicksand isn't far. We turn, run around the edge. Chances are he'll take a straight route.'

'Isobel?'

'If we give ourselves up, we can't help her anyway.'

Fetch nodded.

Reaper had just put his glasses back on. He stroked Isobel's hair then held it tight, yanking her head back. Rock looked on impassively, eyes dark in that weathered face.

'Now,' breathed West.

With that, the pair of them spun on their heels and set off at a sprint. West led the way, heading south-east towards the quicksand. He knew it wasn't far; no more than a minute away. But would they survive that long?

They hadn't taken many paces when Reaper shouted his

orders and the roller's engine roared into life again. The rattle of the tracks told West that it was moving once more and shortly after that the machine guns opened up. Fortunately, his suspicion about accuracy proved correct and they'd covered quite a distance before the bullets even came close.

'You see it?' yelled Fetch, pumping his arms and legs as hard as West.

'Not yet!'

Bullets thumped into the ground ahead of them, sending sand into the air.

'Split!'

The pair veered in different directions and – during a brief lull in the gunfire – West heard Reaper bellowing.

Then came another volley of fire and pain tore into West's shoulder. The shock of it caused him to stumble. He almost fell but then realised the wound wasn't severe. Putting a hand to his shoulder he felt a tear in the fabric. Blood was already seeping out but the pain wasn't bad – yet.

'There!'

West was relieved that Fetch hadn't pointed at the edge of the quicksand. He risked a look back and saw the roller powering across the ground, Isobel and Rock's hair flying out behind them. Reaper stood tall, his hands gripping the turret. The orange blooms at the twin barrels of the machine-gun halted, and West saw the gunner gesticulating to Reaper. Did he need to reload?

When he turned back, West found that Fetch was already sprinting along the perimeter of the dark quicksand.

'Don't get *too* close!' he warned, now catching him up. He hoped that Reaper and his mob would be too fixated on killing them to notice the different shade of sand. Though glad that the gun hadn't started up again, he reckoned the roller sounded a lot closer.

And when he stole another glance over his shoulder, he saw that it was barely fifty yards away. Though the gun wasn't firing, Reaper seemed happy enough. West imagined that crushing he and Fetch beneath the roller would please the raider even more than shooting them.

The machine-gun burst into life again but stopped almost immediately. With a jarring screech of metal, the noise of the tracks suddenly ceased. From the roller came several shouts and a scream from Isobel.

West stopped and spun around in time to see one side of the vehicle lurch downward. A man he hadn't previously noticed fell off the back of the roller into the sand and was struggling within moments. Reaper, Isobel and the others desperately hung on as the vehicle sank further in, the angle already so steep that it looked close to tipping over. A second man at the rear threw himself towards the solid ground. He landed well but in moments his legs had disappeared under him. The roller's engine now spluttered and failed as one set of tracks began to sink beneath the sand.

West might have enjoyed the moment had he not been so concerned for Isobel.

'What do we do?' asked Fetch.

'Wait,' said West, putting out a hand. They were still unarmed. The raiders were not.

The sand sucked the roller further down, crushing the man who'd fallen on the wrong side. Reaper and Rock were now out of the turret, apparently weighing their chances. The big enforcer seemed to have hold of Isobel but she somehow got free. Scrambling to the rear of the roller, she threw herself off.

'No choice now,' said West as he sprang away, Fetch close on his heels.

Even as they neared the foundering vehicle, Reaper and Rock didn't even look at them; they were far more concerned with their own welfare. Along with the gunner, they were desperately tying some clothes together to save themselves. The roller had settled a little but was still sinking with alarming speed, the tracks now fully buried.

West and Fetch passed the first man, who had remained on the surface by spreading himself wide and not moving.

Isobel had not fared so well: her legs had plunged into the

worst of the quicksand and she was already in up to her armpits. Her eyes shone with the same fear that West had felt only a day earlier.

He already had his shirt off and now tied a sleeve to Fetch's jacket. 'Hold on to my legs.'

Starting as close as he dared, he threw himself down and whipped the makeshift rope through the air. It landed a couple of feet short. Though he could feel the sand beneath his forearms giving, West reckoned he could advance a bit further. Blocking out the shouts of the raiders to his left, he tried again.

This time Isobel snatched his shirt sleeve out of the air and soon she had her second hand on it.

'Okay, Fetch. Steady.'

West felt his legs pulled backwards and the strain in his right hand and arm as the 'rope' became taut. The bullet wound pulsed with pain but he gritted his teeth and told himself to ignore it.

Isobel still wasn't moving.

'Stuck,' she uttered, her face covered with sand.

But West had moved back a bit and his knees now seemed to be on solid ground. He put out a hand to halt Fetch and got up, heaving Isobel in himself. As she came up a few inches, she threw one hand onto on the sand. Though it gave way shortly after, she was able to wriggle her waist free. Her legs were still stuck, however, but some slow, strong heaves from West were enough to keep her moving. Soon she was close enough for he and Fetch to grab an arm each and drag her to safe ground. For a moment, the three of them just knelt, trying to get their breath.

'Very resourceful!' shouted Reaper, sounding creditably calm given his situation. 'Now get over here.'

Clad in his vest, West ushered the other two away from the quicksand then stood between them and the roller. Twenty feet away, Reaper, Rock and the two remaining men all had a hand on the turret. The roller no longer seemed to be sinking but they had no way of getting off. The man in the sand below them was waving at West.

'Help me! Please!'

'Shut it,' snapped Reaper.

Rock leaned back against the turret so that he could use both hands to aim his assault rifle at West.

'Get over here *now*!' said Reaper.

'Save you so you can kill us?' retorted West. 'No thanks.'

Reaper's sawn-off shotgun was still in its holster but he nodded to Rock's gun. 'We can still kill you.'

'You can. But then you'll die too. I think they call that a stalemate.'

'Maybe we'll just shoot the girl,' countered the raider.

West shifted slightly so that he was blocking her completely.

It was then that Rock bent over and whispered in his leader's ear. Reaper grinned and gave a nod. Rock handed him his rifle then reached for the driver. Grabbing him by the arm and neck, the big enforcer flung the man off the roller. The hapless raider landed between the vehicle and his struggling compatriot.

'No, wait!' said the gunner, grasping his fate. The oblivious Rock grabbed his belt. With a neat spin, he sent him flying past the first man, his boots landing on his head.

Reaper gave an approving nod. 'Bridges should be nice and stable.'

He emptied half of the assault rifle's magazine into his three subordinates, killing them in seconds. Now motionless, they remained on the surface of the quicksand.

'I'll go first,' said Reaper. While Rock kept his assault rifle aimed at West, his leader sat down on the edge of the vehicle. He dropped onto the legs of the nearest raider and his first step took him onto the dead man's stomach.

'Jesus,' breathed Isobel.

Reaper stumbled a couple of times but made it safely across the human bridge. With a final leaping step that took him onto solid ground, he smiled smugly to himself. Then he pulled his shotgun from the holster. West noted the cartridges on his belt. The weapon had two triggers, one for each barrel. Only two shots. That might give them a chance.

Reaper aimed the gun at the trio. 'What's that saying? Necessity is the mother of invention.' Then his expression changed. 'West, I have to say you are one of the sneakiest sons-of-bitches I have ever come across. Reckon it's over now though, ain't it?'

At a nod from Reaper, Rock lowered himself off the roller, the assault rifle in one hand.

West heard Isobel whisper. 'When I tell you – duck.'

He answered with what he hoped was a subtle nod.

The bulky Rock was not capable of crossing as nimbly as Reaper. As he lurched onto the second body, he was forced to use the rifle to help him balance and the barrel stuck deep into the sand. He overbalanced and planted his knees into the body, which began to sink. Forced to let go of the gun, Rock threw himself forward onto the third corpse. He wasn't safe yet.

Isobel whispered again. West ducked.

Something flew over the top of him and hit Reaper in the chest. Shocked, the raider staggered backwards, the shotgun loose in his grip.

West took the chance, driving off a standing start and bolting towards his foe. He noted the folded-up pocket-knife that Isobel had thrown now lying on the sand. Seeing the danger, Reaper brought the gun back up but by then West was leaping at him, flailing at him with his right hand. He knocked the barrel down just as Reaper fired.

The noise stunned him but he saw the pellets strike the sand so knew he hadn't been hit. His impetus took him into Reaper's knees, toppling him to the ground.

With the crash of the shotgun still reverberating through his ears, West scrabbled forward and made a grab for Reaper's arm. The raider was already lifting the weapon but West was able to grab his wrist and dig his nails in. With a cry, Reaper dropped the gun but his right hand was still free and he brought it across in a punch that caught West on the cheek.

The impact knocked him away and he rolled across the

sand. Righting himself, he noted that Rock had almost reached safety. Turning back, he saw Reaper go for the shotgun. The raider was only inches away when West booted it, sending the weapon flying through the air.

Reaper grabbed his glasses and threw them aside. West saw now that one eye was totally red. It might have distracted him because he didn't move fast enough for the kick that came his way. Reaper's boot caught him in the gut, doubling him over. The next blow was a punch that struck West on the cheek. As he reeled away, dazed, his arms were suddenly pinned behind his back.

Feeling the enormous strength and presence of Rock, he could not defend himself as Reaper kicked him again. Badly winded, West tried to brace himself for the next blow.

It never came.

Fetch and Isobel must have done something, because suddenly West was free. He lashed out immediately with a fist. It was not a strong or accurate blow but it glanced off Reaper's brow and was at least enough to make him retreat.

'Fetch!'

At this cry from Isobel, West almost turned around but Reaper was coming at him again.

He ducked under his right cross but felt his jaw shudder as Reaper followed up with a straight left. West swung wildly and missed. After the run, the bullet wound and the rescue of Isobel, he knew he was tiring. Worse, he hadn't expected Reaper to be this tough.

The raider suddenly backed away, confusing West until he bent down and plucked Isobel's pocket knife from the ground. As Reaper pulled out the three-inch blade, West glanced back to see how his allies were faring.

Isobel was only a couple of feet from Reaper's discarded shotgun but was being held back by Rock, who had a grip on her wrist. He in turn was being held by Fetch, who was also punching him in the shoulder and chest, though his blows didn't seem to be doing a lot of damage.

Though desperate to help them, West had his own problems.

Reaper swept the blade towards his face. West backed away, trying to line up another kick to disarm the raider.

'Always knew it would come down to this,' said Reaper. 'And don't think it will be *one* cut. That would be way too easy.'

Isobel cried out.

West tried another kick but Reaper saw it coming. With his free hand he grabbed West's right boot and yanked it. West came down on his left knee and would have taken the knife to his face if he hadn't got his hands up. Circling Reaper's wrist with them both, he pulled to his left, hauling the raider down with him. They crashed into the sand, wrestling for control of the blade.

As they fought, West heard a shotgun blast, then someone hit the ground.

One hand still free, Reaper jabbed a punch into West's injured shoulder. West heard himself scream with pain and he knew his grip had weakened. Reaper knocked him on to his back. Sunlight glinted off the blade as the raider adjusted his grip and raised it high. With a sick grin, he readied himself to drive it downward.

'Get off my friend!'

Fetch's low shoulder charge knocked Reaper clean off West. Despite the pain splintering through his shoulder, West sat up. Turning, he glimpsed Isobel holding Reaper's shotgun, the second barrel now smoking. Behind her, the huge form of Rock lay motionless on the sand. In the middle of his chest was a ragged, bloody wound.

Hearing a scuffle to his left, West saw Fetch and Reaper already up on their feet and grappling, arms high. Though the smaller and lighter man, Fetch had his hands locked on Reaper's wrists and was just about holding him. Teeth set in a snarl, Reaper glowered down at his former subordinate, red eye gleaming.

'Let go you fool and I might just let you live.'

'I don't work for you no more!'

West hauled himself to his feet and looked for a weapon. But Isobel had fired the second of the shotgun's cartridges; the rest were on Reaper's belt.

Though he had hardly any strength left, West lurched towards the warring pair.

'One last chance, Fetch!' hissed Reaper. 'Remember your place.'

'I know my place!' roared Fetch.

It was only when Reaper kneed him between the legs that West realised the raider still had the knife in his hands. As Fetch cried out and crumpled, Reaper grabbed his neck with his left hand and drove the knife into it with his right.

'No!' shrieked Isobel as Fetch fell, the knife embedded in his flesh.

Pain forgotten, West charged forward, a swinging elbow catching Reaper right on the chin. After three staggering steps, the raider hit the ground for the last time. Before he knew it, West had straddled his foe's chest and pinned his arms with his knees. His first punch broke Reaper's nose, the second cracked bones in his cheek.

West felt nothing. He observed his own actions as if drunk or in a daze.

He gripped Reaper's throat with both hands. The dazed raider could mount no resistance and his pained shout died in his throat.

West squeezed and squeezed and squeezed until his hands ached and that red eye moved no more.

Only his concern for Fetch snapped him out of this vengeful fog. By the time he reached his friend, Isobel was sitting with him, cradling his head. The knife had plunged deep into the side of his neck. Only a small amount of blood was trickling out but his breathing was tortured, his skin terribly pale.

The man knew he was dying. Somehow, he forced a smile.

'You hurt?'

'No,' answered West.

'Miss-'

'Isobel's fine.'

'I'm here, Fetch,' she said, stroking his forehead.

'My ...my ...neck.'

'Do you have anything for the pain?' asked Isobel.

There were the tablets back at the camp but judging by Fetch's breathing, West knew if wouldn't do much good. Suddenly the man was flailing at his pocket. West reached inside, knowing what he would take out. He showed Fetch his sister's drawing, then placed it on his chest.

Fetch put one hand on top it and with the other gripped West's.

'Don't think I've got long. Reckon I'll be seeing Ma and Pa soon. Gabrielle too. West, will you tell me now?'

'Tell you what, Fetch?'

West wished he'd just called him Jake from the start but it was too late for that.

'Where you come from. Who you are.' Though Fetch could barely keep his eyes open, there was a glint to them when he asked that. West didn't hesitate; he owed the man that much.

'I don't know who I am, Fetch. I don't even know my name. About two and a half years ago, I woke up in a field not far from a town called Cleaverton. The first man I met asked me who I was, where I'd come in from. I said West, meaning the direction, but he took it for my name. I guess it stuck. I don't know who I am or where I come from. I don't know ...I thought I might find out more here than about the past. Something about *my* past.'

Fetch squeezed his hand very hard now. His eyes closed and his breathing suddenly accelerated, face contorting with every breath.

'Keep going,' he said. 'Keep searching.'

Fetch's grip weakened until his fingers became limp in West's hand. His breathing slowed and slowed and then stopped.

His eyes did not open again.

CHAPTER 21 - ENDGAME

◆ ◆ ◆

West just sat there for a while. Isobel knelt beside him, arm over his shoulder, her face against his. It was she that stood first before pulling him up beside her.

'I thought they'd shoot you both,' she said. 'I thought they'd kill you then kill me.'

'I'm sorry about ...that.' West nodded towards the visible portion of the roller. 'I didn't know what else to do.'

'You got me out. That's all that counts.'

West found Fetch's jacket and placed it carefully over his chest and face.

'What's that picture?' asked Isobel.

'His family. His sister drew it. It meant everything to him.'

'He saved me,' she replied. 'If not for him, Rock would have killed me.'

Isobel now turned her attention to West's shoulder. 'Got any medical supplies?'

He pointed towards Whiterock. 'Over there.'

'Come on then.'

'Wait.'

West walked first to Rock. Grabbing the big enforcer by the ankles, he dragged him as close to the quicksand as he dared, then rolled him towards it. Then he did the same with Reaper, rolling his body over the top of Rock. The tank had already sunk a few more feet and he hoped now the quicksand would take them. Looking down at their bloodied bodies, he felt nothing, not even a satisfaction that he'd defeated the enemies who had pursued him across the Wasteland.

'Your shoulder,' said Isobel.

'Not yet,' said West, already walking towards Fetch. 'First we bury him.'

It was not an easy job. They first carried Fetch back to their camp in the shadows of Whiterock. West decided that one of their cooking pans would make a decent shovel but it was difficult to shift the sand quickly. After an hour or so he had carved out a large enough section though it was nothing like deep enough. Isobel helped out using a metal plate but it was slow going.

'That shoulder – at least let me take a look.'

West shook his head. 'I can't just let him lie there like that. It's wrong.' He had purposefully worked facing away from his friend's body. He wondered if it was guilt as much as sadness.

By the time the grave was deep enough, he barely had the strength to lift him. He put his jacket on properly and left the drawing within his grasp. Fetch's fingers were already cold and stiff. West and Isobel carried him to the grave and gently lowered him. Covering him took another hour and by then West had just enough energy to gather a few stones from the base of Whiterock. These he assembled into a little pile to mark the grave.

'It's not right. Burying him out here in this ...nothingness. With *them.*'

'We've done the best we can.'

They stood there together, arm in arm.

'Do you want to say something?' asked Isobel. 'If not, I can.'

West took a deep breath and composed himself. Though there was just the two of them in the middle of the bleak desert, he wanted to get this right.

'He called himself Fetch ...but his real name was Jake Gibson. He came from a place called Archer's Ford. There was him and his parents and his sister, Gabrielle. Though they're long gone, I know they were always in his thoughts. I hope he sees them again. He was a good friend. Kind. Loyal. He saw the best in people and the best in the world.'

West had been fortunate. The bullet had missed his shoulder bone and passed through only flesh. Isobel told him that stitching it would be a difficult job but she cleaned it and did just that. He took four of the painkillers beforehand but it still hurt like hell. The impact had taken some material into the wound so the cleaning was the worst part; and at one point he felt he might pass out. But he got through it and soon Isobel was bandaging him up.

As he sat there, back against the base of Whiterock, West watched the roller at last disappear below the surface, taking the remaining dead men with it.

He supposed it wasn't a good thought for a man to have but now he *did* feel some sense of satisfaction at the victory. He hadn't just killed Reaper. He'd wiped him off the face of the Earth.

Isobel finished taping the bandage up. 'Hope it's okay. Never dressed a bullet wound before.'

'Thank you. By the way – where did that knife come from?'

'Stole it from the driver while I was in the tank. I was waiting for a chance to use it.'

'Ah.'

West was still clad only his vest but she helped him pull on his shirt and coat. He dozed off then, the exhausting events of the day finally catching up with him.

When he eventually awoke, the surface of the Eastern Sea was an odd pink, illuminated by the setting sun. As he stirred, Isobel presented him with a plate of food.

'I found this. You should eat something.'

'I'm sorry. I didn't mean to sleep for so long. You never even told me what happened to you.'

'They came two days ago. The day before that, General Dawson had been forced to lead out more reinforcements against the Merciless. I don't even know if ...'

As her voice faded out, she sat on a blanket opposite West. 'There weren't many soldiers left in Blackridge. All the halfies had to go on patrols. I was with one when Reapers Boys hit the south of the town. Word reached me that they were threatening this family and wanted me to tell them where you were. I was with Corporal Cale. She told me not to go but I disobeyed orders. I went to Samuel, made him tell me about this place. Reaper and those other bastards were standing in front of a house, torches ready to burn it. I could see the faces at the windows. Children. I ...told them about you. I just had to get them out of Blackridge.'

'You did the right thing. What about the roller?'

'Sheer bad luck. As we rode out of town we went past the yard where they fuel it. Reaper had forty men with him. There was a gunfight but he had the numbers. He grabbed one of the engineers, made him show him how it worked. But then the Regiment hit back. I'm pretty sure I saw Cale. Reaper told his men to keep them occupied and we left on the roller. They had maps on there. Maps that showed this place. He didn't seem to care about much else other than killing you two.'

'He got one of us,' said West ruefully. 'Wish it had been me.'

'So, you didn't find anything? Samuel said something about some bunker.'

West detailed it all: Station Alpha and Station Charlie, his research with Samuel and his unsuccessful search earlier that day.

Some time passed before she spoke: 'South Common. I thought you just didn't want to tell me about your past. Growing up. I thought perhaps you had your own secrets. But you had nothing to tell me. I'm sorry.'

West just sighed.

'Will you keep looking?' asked Isobel.

He shook his head. 'There's nothing. I think I wanted it

so bad but it makes no sense. Who would build something out here?'

West stood up and watched the last of the sun dip below the eastern horizon.

'There's only one thing.' He turned back towards Whiterock and looked up at the towering formation. 'I can't shake the feeling that I've been here before.'

They agreed to leave in the morning. West thought of only Fetch as he lay there in the dark, Isobel beside him. He was glad to have her there; the loss of his friend would have been harder without her.

He could not dispel that last memory of Fetch: his agonised expression; his tortured breaths. West forced himself to remember better times: the two of them riding together; the meals they'd shared; the night in The Golden Chance when Fetch had enjoyed the music so much.

Somehow, he slept, only to be woken by Isobel.

'West, look! Look there!'

It was still pitch black but as he sat up, he saw instantly what she was talking about.

The distance was hard to gauge but, to the south of their position, two lights were moving in the darkness.

West instinctively reached for his sixer.

'Reaper's Boys?' said Isobel.

'Could be. Don't see why they'd be coming from that direction though.'

They both stood up and watched the lights.

'Seem to be moving west,' said Isobel. 'Towards the quicksand.'

'That means they haven't seen *us*, so let's go take a look at *them*.'

He retrieved the flashlight and put on his coat, which still had plenty of spare ammunition in it.

'Got the rifle?'

'Uh-huh,' replied Isobel, already checking the magazine was full.

'Let's go.'

It was a cloudy night, meaning that the floor of the plain was inky black. As they walked on, West glanced back. At least the great bulk of Whiterock was visible against the night sky so they could easily navigate their return.

With Isobel at his left shoulder, he strode across the sand, eyes fixed on the lights. They seemed to have stopped for a while but – now closer – he could see that they were flashlight beams scouring the ground. It was almost as if they were looking for something – a trail perhaps.

Soon they were close enough to glimpse a figure illuminated by one of the beams. West wasn't sure if it was a man or a woman but he or she was wearing a hood and dark clothing. The pair were certainly studying the ground and now their voices could be heard.

Then West heard another voice. A female voice: calm and assured.

'Drop the guns.'

Then another flashlight beam was activated – this one behind them.

'Do it.'

West turned to Isobel and they nodded to each other before dropping the guns to the ground.

'Hands up. Walk forward five paces.'

They did as they were told and West heard the interloper pick up their weapons.

'Garcia! Trent! Get over here. I've got two.'

The others were already aiming their lights towards the third and now ran towards them.

'Who are you?' asked Isobel.

The interloper's only answer was to walk around until she faced them. She wore a scarf over her mouth and nose so all they could see were her dark, unblinking eyes.

Then her compatriots arrived. Trent and Garcia were both men. The trio all wore the same hoods and black military gear. All three were holding small, unusual guns of a type West had never seen.

'Nice going, Wheater,' said one of them to the woman. 'I thought they'd all gone.'

The second man now aimed his flashlight at West, who was forced to close his eyes and look away.

'Jesus Christ.'

'Garcia?' asked Trent. 'What is it?'

'I know him. Used to be one of ours. Heard he was dead.'

It might have been the impact of the words but West felt immediately that this was a voice he knew. The next words hit even harder.

'His name is Flynn,' added Garcia. 'Kyle Flynn.'

Over the next few minutes, West remained in a daze. He was dimly aware of Isobel holding his hand while the trio escorted them across the plain to a point where the flashlights picked out a specific area. Something about the surface seemed slightly different than the surrounding sand. Suddenly West knew exactly what was going to happen.

Garcia tapped his boot on the ground three times. Seconds later, a wide hatch opened, sand falling from the metal circle. A man appeared, nodded to the others then withdrew down a ladder.

'Do you remember this?' asked Isobel.

'I do.'

And though West couldn't recall Wheater or Trent, Garcia he was sure of.

'Raul. Your first name is Raul.'

The man was about to head down the shaft but now turned to him. 'That's right. I'm glad to see you, Flynn. But be prepared for the fact that I may be in the minority.'

West didn't much like the sound of that but of equal impact was the use of his name.

Flynn. Kyle Flynn.

Like Garcia, it was familiar. But it didn't unleash a stream of memories.

Garcia was already climbing down the ladder. West noted that it was considerably wider than those for stations Charlie and Alpha.

'The Hub,' he said quietly.

Trent answered: 'I believe that was its original name.' Though his tone was not unfriendly, he then aimed his gun at the shaft.

'We're going to have to insist, I'm afraid.'

Though he had spent months searching for this place, West now wasn't even sure he wanted to go inside. Isobel squeezed his hand then let go.

'I'll go first.'

'All right.'

He waited for Isobel to head downward, then walked over to the shaft and lowered himself onto the ladder. He could already hear a number of voices below and now found that his curiosity outweighed his fear. The shaft was also notably longer than those at Alpha and Charlie but he climbed down quickly and was soon stepping down off the last rung.

Here too, the facility was on a different scale to the other stations. The roof was much higher and three corridors led away from the spacious room below the ladder. Having shut the hatch, Trent and Wheater now climbed down to join Garcia.

Then a fourth man appeared from one of the corridors, shutting the door behind him.

'Holy shit. I didn't expect to ever see your face again.'

He was a tall, lean man with an angular, weathered face. He wore a green t-shirt and – like the other three – black, military fatigues with heavy boots. As West gazed back at him, a second name came to him.

'Cou ...Coulton.'

'That's me, Flynn'

Coulton just shook his head. 'I think I might have almost as many questions as you but first things first – decontamination.' He pointed to a door to the left. 'Strip and leave the clothes on this side of the showers. I'll have some clean gear put our for you.'

'How do we know we can trust you?' asked Isobel.

'You don't,' said Coulton. 'But we have a lot of vulnerable people in here – people who haven't been exposed to the same bacteria and agents as you. It's not a request. You want to go inside, you go through decon.'

West was still adjusting to this new environment, some of which already seemed familiar; even the word, "decon".

'It's all right,' he said to Isobel.

He entered the room first. It was a narrow space and ahead were six cubicles, each equipped with a shower. A chemical smell washed over him, sparking memories of being here before, many times. Isobel joined him and shut the door.

She began to undress, prompting West to do the same.

When they were down to their underwear, she gestured to the showers. 'Girls left, boys right?'

'Sure.'

'You go first. Promise I won't look.' She managed a grin but West couldn't match it. When she turned away, he removed his boxer shorts and entered the furthest shower on the right. The water was cold to begin with but swiftly became warm. Once under it, he detected a strange odour but being under the water was a pleasant feeling. Though careful to avoid his bandaged shoulder, he used this rare opportunity to clean himself properly.

When he was finished, he hurried through to the last section where towels and clothes had been put out. He swiftly dried himself and started dressing.

'Coming out,' announced Isobel, already on her way.

'Sorry,' said West, when he inadvertently glimpsed her exiting the shower.

In five minutes, they had put on the clothes: military fatigues and boots. Whoever had selected the sizes had done a good job.

When West opened the door, Coulton was waiting for them in another narrow space. One thing had changed; he now had a holstered quick on his belt.

'Feeling better?'

'Cleaner,' said Isobel. 'Better? I'll let you know.'

'Unfortunately, we have to go through some busy areas to reach Mason and Barnes. Don't worry if you get some stares. We don't get all that many visitors.'

Mason. Barnes. West felt pretty sure that he knew those names too.

Coulton led the way out into a corridor and to the left. Here they passed through a command centre not unlike that in Charlie and Alpha. Incredibly, some of the systems were active, with two screens displaying rows of figures. Two middle-aged men sat there, wearing civilian clothes. They turned in their chairs to watch the new arrivals but Coulton kept moving.

They emerged into another corridor and turned right past a man sitting against a wall. He had opened up a panel and was studying a mass of multi-coloured wiring. The trio then passed several doorways; inside were bunks and other furniture, all neatly arranged. The corridor then curved around to the right and here were windows on either side.

To the left was a large, open area. A dozen or so children were sitting, listening to a teacher read from a science text book. When the first of them saw West and Isobel, they got up, ran to the windows and gazed at the interlopers, eyes wide.

'Hey,' said Isobel warmly.

'Hello!' replied a pair of little girls with enthusiastic waves. As they passed the classroom, a barrage of excited comments and questions broke out. There were also adults there, working at their own tables; they too studied the new arrivals.

The windows on the other side of corridor offered an even more remarkable sight. Here was a massive room, fifty feet across at least, with a very high ceiling. Rows of vegetables and fruit were being tended to, some under intensely bright lights. Another twenty adults looked up from their work and West felt numerous eyes upon him.

'Do you remember any of this?' asked Isobel as she walked

along beside him.

'I ...I don't know.'

'What about these two?'

West looked forward. At the end of the corridor, a man and a woman stood outside an open door. The man was frowning; the woman was simply shaking her head, a slight smile upon her face.

The man looked to be at least seventy and his long, white hair was tied in a tail. He was holding a walking stick. The woman was younger, her grey hair short and spiky. She wore the black fatigues and a green jacket. She also had a gun on her belt, this one a sixer with what an embossed silver handle.

'Welcome home, Kyle,' she said.

'Barnes.'

She offered her hand and he shook it. Though he looked into her eyes, no more memories came.

'You remember, Mason?' she said, nodding towards her companion.

'I think so.'

Mason stepped around them and held up both hands. West turned to see that the corridor was filling with the Hub's inhabitants.

'It's all right,' he said in a loud but calm tone. 'We'll see what's going on and brief you all later. Please, go about your work.'

Some – but not all of them – followed this instruction.

'We should go inside,' said Mason, gesturing to the room beyond the door.

West entered first. It was a confined space, the walls lined by metal cabinets and full bookshelves. In the centre of the room was a table with two chairs on either side.

'Here,' said Coulton, gesturing to the chairs facing away from the door he had just shut. West and Isobel sat side by side. He saw her shiver. This part of the Hub was cold and her hair had not yet dried

Coulton took up a position in a corner. Though he leant

casually against the wall, he put his hand on his belt close to his gun.

The aged Mason winced as he lowered himself onto the chair using his stick.

Once beside him, Barnes leaned onto the table, gazing intently at West. 'We heard the battle. As you're the only ones left, I guess you won. Who were you fighting?'

'Raiders,' said Isobel. 'Reaper's Boys.'

'They're a long way east,' said Barnes.

Isobel nodded towards West. They were after *him*. They took me hostage.'

'What was the vehicle?' asked Barnes. 'We've never heard an engine like that.'

'They stole it. It's called a roller. I believe they were also called tanks.'

'The Last Regiment?'

Isobel leaned forward. 'You know it? You know General Dawson.'

'We know *of* him,' said Barnes. 'He doesn't know us.'

'Who are you? How long have you been here?'

'All in good time,' Mason told Isobel, though his eyes remained on West. 'How did you find your way back here, Flynn?'

'Long story. But what interests me is how I ended up hundreds of miles away. With no memory.'

'That's another long story,' said Mason evenly.

'I don't mind going first,' replied West. 'But when it's your turn, I want the truth.'

'That seems fair.'

And so West told his tale. He avoided mentioning some of his more ruthless and violent acts but was otherwise honest. The four others listened attentively but asked nothing, allowing him to go at his own speed. And that speed was pretty fast; because West wanted the answers he had travelled so far to find. But when he concluded, Mason was interested in something else.

'The rest of Reaper's Boys – might they come here?'

'I doubt it,' said Isobel. 'He left them back in Blackridge. They couldn't keep up with the roller over distance anyway.'

'But in time they might come looking,' replied Mason, his tone anxious. 'They know about Whiterock now. So does Dawson.'

'True,' conceded West. 'But I didn't find this place so I don't see why they would. Anyway, I'm done. It's your turn.'

Mason sighed. 'I don't know where to start.'

Barnes interjected. 'I expect you'd like to know if you have any family here.'

'More than anything,' said West, surprised by the weakness of his voice.

'You were born here, thirty-six years ago. Your mother died fifteen years ago. It was a bad year for us here.'

Though he still could not picture her, West did remember something.

'The pipes,' he said. 'The air.'

Barnes' expression darkened. 'We lost nine, all told. Bacteria within the air-recycling system. In time, we worked out the cause and fixed it but by then...'

West didn't hear all of this. The next memory that struck him was horribly clear:

His father, in bed, terribly pale, barely able to speak.

'It was his heart.'

'Your father?' said Barnes. 'Yes. I'm afraid so. Six years ago.'

West recalled his father's eyes closing for the last time, remembered the others wrapping his body.

'Where is he buried?'

'Up top,' said Barnes. 'Like all of them. About a mile to the east. You'll find no trace on the surface but we know exactly where they are. Every single one.'

For a time, there was silence.

'How long have you been here?' asked Isobel eventually.

Mason answered: 'When the Cataclysm occurred, there were thirty people here. Some army personnel, some scientists conducting research. Every person here is one of their descendants. After a few months, they ventured outside. When they saw the state of the world, they decided to remain down here. It's never been easy but over the years we've worked hard to keep what we have. We had the knowledge we needed to retain the geo-generator, to grow food, sustain ourselves. Over the years, our population has grown to almost a hundred. We have our challenges but-'

'-Mason would stay here for ever if he could,' interjected Barnes. 'And he has his supporters. But I've always been more of a realist. I knew we had to look beyond this place; look for a different way, look to the future.'

West heard all this but he searched his memory for his mother's face. He could not find it.

'Back up a bit,' said Isobel. 'If people were here during the Cataclysm and this was a military base ...do you know? Do you know what happened?'

'Communications were severed only minutes after the first attack,' explained Mason. 'We have ... theories.'

'Everyone has theories,' replied Isobel.

West's thoughts had moved on again. 'I worked for you,' he said, eyes fixed on Barnes. 'You sent me out.'

Barnes gave a grim smile. 'You were the best I had, Kyle. You went further than anyone. You knew how tough it was but you saw that others were surviving. You said we had everything down here except the thing that counted most – freedom. You wanted it for all of us. So did I. But we were in the minority. We tried to-'

Now came Mason's turn to interject:

'You two saw the garden? We gather there sometimes. We were there one night when you came in.'

West had no recollection of this event but he could see from Barnes' expression that it was true.

'You told us all that we were weak,' she said. 'That we deserved to die down here. We managed to calm you down that night but you just wouldn't leave it alone. You became more and more confrontational. Angry. Unpredictable. One night the decision just got made. You and Coulton were sent east.'

She paused, composed herself. 'He had orders to kill you, to prevent anyone else learning about this place.'

At that moment, West couldn't summon much anger. He was just relieved to finally know.

'I gave that order,' said Mason, 'and I don't regret it. I had to consider the greater good.'

'I was outnumbered,' said Barnes. 'But there was no way I was going to let them kill you. We have a supply of drugs. Over the years, we've developed certain cocktails for certain purposes. One of them causes severe loss of memory. I made a highly concentrated dose. Just know that it was not something I wanted to do.'

'Cleaverton,' said West, now looking at the hard features of Coulton. 'That's where you did it. That's where you left me.'

Coulton was still leaning back against the wall, arms now folded across his chest. 'I checked you were breathing, covered you with a blanket, rode off. I'm glad to see you alive, man. I mean that.'

'Me too,' said Barnes. 'In the time you've been away, it's becoming obvious – to everyone – that we can't stay here forever. These lands could be overrun.'

Mason made no attempt to disagree.

'You're talking about the wraiths,' said Isobel. 'What do you know about them?'

'Very little,' replied Barnes. 'Only that they come from the west, and that they have equipment and weaponry far more advanced than anything we've ever seen. The first sighting of them was eighteen months ago. We've observed them moving east with alarming regularity. It looks like reconnaissance.'

West noticed that Coulton was nodding.

'I believe we may have to fight.' Barnes reached across the table and gripped West's hand. 'And I know of no better fighter than you. What do you say? Are you with us?'

Printed in Great Britain
by Amazon